ADVANCE PRAISE

"Quinton Skinner is like a miner, digging deep into the lives of one family for treasure, and offering it up in lyrical and graceful prose. The characters are endearing and maddening, funny and profane, tender and hopeful—and in *Odd One Out*, the reader is given both a unique family story and a universal one."

— Lorna Landvik, author of *Once in a Blue Moon Lodge* among many other novels

"Quinton Skinner has written a tragic, antic, unhinged domestic drama filled with pratfalls, puke, and dysfunction galore. Also, it's funny. You know, just like family. *Odd One Out* is a delight."

— Christopher Noxon, author of *Plus One*

"Quinton Skinner has imagined a genuinely and self-consciously exceptional family, and has honored them by writing an exceptionally humane, frank, and funny novel. A triptych of perspective and form, *Odd One Out* ranges from picaresque to stream-of-consciousness, but it's most of all a novel of detection about the exhausting and sustaining mysteries of familial love."

— Dylan Hicks, author of *Amateurs* and *Boarded Windows*

D0933044

ODD ONE OUT

Quinton Skinner

Prospect Park Books

Published by Prospect Park Books
2359 Lincoln Avenue
Altadena, CA 91001
www.prospectparkbooks.com

Distributed by Consortium Book Sales & Distribution
www.cbsd.com

Library of Congress Cataloging-in-Publication Data

Names: Skinner, Quinton, 1968- author.
Title: Odd one out / by Quinton Skinner.
Description: Altadena, California : Prospect Park Books, [2017] |
Description based on print version record and CIP data provided by publisher; resource not viewed.
Identifiers: LCCN 2016037563 (print) | LCCN 2016031530 (ebook) |
ISBN 9781938849961 () | ISBN 9781938849954 (pbk.)
Subjects: LCSH: Domestic fiction.
Classification: LCC PS3619.K565 (print) | LCC PS3619.K565 O33 2017 (ebook) | DDC 813/.6--dc23
LC record available at https://lccn.loc.gov/2016037563

Cover design by Laywan Kwan
Book layout and design by Amy Inouye, Future Studio
Printed in the United States of America

For Maureen

ALSO BY QUINTON SKINNER

14 Degrees Below Zero:
A Novel of Psychological Suspense

Amnesia Nights:
A Novel of Psychological Suspense

Do I Look Like a Daddy to You?
A Survival Guide for First-Time Fathers

Casualties of Rock (Behind the Music)

The Day the Music Died (Behind the Music)

"Suppose all the lions get up and go,
  And all the brooks and soldiers run away;
  Will Time say nothing but I told you so?
  If I could tell you I would let you know."

— W.H. Auden, "If I Could Tell You"

PART I

1

BEING TOLD THAT OUR NUMBERS HAD DWINDLED

IT STARTED WHEN MY FATHER WOKE US ALL IN THE MIDDLE of the night—at least it seemed like the middle of the night; I was a child. For all I know it was ten p.m.

"Jesus!" he shrieked, holding a piece of stationery in his shaking hand. "She's left me! She's left *you*, too! This is . . . it's . . . *abominable!*"

I was used to watching my father tremble while searching for the right adjective. But this moment seemed to foretell something uniquely ominous, and I sensed that something real was unfolding that eclipsed his usual talent for hysteria.

Even then I knew right away that the fuss had to do with the mystery that took place between men and women. It was tied away into the afternoons when Mom and Dad would park us in front of the TV and instruct us not to come into their room because there was a matter they had to discuss. It had to do with the years to come, when I would make girls cry, wishing they wouldn't, wishing I hadn't.

"Get your things!" my father shouted in the white hallway of our two-story home. "Get your shit! Grab what matters! We have to go!"

He was wearing brown wool slacks and a green shirt untucked; his ample black hair was displayed in its usual Einsteinian disarray. A couple of hours before he had dispensed us to our beds while ostensibly waiting for our mother to return home from a night out with her female friends, a group that included the mothers of some of my classmates.

"Daddy?" my little brother Daniel said, emerging sleep-faced into the hall with his long uncut head of hair forming a halo around his face.

"Danny," my father barked, "we're leaving. Get your Poké-mon cards, or whatever the fuck it is, and pack your bag."

Daniel unleashed an expression of benign confusion while fondling his penis through his pajamas. I reached out for the supercharged form of my dad, feeling that somehow I should be responsible for calming him.

"Daddy?" said my big sister Sam, emerging from her room, a kingdom to which she had recently, trium-phantly, staked her claim, leaving me and Daniel to the brutal negotiations of a small, shared space. "What's going on?"

"What's going on?" my father repeated, as if asking some other, invisible adult in the room. "What's going on is that . . . your *mother* . . . your *mother* . . . she's, well, she's . . . *left me.*"

Sam fixed her thirteen-year-old gaze on my father and slipped into a familiar, skeptical pose with her eyes drawn down. "Dad, be calm," she said with dripping dis-dain. "What time is it? Where's Mom?"

"Not *here,*" my father said, raking his hand through his hair, waving the piece of paper as though it were a death certificate (which, in a way, it was, though I never actually read it and don't know what it contained). "She's not here, Sam. That's what I'm trying to tell you, honey. She's not coming back."

My father never was able to hide the fact that Sam represented a unique and revered position in his life. His relationship with my mother was, even to my own unschooled eyes, fraught with misplaced conflict, but he always maintained a consistent deference to my sister's authority and instincts. He spoke to her now as an ally, a confidante, and I remember that in that moment his fleeting collusion with me broke to pieces now that Sam was there.

For her part, Sam looked surprisingly taken aback. With her sandy brown flip-do, big eyes, and porcelain features, she tended to reign over the household like exotic royalty, ceding power only to my mother in some unspoken parliamentarian agreement. Her feet came together and her back stiffened; just a few years before, her thumb would have snuck up toward the corner of her mouth.

"Dad," she said quietly. "Maybe you didn't understand what she meant."

The Burns household was one that had, for as long as I could remember, maintained a heartening level of daily resolution, while simmering just below the surface were all sorts of matters that were simply not to be discussed—at least not in front of us children. My father was unspeakably brilliant, as far as I was concerned (and the hands-off treatment with which my mother largely dealt with him seemed to confirm his exalted status), though he often seemed preoccupied with the question of why the larger world didn't share this opinion. He wrote for magazines and newspapers in Minneapolis— the only home I'd known. We had, in fact, lived in the same house my entire life, which gave us kids a sense of solidity and privilege, though a trip to Davanni's Pizza was a big deal and our cable TV came and went like the passage of the seasons. I know now that he must have earned disgracefully little money, considering his age and the range of his education and interests, but he and my mother did such a crackerjack job of keeping this information from me and my siblings that we considered him not only our resident genius but the driving engine of our five-person world.

However, it seemed that our numbers had dwindled.

"I don't understand what she means," my father said, dropping to his knees, sort of holding out the letter for Sam to look, but maintaining enough good sense not to let her actually see it. He turned grave. "I think I do. I really think I do. Your mother has decided that life with me is intolerable. That's the *precise* word she used, Sam. Do you know what that word means?"

Sam was standing right next to Dad, and his comment allowed her to return to her comfortable disdain.

"Yes, I know what that word means." She paused and adjusted the waistband of her pajamas. "It means she thinks you suck."

My father's face flattened, then he frowned deeply, and then he showed us something like a smile.

"Yes, that's precisely what she's saying," he allowed. "And now the cogent question, I suppose, is whether or not she's right."

"Daddy!" Daniel called out from the bathroom,

where the door was partway ajar and the light from inside made me realize we were all conferring in semidarkness.

"You don't suck," Sam said, moving a little closer to him. My father took this in, nodding slightly, then looked over at me.

"Daddy!" Daniel said again. He was only six, just finished with kindergarten, a magician of chaos and charm who filled me with resentful jealousy and unlimited irritation.

Dad was still looking at me. My position felt tenuous; Daniel was calling from the toilet with some undoubtedly exotic disaster, Sam had just firmly weighed in with Dad's non-suckitude, and the Big Guy was looking for an Amen. The stark lines of his face held angles of peril and slopes of disapproval. His eyes bored into mine, and he started to move that damned letter back and forth just below my eye level in an urgent tic.

"I love you, Dad," I said to him, and I profoundly meant it. I felt worshipful in his presence, and thrillingly frightened, like a startled ancient peasant quaking gleefully in the presence of a king.

Dad was kind of tearing up, I remember now, firmly nodding as though securing my support had been precisely the factor that he required in order to move forward.

"Daddy!" Daniel said, now starting to sound more than a little defeated.

"Dad," Sam pronounced, "we really better check on him."

Daniel's toilet crisis was indeed urgent and pungent; it took what seemed like a week's supply of toilet paper and wet wipes before a warm bath could take care of the rest. Sam hung in there and administered an on-the-spot lesson in back-door hygiene. She must have learned this from someone, one of our parents, maybe both. We had long run a de facto nudist colony in our house, although Sam was on the verge of puberty and had recently dropped out.

Dad was on his knees drying Daniel. The letter lay on the floor out in the hall, and Sam and I both eyed it.

"Read it," she commanded. "Tell me what it says."

"No way!" I whispered with an anxious glance back at the open bathroom door. Dad was whistling, a sure sign his nervousness was building.

"Chickenshit," Sam said.

She could call me whatever she liked, but even at ten I knew that there were vast swaths of life that were best left untouched by me. That is a wisdom I could stand to re-learn, come to think of it. Whatever was in that letter was in the private language between my mother and father, a glossolalia that encompassed all the factors beyond my control and that led, in my mind, to the inevitable specter that I constantly fought to keep at bay: death—my mother's, my father's, my sister's, my own. Daniel, oddly enough, was somehow exempt. He always seemed untouchable by fate.

"It's all so fucking relative," Dad said, out in the hall again, with Daniel in his arms.

"Don't swear so much," Sam said.

"Pardon me, Duchess," Dad replied. "Desperate times call for profanity. But back to my original point: how relative it all is. You say I don't suck, for which I thank you, by the way. But in your mother's eyes, I obviously do. It's not that I didn't suspect it. But it comes as a shock to have it presented to me in such glaring and dramatic terms."

"Dad, Daniel's going to get cold," I said.

"Oh, right." Dad looked down at the naked six-year-old in his arms. Daniel was small for his age; he could have easily passed for two years younger. "Let's get you dressed. Then we have to get back to packing. I want us on the road within half an hour."

He started throwing open dresser drawers in the room I shared with my little brother. "Kevin," he barked at me. "Make yourself useful. Pack a bag for yourself. We're each going to need a week's worth of clean clothes. And toss some books in. We're going to be spending a lot of time in the car."

"Dad, don't be crazy," Sam said from the doorway. Her voice sounded defiant but I could see her beginning to chew her lower lip. Dad stared her down for a good thirty seconds, until she stalked off. A moment later I heard the door to her room slam behind her.

"She says it's intolerable," Dad quoted. "What a statement to make. Not, 'Glenn, there are some things you need to work on.' Or, 'Glenn, maybe we need to reconsider our domestic arrangements.' Or, 'Glenn, duck fast, because I'm about to throw something at your head.'"

Daniel and I were staring at him. Dad wasn't looking at either of us, and as was not infrequently the case, I felt as though I were eavesdropping on him.

"No!" he said, holding a pint-size Batman shirt up to Daniel without putting it on him. "Instead it's, it's . . . "

Dad crab-walked out to the hall, where he found the letter from Mom on the floor. As he unfolded it, I saw big water stains where Daniel had dripped on it. Or else they were from some earlier bout of tears, though that didn't seem likely. I had never seen Dad really let go and cry, not even when his mother died.

"I really feel that the situation with you has become intolerable, and I no longer hold out hope for improvement," Dad read aloud. My brother and I avoided each other's eyes; Daniel slowly slipped on his shirt. *"I know this is happening very suddenly but if I don't do this now, I will almost certainly lose my nerve. I know the children will be in good hands with you until we sort out the immediate future. For the moment, I need to get away from you. Please don't come looking for—"*

He broke off in mid-sentence, looking up at us uncomfortably. I heard the sound of drawers sliding in Sam's room, as well as a couple of heavy thuds, which meant that she was throwing things around angrily. I would have worried about her but it was pretty much standard procedure for Sam to be throwing things around angrily. For once I wasn't in the line of fire.

"Are we going to find Mom?" I asked. "Because that letter seems to pretty clearly spell out that—"

"Tut! Tut! Tut!" Dad barked, his finger to his lips. "I'll be in charge of tactics, thanks very much. Like I said, it's all relative. Your mother left in haste because she knew it was the wrong thing to do. By the time we get to her, I'm willing to lay big money that she will already be regretting the whole thing. We'll collect her in the old Subaru, have a big laugh about it, and get a pizza. Bang! Back to old times."

"How do you know where she is?" I asked.

"There's only one place she would have gone," Dad said, folding his arms triumphantly and squinting like a cop on TV.

"Aunt Beth's house?" Daniel asked.

"We wouldn't need a week's worth of clothes if we were going to Aunt Beth's, dumbass," I said.

My father flashed me a look of silent reproach over my word choice, though Daniel wasn't fazed in the slightest, probably because he saw my point. Aunt Beth, my mother's sister, lived a twenty-minute drive away, in Plymouth. Dad called it the place where you needed to take your Soma every day, a reference that I didn't understand until years later and which he never bothered to explain to me.

"Not *Aunt Alayne's*!" Sam blurted from the doorway, startling us three boys. She had balled-up clothes clutched in each fist. "Dad! We have to go to school!"

We were indeed in the meaty part of the school year, and Aunt Alayne's house as a destination had the distinct disadvantage of being in Southern California.

"I've thought of that," Dad said. "I'll call the school from the road and say there's been an emergency. I'll have your teachers email me your assignments and you can work on the road. Anyway, we're not going to stop much. I can have us there in a couple of days, then a couple days back."

Sam looked at my father as though he had just sprouted wings or informed her that he was, in reality, a woman. For me, the prospect of missing a week of fourth grade was at worst a value-neutral proposition. Now that I thought about it, I wouldn't mind at all a week away from Ms. Salveson's high-strung attentions (she was just a year or two out of college, and from her behavior to date, she regarded the year we were spending in her care as the most crucial and formative of our young lives). Daniel was in first grade, already at

least a year ahead of his classmates academically, so he
could pretty much fall into a well for six months and not
miss much. Sam, however, I understand now, was swimming in the cusp-of-puberty waters of middle school.
I saw the look of horror in her eyes, and understood that
being absent for a week, over a *family emergency*, no less,
entailed the prospect of being branded weird, unfit,
and might well result in losing precious points in her
social standing.

"Dad, if you have to go, leave us with Aunt Beth,"
Sam said, speaking very slowly in that hypnotic mode
she employed when trying to talk Dad off the ledge.
"They have three cars and she doesn't work. She can
drive us to school. If you explain things to her, she
might even come stay here with us until you get back."

"Not an option," my father said.

"Dad!"

"Sam, that is not an option." Dad left the room,
nudging past Sam and moving down the hall to his own.
He lurched into the closet and produced a soft-sided suitcase. The three of us followed him; I turned on the overhead light so he could see what he was doing.

"Dad, listen to me," Sam pleaded. "I really don't
want to—"

"First of all, I would like to leave your Aunt Beth
out of this, if it's at all possible." Dad indiscriminately
snatched a handful of balled-up socks from a dresser
drawer and tossed them into the suitcase. They were all
different colors; Dad had a thing about never wearing
plain white sweat socks, even when he was exercising.

"Why?" Sam demanded.

"You will have to accept the reality that there are

things going on here which you do not know about, and which you would not understand," Dad said, slowly and precisely.

"How do you know?" Sam shouted. "How do you know if you don't try me? Maybe I would understand perfectly well—"

"You children are not going to be privy to the intimate details of my personal life." With that, Dad started to take out shirts from the closet; he threw them into the suitcase while they were still on their hangers.

"Dad, this is all pretty personal," I said. "You have to admit."

"Yes, and it's more than you should have to deal with, and I'll probably be apologizing to you for this for the rest of my life." He was throwing jeans and corduroys on top of the shirts and socks. "If I could completely shelter you from this, I would, believe me. I'm tempted to assign the lion's share of the blame to your mother, what with her *abandoning* us and all, but she's not here to defend herself."

"You," Daniel said, in his high-pitched voice.

"Pardon?" Dad said, looking down at him.

"She didn't abandon *us*," Daniel corrected; in his child's accent, the word sounded something like *a-dan-dun*. "She abandoned *you*."

Dad stared at Daniel for a while, with a look on his face as though someone had slapped him with a damp fish. A few moments later a smile curled the corners of his lips and he affectionately ran his hands through Daniel's hair.

"That's my boy, Danny," my father said. "Be precise. Always be *precise*."

"How about if we be precise *here* instead of in LA?" Sam asked, putting as much ice water into her tone as she could manage, though still visibly spooked and—I thought—aware that she was fighting a battle already lost.

We followed Dad down the hall, where he busily started to fill up a little leather bag with his razor and toothbrush. Sam stood in the doorway breathing heavily and theatrically, as though she would somehow respire Dad into changing his mind.

He looked up. "Stop staring," he said. "And get your shit together. We're losing time."

The battle was lost. In truth, I wasn't all that broken up about the prospect of a car trip. True, I would be stuck with Daniel in the backseat most of the time, and I would have to deal with Dad without the mitigating influence of Mom. But I was still at a point at which Dad also represented a good deal of dangerous fun. And I was also getting the picture that we, the children, were an integral part of Dad's desperate bid to keep the family together. It hadn't really occurred to me until then, what with all the panic, that there was a very concrete possibility that our lives had changed irrevocably. The realization gave the moment a gossamer, liquid quality, as I felt my reality oozing outside of its usually sturdy frame.

"The important thing is that we stick together," Dad was saying, from seemingly someplace far away. A strange feeling had started in my gut and radiated upward. The light fixture in the bathroom danced a little, and silvery shards of crystal light began to emanate from its center.

"If we can just stay together, we can restore the balance," Dad said. "Some day this will be something we'll all laugh about together. Along with your mother."

I reached out and put my hand against the door frame. For no reason at all I was thinking about my daily school lunch, and how my mother had started to half-fill my water bottle at my request, so that my backpack wouldn't be quite as heavy. It was just the sort of thing I could never count on Dad to remember.

My dad was calling my name. "Kevin?" He sounded as though he was calling from the bottom of a well. Or was I the one at the bottom? That would certainly explain the way my field of vision was narrowing into a circle of visible things (the toilet, the magazine rack beside it) while deep, rich blackness closed in from all sides.

"Glenn," I said, and it took a moment to realize that I had said it. I never, ever, called either of my parents by their first name.

Someone was holding onto me, probably Sam. There was a rush of voices, and I heard Daniel shriek and, I thought, run back down the hall to our room. That was probably a good idea, I thought. It was certainly for the best that he not be around to see what was going to happen next.

I was on the floor. I saw my father's brown eyes widen in horror as he stood over me, and felt intensely sorry to be adding to his troubles. Childhood emergencies were not something he handled with particular aplomb, as demonstrated by Daniel's potty accident. It occurred to me that Daniel must have panicked when Dad woke us up, that must have been why he had shit all over himself. I also felt intensely sorry for, and protective of, my little brother. No one should have to be so frightened that it makes them shit. No one.

And that was about it. I started to panic along with Sam and Dad over what was happening to me, and then it didn't seem to matter anymore. I effortlessly cut the cord that connected me to the world of things and people, and began to drift with the most enveloping and welcoming feeling of bliss. That's about all I remember.

2

SOMEHOW LIKE BEING BACKSTAGE IN LIFE'S DRAMA

I HAVE TO GIVE DAD CREDIT: HE RECOVERED QUICKLY FROM my episode, efficiently dispatching the puke I'd spewed all over myself. Fortunately I didn't remember doing so, having a family-famed aversion to throwing up. He got me cleaned up, and even packed for me. He had the presence of mind to bring my copy of *Total Baseball*, which contained stats for everyone who had ever played the game, and with which I could have entertained myself for a thousand years in Limbo.

The evidence that I had vomited was abundant in the crust around my molars—Dad's rallying me, unconscious, into the car had included brushing my teeth for me—and the rest I pieced together from a backseat conversation that went something like this:

ME: What happened? Where are we?
DANIEL (Staring into the lit screen of a handheld car-racing videogame that Dad had bought on impulse while paying for gas at the SuperAmerica by our house): In the car, stupid.
ME: I can see that. Are we going to California?

DANIEL: I hope we go without you.
ME: You're a little shit, you know that?
DANIEL: So? You're a big shit, then.
ME: Daniel. Seriously. What happened to me?
DANIEL: You fell over and puked all over yourself. You smell gross. I wish I didn't have to ride back here with you.

It was totally black outside save for the fleeting glare of headlights passing in the opposite direction. We had made this trip several times before, under far better circumstances, and I caught a glimpse of a sign signaling that Albert Lea was ten miles off. That meant we were still in Minnesota. We were just getting started.

Dad had both hands on the steering wheel. He was a cautious, sometimes tremulous, driver, and his fallback attitude was to regard everyone else on the road as either homicidal or criminally negligent. I peered over the seat and saw that we were speeding along at close to eighty. That was pretty unusual; Dad was a pretty staunch speed limit kind of guy.

Sam had a pillow wedged between her head and the passenger-side door, but I could sense that she was awake. I leaned over the backseat, rummaged around in the hatchback bed, and found an old Mexican blanket and wrapped myself in it. The car was chilly inside, and the steady purr of the wind outside sounded as though it was insinuating itself through some remote mountain pass.

"You okay back there?" Dad said, glancing in the mirror. I took in his big mess of hair, his big veined hands on the steering wheel.

"Fine. Sorry about what happened."

"Don't apologize," Dad said. I saw his eyes blinking in

the mirror. "I freaked you all out. I'm sure you can appreciate that I've never been in this kind of situation before."

There wasn't much that I could appreciate about it, actually. My parents' lives, as far as I was concerned, began with my birth, but I was also dimly aware that there were things that came before even their meeting—romances, agonies, bliss, things for which I had no context or understanding. For all I knew, Dad had been abandoned before—but never with three children.

"You children should know that I love your mother very much," Dad said in his lecturing tone. "And she loves me. And we love you. Your mother and I . . . well, you know, sometimes things happen. People forget how much they mean to each other."

"*Dad*," Sam moaned without moving. She was looking the opposite way from him, staring out the side window.

Dad took a big swig from his jumbo Styrofoam cup of coffee. Strange, I hadn't been able to smell it until I saw it, but I surely did then: bitter, acrid, grown-up.

"Well, it's true." Dad sounded as though he had settled some important matter within himself. "Just think about the way people treat each other. The people who are the most important to us are the ones we inflict all our shit on."

"Stop swearing," Sam said.

"I can't imagine doing without any of you," Dad said. "And yet think about what our communication consists of. Clear your place at the table. Take a bath. Do your homework. Homework? What the fuck do I care about homework? From now on, fuck the homework. You know? Really. Do your homework if you feel like it. It's not like it's going to make you a happier person if

you go to Yale and get a job making two hundred grand
a year. In fact, if that happens, your odds of being happy
are probably more stacked against you."

"You don't even mean that," Sam murmured.
"You're still going to make us do our homework."

A long pause. We were really chewing up miles, cat-
apulting through the night. I thought about my friends
getting up and going to school in a few hours. I wondered
how long it would take them to notice that I was missing.

"Yeah, I probably will," Dad admitted. "And then, someday, we'll all be dead, and none of it will have mattered."

"Dad, you're so *maudlin* sometimes," Sam said.

More silence. I glanced over and saw Daniel asleep,
slumped over and looking positively angelic. The more
he slept, the better for me. I knew that over the next couple of days I was going to be trapped in the backseat with
him, his energy coming at me, his endless verbiage driving me to desperation. I might as well have been caged
up with a small monkey.

I gave a little start and realized that I had been dozing. It was still nighttime, and from my semi-reclining
position I saw Dad's profile: his big bony brow, the slope
of his slightly asymmetric nose, the edge of his jawline
glowing from the dashboard lights.

"I wish you could have seen us back then," he was
saying to Sam. "I mean, it's impossible for you to understand, of course. It's the nature of things that you have to
see us as types, rather than as actual people with actual
stories. Still, I wish you could have seen me and your
mom when we were young. When it was just us. Christ, I
know you'd like us a lot better."

"You know, Dad, our relationship would run a lot

smoother if you didn't keep reminding me about what you think I don't understand," Sam scolded quietly.

"Look, I didn't invent the system," Dad replied. "And it goes both ways. Do you think I'll ever be able to understand you as a person the same way as, say, a best friend? Or a lover?"

"A *lover?*" Sam sounded as though she was repeating a dirty word. "Dad, you can be so completely repugnant sometimes."

This was thrilling beyond compare. Listening to the two of them in unguarded talk was somehow like being backstage in life's drama, like being invisible at a secret meeting where the future was being planned in meticulous detail. I shut my eyes and remained completely motionless. The world thrummed.

"What?" Dad replied. "Are you telling me you aren't interested in boys? Not at all?"

"No, I'm not—" Sam exhaled heavily. "I *am.* I mean, sometimes I . . . You know what? You are the very last person I want to talk to about this right now."

"That's kind of sad, isn't it?" Dad said. "I mean, I understand where you're coming from. Sure do. But if there's anyone who has your best interests at heart, and who knows a thing or two about—"

"Tut. Tut," Sam said, making Dad's trademark little shut-up noise.

"Fine." Dad reached for his coffee. I felt a slow centripetal pull as we changed lanes.

"But you see, this makes my point," Dad finally said. Daniel groaned from the darkness across from me.

"And what point is that, O Wise One?" Sam asked. She sounded infinitely weary.

"About people," Dad replied. "You can't talk to me about boys. Okay. Big surprise. But why is that?"

"Because the idea of doing so is icky and repulsive beyond all imagining?" Sam asked in a sweet voice.

"Because of our *roles*," Dad answered as though she had said nothing. "I'm your *father*. You can't talk to me about puberty, or liking boys. Or girls. Or whatever you're going to be into once your hormones are good and revved up."

"Kevin already puked once tonight," Sam told him. "Are you going for the twofer? Because I'm about to lose it over here."

"Stay with me here," Dad went on. "I'm your father, right? Not Glenn. Not a forty-one-year-old person. I'm Dad. All the symbolism, all the weight of our shared history—you'll never be able to shake it and see me for who I really am."

Sam was silent now.

"And that's what I was trying to explain about your mother and me. We've been together for more than fifteen years. And though you'll never be able to understand it, we're just two people. It's our nature to take each other for granted, to stereotype each other, to twist each other's words and intentions to fit whatever script we're playing out that particular day."

"You mean like when you and Mom fight?" Sam asked.

"Sure. And also when we get along, if you really want to know the truth. But getting along is more pleasant all around than not. It's just that people forget that sometimes."

"And then we get into situations like this?" Sam asked.

I half-opened one eye and saw Dad staring at me in

the mirror. It was dark, though, and he couldn't see that I was awake. I knew the nature and tone of the conversation would shift tectonically the moment he learned that I was listening.

"Sure," Dad answered. "That's a big part of it."

"Bullshit," Sam said, sitting up in her seat.

"Would you mind repeating that?" Dad said.

"I said bullshit, Dad. You heard me the first time."

Normally when this kind of moment occurred, say, around the dinner table during a spat over whether Sam could go to a party on the other side of town, or out on a shopping trip when she wanted an expensive pair of jeans, I would metaphorically take a ringside seat and savor the action to come. My dad versus my sister was one of the great matchups of the first year of the new century. It was great because, while Dad could be as authoritarian as Pol Pot, in his core he had a quaking fear of Sam's righteousness, and the unflinching nature of her will. But this was something different. Sam calling bullshit on his explanation for Mom's leaving seemed cruel, and wrong. More than anything else, I wished I didn't have to be listening to this.

"Care to expand?" Dad said in a tight voice.

"You're describing things that happen every day." There was a trembling note to Sam's voice; she understood very well that she had climbed out on a ledge and had to work her way back without a misstep. Calling bullshit was a very big deal indeed in our family. You could do it, but you had better be able to back it up. "None of that is enough to explain why Mom would just leave us. And without telling us where she went. From what I understand, we might get to California

and find out that she went to New York or something."
"Don't try to cloud the issue," Dad said. "You know,
I really don't appreciate this. Here I am trying to explain
something to you about what goes on between people, about
how the world *works*, and you're telling me it isn't enough."
"Because it *isn't*." Sam was trying to keep her voice
down, in deference to the backseat contingent, but she
was getting heated. "You know my friend Gabrielle?"
"Curly blond hair. Annoying voice."
"That's her. Did you know her parents split up six
months ago?"
"I remember something about it," Dad said, transparently lying.
"Do you know why?"
"I don't presume to know about anyone else's marriage, honey."
"Because Gabby's dad had cheated on her mother,
like, five or six times, and he kept getting caught. And
he drank too much, and he was really mean around the
house, and he treated the kids like shit, and he generally
made everyone in the family miserable."
"So she left him?" Dad asked.
Sam gave a world-weary chuckle. "No way. He left
her. He got an apartment with his girl who's, like, twenty-two
or something. It's disgusting."
"So what's your point?"
"That this stuff happens for a *reason*," Sam explained. "You can't just spout off about people not really
knowing each other and expect me to nod and thank
you for your insight. I mean, you and Mom might
not have been Romeo and Juliet lately, but it's not
like you've been fighting all the time or anything."

The wind and the tires on the road reverberated through the car and gave me a low-level feeling of electricity, like a prolonged cosmic exhalation that ran through the body and spirit of things. With each mile that we traveled (I knew that we were moving at well past a mile a minute), I began to imagine a doppelgänger of myself about to wake in a couple of hours. He would head off to fourth grade at Jefferson School, maybe stopping at his locker to tell Eli or Gus about the weird dream he'd had.

Sam and Dad had settled into silence, and now I started to convince myself that my fantasy was true. In fact, there was an entire family of doubles: Mom and Dad, me, Daniel, Sam. They were sleeping peacefully under the high, steep roof of our house, completely oblivious to the black Subaru that was speeding through the night from Minnesota into Iowa. They would wake, eat breakfast, and go about all the little routines of our lives. They would even think they were the real us, and everyone would assume they were the real thing. But no: *we* were real, shooting into the great question of the future. But when we got back, if we ever did, our old lives would no longer be waiting for us. They would be taken away, and we would never get them back.

"True, we don't fight that much." Although at least two full minutes had passed, Dad had this habit of picking up a conversation as though no time had elapsed. "But you can't go by that. Sometimes it's healthy to fight. A lot of couples who are really happy fight all the time. It's just a matter of style, really."

"But everything has seemed so normal," Sam said.

I felt the heavy pull of sleep behind my eyes. I

wished I had brought my watch, but it was back home on my nightstand, where my duplicate would don it in the morning, his perception of time eclipsing my own. Morning couldn't be far off.

"Normal. Sure." Dad sounded unconvinced.

"Aren't I right?" Sam asked.

I was being pulled under by the combination of fatigue and intoxicating motion; there must have been an autumn breeze in the night, because I felt the car undulate slightly from side to side as we glided ahead. In years to come I would always recall this night, and the ones that followed, whenever I was a passenger on an airplane, borne on the cushioning air, the soporific pull of airborne motion overruling any anxiety my naturally fearful tendencies might have produced.

"People get into ruts," Dad told Sam.

"What does that mean?"

"Like I was saying," he said slowly. "They don't see each other the way they used to. They *can't*. All they see when they look at the other person is all the ways they're frustrated with them. Or they look at that person and all they can think about is how they don't have as much money as they wish they had. Or all of the things they might have been, or all of the things they might have done, if they hadn't put their trust in that person."

"Is this about your job?" Sam asked. "Because it seems like you've been really busy lately."

"Well, there's busy," Dad said, "and there's earning money. The two aren't always the same thing in my experience."

When I'd reached in the back of the car for the Mexican blanket that was now pleasantly abrading my cheek as my lids grew heavier still, I had seen the big black shiny valise where Dad kept all his papers and his laptop computer. There was no equivalent object in our universe to that case and its fraught symbolic import. It contained at least two unfinished book manuscripts, folders full of clippings and notes for various long articles he was either working on or planned to pitch to assorted publications, and a panoply of free books and CDs he'd gotten in the mail and had either been hired to review or for which he hoped to find a place in print for his musings. Packed imposingly tight, I always thought of it as an exterior manifestation of Dad's brain: full of an infinity of information, hopelessly disorganized, and redolent with an alarmingly vivid tinge of purposeful futility.

None of which is meant to imply that Dad was misguided, or inept, or lacking in talent. Looking back, I think it was his real and palpable talent that probably contributed most to his unease and inability to lock into the main currents of life and locate his own brand of contentedness. He was good but not great, and at times that constituted a curse. Once, years later, when I was helping him move into an apartment smaller than the one in which he had been living, I came across an old paper carton full of magazine and newspaper articles he'd written. They were meticulously clipped, albeit stacked haphazardly. I read through a few of them: book reviews, a theater review, a couple of profiles of local artists whom I barely remembered and who were no longer on the scene.

It chilled me to dip into these word streams and hear my father's voice: skeptical, articulate to a fault, childishly passionate. I realized that these bits of ephemera were what Dad had been plugging away at all those years, in that little cubbyhole downstairs jam-packed with papers and books. None of it amounted to much. But it was pretty good.

"—not telling me the whole story," Sam was saying; I realized that I had nodded off. "And you have no idea how frustrating that is. I mean, here we are in *Iowa* in the middle of the night, and I don't even understand why."

"You want to *understand?*" Dad replied, with a brand of sarcastic venom he rarely employed on his children. "What a fucking joke. If you're waiting for *understanding*, little girl, you just keep right on waiting. I got news for you. I don't understand any of this shit, either. I just want my wife back."

Well, that silenced her. I lay there in the dark feeling a swell of painful sympathy for my older sister. She'd tried to get a straight answer out of Dad's mountainous self-preserve, and come away stung with the kind of sentiment none of us were really prepared to deal with (Dad included, probably).

But it was liberating in its way. Sam didn't understand, Dad said he didn't understand. *I* sure didn't. Whatever was unfolding was too vast and dark to bear much contemplating, and I drew upon what I knew were my final seasons of the child's prerogative: to pretend to know less than he knows, to protect the self by feigning the simplicity adults assume lives in his heart. I had no interest in knowing precisely why a woman would leave a man and her children behind, because the answer was surely too monstrous to look upon directly. In the moments that I allowed the demonic thoughts to slip past my barriers, I even contemplated whether my own behavior might have been to blame. I talked back, I argued, all in tacit service and tribute to my father, but Mom never seemed to really enjoy playing that game as much as her husband and kids. Maybe my father had been right in his first panicked exclamations after finding his wife's good-bye note. Perhaps she had indeed left us all.

It was a thought that I tidily tamped down, along with a galaxy of others, as I slid into the enveloping silence. Sam was either asleep by then or too tired to seek answers from Dad. Daniel snored beside me. The night became like any other night, at any other time: becalmed, purposeful, unspeakably fragile.

3

"CUSSIN' LIKE THAT MAKES A BOY HUNGRY!"

I OPENED MY EYES TO A SENSATION OF ALMOST INDESCRIB-able staleness. The taste in my mouth had transformed into something that was somehow both organic and metallic, deeply unclean and with a tinge of shame. The inside of the car smelled of coffee and unwashed bodies, of worry and tedium. I felt enveloped by an enormous silence as I tried to open my eyes; then a thunder erupted next to my ear and I sat bolt upright, an involuntary squeal coming from me that I immediately and fervently hoped no one had heard.

Sam was standing right outside my window, laughing her ass off. She rapped on the window again and said something I couldn't hear on the other side of the glass. Dad was standing close by with his shirtsleeves rolled up, stretching his back and wincing in the morning light.

Salvaging dignity was going to be quite a project, I immediately understood, as I tried to focus my vision. Something was wrong with one of my eyes. The left one seemed to be in good working order, but as I ran my just-waking inventory of all my parts, there was no mistaking that something was amiss.

Now Sam was noticing that something wasn't quite right; she nudged Dad on the arm. He stooped over a little, one hand cupped over his eyes to shield himself from the glare on the window. He motioned for me to get out. I got the door opened and lunged out, immediately executing a drunken-style reel across a stretch of parking lot asphalt. I focused my one good eye on my surroundings and took in the gaudy twists and intestinal labyrinth of a kid's play area. We were at a McDonald's someplace. The sky was fresh-water blue with that optimist's cast of breakfast-time sun.

"What's with you?" Sam jeered. "Jesus!" she added as she took a closer look at my face. "That's disgusting!"

"Kevin, come here," Dad ordered, reaching out a hand to brush hair from my face. "Are you feeling all right, son?"

"Gross!" Daniel called out. I glanced over and saw him sprawled on a patch of grass next to a trashcan burgeoning with wrappers and cups.

Dad's big face filled my field of vision, and I saw him suppress a flash of panic. He hadn't taken me to the doctor after my episode the night before, and that might have been negligent—I saw this realization flash across his face, in the instant before he dismissed it and moved on to more pragmatic concerns.

"Son, your eye is really goddamned goopy," he declared with considerable sympathy.

I turned around to see my reflection in the car window. This was the same old face I knew quite well—at least ninety percent of it. My right eye, on the other hand, was a mess: swollen, the white a vivid red, a greenish-yellow crust having invaded all the territory around its contours, making it impossible to open it all the way.

"Pink eye!" Daniel shouted with ample delight.

I started to touch it but Dad brushed my hand away.

"Um, I don't really think you want to be touching that too much," he said delicately. "I think you'll spread it around. You might get it in the other eye."

"Yeah!" Daniel said. "Double pink eye!"

"You are so disgusting," Sam pronounced, taking a step away from me, without words pronouncing me as infected with the profoundest strain of cooties.

"Stop making fun of me!" I yelled out, suddenly aware of another family getting out of their minivan a couple of spaces over. "Do you think I want to wake up with my eye crusted over with this *shit*?"

"You know," Sam said with a little smirk. "I think there's been way too much profanity floating around this family lately."

"Shit shit shit!" I shouted. "Mothersucker! Ass! Jesus Christ! Butthole! Piss! Fart! Double fucking shitty shit!"

Dad's expression of surprise almost made my explosion worth it; Sam was doubled over at the waist, laughing so hard that no sound came out. The family in the van stopped their elaborate process of disembarking their vehicle to stare at us slack-jawed. They were all kind of overweight, dressed in the bland sweats and T-shirts that comprised the uniform of the normal family enjoying a vacation together. I looked at us. Sam was wearing rainbow tights and a shawl she'd knitted the summer before. Dad's hair was every place at once, the knees of his slacks shiny with wear. Daniel was smiling with beatific malevolence at us all. And me, with my eye, and the hair I inherited from Dad, and the posture of profound discomfort with the world that I knew I would never be able to hide. It felt as though we had just been transported from some other marred and profoundly imperfect world into a realm of normality that did nothing but accentuate our aberrations.

Of course I couldn't just shout every profanity I knew at the top of my lungs without there being repercussions. Dad glanced over at the other family ruefully; sure enough, they were frozen there, waiting to see what Dad would do. In the quiet morning air the question of my punishment hung over us like a Pinter-pause written into a play. Dad was in the lead role, and he would determine the course of action to follow.

He folded his arms and squinted into the sun.

"Well, son," he said in an exaggerated hillbilly accent. "That's some *damn fine* cussin' you did just there. Keep up the good work, boy."

A stifled gasp came from the precinct of the minivan. I didn't dare look, instead I stared dumbly at my sister. Sam flirted with outrage for an instant—seeing me in trouble was one of her greatest and subtlest pleasures, and she savored all its varieties—but then she took in the other family and a look of comprehension played over her mouth and eyes. She gave a little smile of satisfaction.

"Cussin' like that makes a boy *hungry*," Dad added with a big, goofy smile. "I bet you need you some *hash browns*."

"An Egg McMuffin would be good, actually," I said quietly, not sure how deeply I wanted to tread into the territory of Dad's joke. His punishments were never severe, but the intensity of his disapproval was enough to roil my guts and send a shot of adrenaline into my system. I had gotten away with a pretty big one. Swearing and generally acting like a lunatic were pretty much fine

in our home, but our sense of the public/private distinc-
tion was finely honed and profoundly followed. It was
never explicitly stated, but put simply: we weren't supposed to let outsiders see how bizarre we really were.
I had transgressed, but Dad had closed ranks. I could
have kissed him.

Dialogue from my boyhood:

ME: You're the greatest Dad ever. And I'm the worst son.
DAD: Stop it, Kevin. Don't say that.
ME: It's not your fault. Nothing is your fault.
DAD: Jesus, Kevin, son, you know I love you. Right?

Inside I was dispatched to the restroom while the
others ordered our food. The bathroom was dingy
and smelled of cleaning solution, but it had the distinct
advantage of being empty. Thus I was able to take a full inventory of my eye, and the news was anything but encouraging.

I took a paper towel and wet it down with warm water. After a couple of strokes I was able to clear away a
good deal of the yellowy crust that had accumulated in
the short hours I was asleep. It came off in thick chunks,
and it hurt, but at least I was finally able to open my eye
three-quarters of the way. I couldn't see very well out of
it, though, and now that it was fully exposed, I saw that it
was a very angry red, and shiny, and really quite nauseating to behold.

When I walked back out, it felt like everyone was
staring at me: the diners, the mix of young and elderly
workers behind the counter, and (especially) the mom,
dad, and two kids whom I had outraged in the parking
lot (my counterpart in the family, a boy about my age,

looked at me with bovine superiority, incapable of hiding his fascination with my mark of affliction).

Dad had just paid for our food with a credit card. He gave me a brief look of sympathy, then his patented tough-it-out tap on the shoulder. "That doesn't look so bad," he said. "Maybe it'll clear up as the day goes on."

"It looks horrible," Sam said.

"Are you going to go blind?" Daniel asked.

"No one is going blind," Dad pronounced. "Dr. Dad diagnoses a little harmless conjunctivitis. No lasting effects, contagious as all heck, though. Keep your fingers away from your face, Kevin, or else you're going to have a matching set."

Dad was very skilled at holding back sympathy when he sensed it would force one of his children to hold it together rather than succumb to an attack of childhood despair. It was mostly self-defense on his part; while he had little patience for the ambient bickering and inane chatter of his children, which manifested almost daily in his semi-comic (for us) attacks of fleeting rage, he reserved his deepest bumbling and discomfort for our sadness. Sam used to be prone to epic crying attacks over perceived slights and injustices, and I had my own particular talent for panicky breakdowns from which only Mom could talk me down.

The unintended effect of Dad's appeal to my toughness, as was often the case, was to remind me that I had cause to, say, begin crying uncontrollably. My mother was gone. I was somewhere in Iowa. I was disfigured. Back in Minneapolis my world was starting its clockwork machinations without me. My imposter was rising in my bed, yawning, so immersed in his role that he wasn't aware of his own fraudulence.

We got a table by the window, where the sun's glare was magnified with laser-like focus on my raw, aching eye.

"I don't even know the name of this town," Dad said between bites of his coffin-shaped slab of hash browns. "We got through Des Moines before the morning rush, that's all I know. Des Moines. Jesus. Who in the hell thought that place was a good idea?"

Dad looked haggard and wan even by his own considerable standards of wear. His eyes were glass-shiny—no match for my own right orb, but still—and his hand shook as he reached for more coffee. I wondered how long he was going to be able to make it without sleep.

"We'll drive as long as we can," he said, looking directly at me as though listening in on my thoughts, a disconcerting habit of his. "Then we'll get a hotel tonight. But I'm going to need some help before then. Sam, you think you can drive a few hours while I catch a little shut-eye?"

"*Dad!*" Sam said, putting down her sausage biscuit.

Dad leveled her a stony, sober look, and Daniel and I ping-ponged back and forth between him and Sam. Dad wasn't letting on, but there seemed to be about a twenty-five-percent possibility that he was serious.

"Your legs are long enough to reach the pedals," he said, dipping his hash browns in ketchup. "And it's a standard transmission. Seriously, all you really need to do is point it in the direction you want to go and keep your eyes on the road."

"All right, fine," Sam said defiantly. "You're on. In fact, you know what? I'll drive the whole way. What do you say to that?"

"Hmm," Dad muttered appreciatively.

"So cool!" Daniel erupted. He had been busily employed with turning his pancakes and syrup into a revolting paste, but this new development so distracted him that he actually forked a big wad of it into his mouth and started to chew.

"Dad, you're not serious," Sam said.

"This is getting me to thinking." Dad leaned back and took in our fluorescent-sharp environment. "Why can't Sam drive the car? Why couldn't Kevin, I don't know, take the bus downtown on his own and go to a movie? We've *constricted* you children in this society. You're never allowed to do anything on your own."

"I don't want to," Daniel interjected, wide-eyed and obviously terrified by this sudden expansiveness on Dad's part.

"Sure you do!" Dad said, a little too loud for Sam. "I was just talking to Sam about this last night, even if she didn't want to listen. We all constrain each other too much. We assign each other these roles, and then insist that they play out in just the right way."

"Dad, don't start," Sam sighed.

"But why does it have to be this way?" Dad asked. "How much energy do your parents spend in keeping you acting like children? Who knows what you're really capable of?"

"Dad," Sam said, firmer.

"Who's to say we can't break out?" Dad held his hands up in front of him, curled as though wrapped around invisible prison bars. "We can be anything! We could get up in the morning and decide to be an entirely different person, if you really stop to think about it."

"That's enough, Dad," Sam said.

My father's eyes widened with sincere offense. "Sam, what is so obnoxious to you about what I'm saying? Don't you have any sense of *possibility?*"

"You're upsetting Daniel," she said.

Dad looked at my little brother. "Daniel is perfectly fine. Aren't you?"

"I don't know," Daniel said, his fork still churning his pancakes.

"All right, then," Sam said between tight lips. "You're upsetting *me*. All right? Will you stop now?"

"Sam, what is it?" Dad asked.

"Well, golly, Dad, I don't know," Sam barked. "Maybe it's because you're dragging us out of school and across the country—"

"I'll have us all back in—"

"Let me finish. You're dragging us across the country so that you can try to get your wife back. So that you can be a—"

"I don't have to—"

"So that you can be a husband and a father in a family again," Sam said, steely and cold. "So that things can be *normal*. So that you and everyone else can play these *roles* that you keep criticizing. We're coming with you, we're going to try to help you fix whatever it is you messed up, but I really don't need to listen to how *limiting* it is to be with us. Because Mom's the one who really seemed to have gotten that memo, don't you think? She isn't being *Mom* today, is she? Now there's someone who knows how to throw off these *constricting roles*."

That pretty well made a light breakfast impossible. Dad stared at Sam for a really long time with absolutely no expression on his face. An elderly couple in the booth across from us, who had listened to Sam's every word with horrified fascination, began to gather up their greasy wrappers and polish off their morning coffee. Daniel stared glumly into his pancakes. I don't remember doing much of anything, other than fervently wishing that none of this was happening or, at the very least, that I didn't look like a circus attraction (Cyclops Boy: A Tragic Tale of Perseverance).

"Well," Dad said sharply, as though concluding a round-table discussion on gun control or something. He managed to fold his arms and down his coffee in a single gesture, then fixed his gaze in the general direction of the front counter with a look of generic amiability.

"I'm sorry, Dad," Sam said, close to tears.

"These are trying times," Dad said, not looking at her. "Things get said, don't they? It's not like I can argue."

"Dad, I didn't mean anything." Sam's alabaster complexion had turned flushed; she reached across the table toward my father.

Dad got up from the table with a little groan; his knee popped. "Time to get back in the chariot," he said. "All matters will eventually be settled one way or the other."

"I'm not done!" Daniel protested.

"Everyone take a quick bathroom break," Dad said. "I want to get some serious miles behind us before we make our next pit stop."

"Dad, we can still turn around," Sam pleaded. "Maybe Mom will come back on her own."

Dad moved his jaw around thoughtfully and looked into the near distance, pondering what Sam had said. He gave a little appreciative nod, as though to acknowledge her optimistic sentiment, yet in the same instant dismissing the notion entirely.

"That's not the way this one is going to play out," he finally said. "Your mother is royally pissed at me. Too much has gone down."

"What do you even mean?" I asked. "You said last night that you and Mom don't even fight that much. So why did she go?"

I had seriously overplayed my hand, I realized at once. Dad looked at me as though I were a spy in his midst, and I saw that he realized I had been listening in on him and Sam a few hours before.

"There are some things that you won't understand until a lot later," Dad said to me. "If ever. You heard it here first, Kevin. Hate the game, don't hate the player."

And with that, he went outside to wait on us to finish going to the bathroom. He hadn't gone the entire time we were there, and he often went what seemed like days at a time without stopping to take a leak. It was one of those little things that made me wonder whether he was even human at all.

4

NOT BAD, BABY DOLL

BY THE TIME THE SUN WAS HIGH IN THE SKY WE HAD MADE it into northwest Missouri. I'd saved my placemat from Mickey D's (*can YOU find Mayor McCheese before the Hamburglar does? Shit,* I thought. *Who cares?*) and started inking down the names of the towns we passed through without stopping to see: Coffee, Winston, Kidder, Turney, Holt, Kearney. Far from inviting fantasies, the way little towns usually did for me, in the weekday autumn haze all I could make out were strip malls and fast-food joints, gas stations and drive-throughs. There was a sign announcing a turnoff for a Mormon Shrine, whatever that entailed, but there was no stopping Dad.

We had stepped squinting into the glare of a new order, and we all knew it. Whatever solidity our lives had had the day before, when we had talked about the Vietnam War in history class, and for lunch I'd had the burrito with rice, was now firmly in the category of the past. In the passage from Tuesday to Wednesday, none of us could ever again be the people we were. Everything that passed by outside my window seemed ephemeral and anemic, unaware that soon enough its glossy color would fade, that the tin and plastic would strip away, and the foundations erode to instability. I felt as though I alone was privy to some dark secret, but then I wasn't alone at all. All four of us in the car were surely thinking some version of the same thing.

"Who's up for a sea chantey?" my father roared after about fifteen minutes of stony silence.

"What's that?" Daniel asked.

"You know." Sam looked over the seat at us. "Yo ho ho and a bottle of rum. That kind of thing."

"Like SpongeBob?" asked Daniel.

Dad looked in the mirror for a second. He was weaving from lane to lane, driving uncharacteristically faster than the flow of traffic.

"Yar, matey!" he bellowed.

It only occurred to me much later that our trip to California was the product of a particular sort of intuitive genius that my father possessed in those days. It was probably the beginning of the end of that scary flame he evinced at times without warning, searing to the core of ideas or events and coming away with a truth that was greater than the sum of the information that was made available to him.

He had no firm evidence, for instance, that my mother had gone to her sister Alayne's house in Los Angeles. Much later I would find out that she had bought a ticket to LA on a credit card and had, in fact, never showed up for her ladies' night out with her friends (whether any of them were complicit remains behind the veil of adult secrecy). When the four of us were having pizza that night, Mom was clearing airport security and making her way to her gate. By the time Dad tucked us in, my mother was in the sky. Up, up, and away.

But none of this would become clear until later. For the moment all Dad had was my mother's admonishment not to come looking for her. Which, knowing Dad as she did, was pretty much a direct command that he *should* come looking for her, but I realize now that she was improvising in a difficult situation. I think she probably hoped Dad wasn't crazy enough to come after her, and that he would be bogged down sufficiently with the weight of the children to come to at least partial terms with her leaving him. It was a gamble, which was unlike her.

For his part, he had told us children more than once that he firmly believed that God *did* play dice with the universe. He also credited Einstein with re-establishing the primacy of a four-dimensional universe, with each moment everlasting, a secret he claimed was part of the New Testament and had been passed down to the rabbi Jesus in a line of knowledge originating in ancient Egypt. It was just the kind of thing you really didn't want to let him get started on. Most of the time he lived what could be considered a conventional and rational life, at least in public, but it was mostly out of obligations to family life rather than any real taste for normality.

For a time I figured that Dad had some piece of evidence, some trace of Mom's journey that led him to California. He had no such thing. He wanted to avoid Mom's sister Beth at all costs, for reasons that weren't clear to me, but he knew my mother was closer to her sisters than most. So Alayne it was. He apparently simply knew where to go.

My Dad's sea chantey idea didn't really take hold. The radio was playing country music, which was all that was available if you didn't want to listen to political

commentary—and thankfully my father didn't, because
once he became incensed about talk radio he would go on
for an eternity. It seemed like every other song was about
a couple breaking up. I wondered if my father noticed.

"I hate this music," Sam said. "Can I go on the record
as saying that I really, really, hate this music?"

"You shouldn't be so small-minded," Dad said, staring at the road.

"Small-minded!" Sam yelled. "Dad, this song is about
some guy's *pickup truck*. I'm the one who's small-minded?"

"I hate it, too!" Daniel piped up.

"What about you?" Dad asked, eyeing me in the mirror. I was growing to resent his ability to check up on me
any time he wished. And though I was struggling might-
ily not to think about it, the car was beginning to feel
oppressively small.

"I don't know," I said. "It's okay, I suppose."

"Country is a kind of soul music," Dad announced
to no one in particular. "You can trace its roots back to
the same source as R&B. You know, for a while black
people and white people made music together, then for
a while they didn't. Which is kind of sad. Now it feels
like people are coming together again, and that makes
me happy. I can't really relate to much of the new music
today, at least the pop stuff, but it feels like black people
and white people are in the same room again."

None of us was really listening. Daniel was industri-
ously mining his nose, which he had been doing all morning, rubbing what he produced into the carpeted space
between the car seat and the door. I would have preferred
he didn't, but I knew there was no stopping him.

"I'm bored," he said to me.

"There are no boring situations—" Dad began.

"Only boring people!" Daniel finished Dad's old and increasingly annoying pet saying for him, adding a frightening note of malevolence into his self-consciously bratty tone.

It was just the kind of outburst that would normally have provoked intervention from Mom; Dad's behavior practically invited insolence a lot of the time, but my mother was always quick to clamp down as part of her general campaign to protect his dignity. Instead Dad just looked sort of puzzled into the mirror at Daniel.

"Danny, Danny," he muttered meditatively.

The air inside the car was dry, which only seemed to further irritate my angry eye. By then every blink came accompanied with a raw scraping sensation, and the entire surface of my eye felt as though a sensitive layer had been scraped from it by a careless if not malignant surgeon.

"Do you think we ought to get Kevin to a clinic or something?" Sam asked Dad without looking at me.

My father was in the process of roaring past a semi; he held onto the steering wheel like a fighter pilot in a World War II movie.

"What kind of clinic?" Dad asked her. "A VD clinic? Kevin, is there something you need to tell me?"

"*Stop it*," Sam said. "I'm serious, Dad. His eye looks even worse than it did when he woke up. What if it gets infected? Mom's going to be really mad at us if we show up and Kevin's eye is hanging out, or if it spreads all over his face and leaves him *scarred* and *disfigured* for life."

"Shut up!" I smacked the headrest she was leaning against. I knew she was kidding, or at least I was almost certain she was, but more than anything I resented the little smirk she was wearing.

"Poor Kevin," she said, all mock-lachrymose. "I remember when he looked normal. Now no one can even stand to look at him."

"You ought to talk," I spat out at her. "Fat ass. I saw how you acted when we ran into David Glass at Rainbow. He doesn't give a shit about you, you know. No boys are even interested in you."

Sam stared at me over the headrest. I had amazed even myself, how quickly I had ramped up the atmosphere of sibling cruelty.

"*Hey*, now," Dad said. "That's too much. Sam, quit picking on your brother about his goop-eye. Kevin, apologize to Sam."

"I'm not going to!" I wailed. "She's the one—"

"Yes, she started it," Dad interrupted. "But you took it to an unacceptable level. That's what you need to apologize for."

"All right," I said. "Sam, I'm sorry you're a fat ass who no boy is ever going to like. I really am."

Sam launched a fist into the backseat. Dad said, "Whoa," and the car swerved in the passing lane. I easily dodged her fist, feeling absolutely horrible and sick inside. Sam settled back into her seat and Dad righted the ship. We traveled on in silence for a few miles.

Finally my father let out a big sigh. "Sam, you're a beautiful girl and you're going to be a beautiful young woman very soon," he said softly. "You know that, don't you? When have I ever lied to you?"

Sam said nothing, and from the way her head was turned to the side window I suspected that she was crying.

What I wanted to say, and what I of course couldn't possibly say, was that Sam was pretty much the epitome of female beauty in my eyes. Sure, she looked like Mom, with her big eyes and fine jawline. But Mom always joked that, in mating with my father, she had produced a far more aesthetically pleasing version of herself. Dad said the same thing about me; the jury was out on Daniel, whose pixie charms were impossible to speculatively project into his future manhood. Sam was somehow both delicate and strong, inviting and distant. Sometimes I would lose myself in her brown eyes, until she would notice me looking and I would have to insult her to cover up my adoration.

Dad had found some station on the radio that was playing rock songs from, presumably, the time he grew up. To my ears the music sounded grandiose, even vulgar, full of airs and ambitions that led people to places like this stuffy car.

I slipped forward in my seat and started snaking my hand through the space between the front seat and the door. I finally found Sam's form; she twitched in surprise, but allowed me to reach forward until I grasped her hand held low by her side. When I slid mine into hers, she squeezed back. For a fleeting moment, all was right in my world.

● ■ ●

At some point I must have fallen asleep. I came to with my eye crusted shut again, a sheen of oily sweat on my face, and a chill. I held my hand up in front of my face and saw that it was shaking.

"You don't look so hot," Daniel said, with a tone of

respect that verged on admiration.

His little video game was on the floor (I always found that those things produced, at best, about four hours of amusement before they instilled a feeling of worthlessness and self-loathing), and he held his huge spiral notebook on his lap, the one that contained hundreds of Pokémon and Digimon cards preserved in plastic sheets. The little cartoon monsters stared out from beneath their glossy covers, wearing expressions of mock fierceness that failed to conquer their innate cuteness, their intentionally created air of harmlessness.

I didn't feel so hot, come to think of it. My nose was clogged up, and a wire of pain ran from my sinuses through my eye socket to my right ear. The State Route signs still bore the marker of Iowa, but billboards had begun to advertise hotels and places to eat in Kansas; the border couldn't have been far off. I reached into the hatchback for my copy of *Total Baseball*, feeling a surge of righteous irritation that no one in the front seat contingent had bothered to notice my worsening condition.

With the giant brick of a book in my lap, I flipped to a random page. There in the middle was someone called Baby Doll Jacobson (born William Chester Jacobson, but once you're called Baby Doll, what are you going to do?). Born in Illinois in 1890, died there in 1977. He made his Major League debut on April 14, 1915. In an eleven-year career that seemed to encompass a few trips down to the minors, he ended up with 83 home runs and a .311 batting average. Not bad, Baby Doll.

I always imagined *Total Baseball* to be like the giant book St. Peter was supposed to consult when people arrived at the pearly gates. All your sins, all your good works, all your coveting and selfishness and selflessness would not only be there, they would be translated into incontrovertible stats. *Extramarital affairs: 5 contemplated, 2 attempted, 1 consummated, 1 time caught. Lies: 3,210 minor, 1,147 major, 587 times caught, 129 times caught without knowing.*

The sky outside had clouded up, all gray and washrag dingy. It came to me that this was the sort of sky reserved for the dispossessed, those consigned to in-between states, children of divorce. I knew other kids whose parents' marriages had either exploded violently or anemically deflated into nothing. Sometimes they had to endure the horror of horrors: stepparents. It wasn't always bad, of course, and sometimes in the initial flush of courtship—because the prospective stepparent was always in the unfortunate position of courting the children along with their mother or father—the whole situation looked like an upgrade: trade a surly semi-alcoholic for, say, a good-natured outdoorsman who liked to go out for ice cream. Such cases were always a little scandalous all around, and in my mind always forced the children to confront their hidden desire to be rid of one, or both, or their parents once and for all (it was the ultimate taboo, the way we both tremble and thrill at the thought of one another's deaths).

But like any new love, reality always set in. I had seen it more than once. The stepparent, often excited by the prospect of a ready-made family—that's if they were childless, if they had children of their own the situation was always impossibly complicated and dogged by constant negotiation—might leap in at first with the enthusiasm of an Irish setter plunging into a river on a hot day. But children were children: selfish, error-prone, raw

with the clay of what would someday become ossified
patterns of self-negation and defeat. And the adults were
on the other end of that hardening, unable to change,
packed thick with all the days behind them and living
out days now that they never thought would come. Ulti-
mately no one was ever all that much happier; they were
simply freed from an old arrangement and mired in the
disappointment of the new.

"You have a funny look on your face," Daniel said,
looking up from his cards.

"I was just thinking," I said.

"About what?"

"You don't want to know."

Daniel shrugged and returned to his perusal of
Charizard and Mewtwo. I planned to return to my
study of *Total Baseball* but, as was sometimes the case,
it was all too much for me. Poor Baby Doll Jacobson,
for instance. All that work and toil, all those optimistic
afternoons at the ballpark with the businessmen and the
children cheering as he stroked a clean drive down the
line, rounded first, and slid into second just in time to
beat the throw for a hit and an RBI. I imagined Baby
Doll, tall and handsome in my mind's eye, doffing his cap
humbly to the crowd, squinting into the outlines of the
future to come, with no idea that he would die in 1977.

I closed my eyes. It wasn't always like this. Sometimes
I would read about the tidy, compact career of a player
and marvel at how his feats had been preserved. Sure,
they were just lists of numbers, but they were there for
me to see. When Baby Doll stood up and brushed the
dust off his uniform after that sweet double, maybe for
an instant he could conceive that his exploits would be

remembered. Someone, in a car in Iowa almost a hundred years later, someone was thinking about Baby Doll. There. That felt better. I never talked to anyone about any of this stuff. Where would I start? Once or twice I started to talk to Dad about death, or God, but that would just set him off—it would be a good half an hour before he would calm down enough to let me say anything. I wondered all the time whether I was going to end up like him someday, once I was big enough that there was no one around to talk over me. Maybe all of these thoughts were just going to come spewing out and, like my father, I would turn into an interesting bore.

"Well, did you?" Sam was asking in a low but insistent voice. I realized that they thought I was asleep. Daniel was so engrossed in his own fantasy world that he was paying no attention at all to what was going on around him. Or at least that's how it looked.

"God, Sam, you know, you can really be inappropriate sometimes," Dad replied, his voice barely above a murmur. "Have I ever told you that? I mean, I am your *father,* for chrissakes. There are certain lines we shall not cross. And all that."

"When it comes to being inappropriate, let's just say I learned from the master," Sam replied. "So come on, tell me. *Did* you?"

"I did not. My heart has not always been true, but no. Not that."

A beat of quiet. A few splatters of rain on the windshield. My father busied himself with setting the windshield wipers' speed, as though we hadn't had the car for almost ten years and he hadn't set them hundreds of times before.

"You have to be careful about what questions you ask, though," Dad added. "You know that I'm pretty much constitutionally unable to lie to you and the boys. By the way, is Kevin asleep?"

"He's out of it," she replied conspiratorially.

I opened my one working eye into a squint and saw her face, in profile, with her full lips set in an angry pout.

"What do you mean about not being true in your heart?" she asked pointedly. "What does *that* mean?"

"Sam, I am realizing that I have made a huge strategic error in even answering your little question," Dad told her. "But I have to admit, you staged such an effective and relentless assault that you finally wore down my defenses."

"Don't dodge, Dad."

"I'm actually being quite sincere," he continued. "Have you ever thought about a career in the law? I'll bet you could really devastate someone on the witness stand. You just did a real number on me. Sure, I'm a little distracted, what with keeping my eye on the road, and with part of my mind preoccupied with my wife leaving me, but boy howdy you really got inside my defenses."

"Oh, shut up," Sam hissed.

"On second thought, scratch that," Dad said with great conviction. "I know a few lawyers. Almost all of them hate it, wish they'd done something else with their lives. They go through school for three years, land a good job for a lot of money, and within a few years they feel like they're spending their days in a cage. Like a little parakeet, except the bars of the cage are made of gold. One thing's for sure, Baby Doll, when someone pays you a lot of money, they expect a lot in return. They pretty much expect you to give your life and your mental well-being for that fat paycheck. Not that I've ever experienced anything like that, of course."

I tried hard not to react. I had never heard my father call anyone "Baby Doll" before.

"You know, Dad, it's thanks to growing up in this family that I had to learn the meaning of the word *fili-buster* at a very early age."

Dad laughed. "But it's such an effective strategy when you really, really, really don't want to deal with something."

It had started raining harder. My father tightened his grip on the steering wheel. I watched the back of his head through a constricted eyelid. Though I couldn't see his face, I could see the outline of his jaw working as though he was chewing gum. And he never chewed gum.

"Whatever I mean, nothing like that has any bearing on the current situation," my father told my sister. "You'll have to take that on faith. And now that I've revealed the secrets of my life to you, I hope you'll respect me enough—and sufficiently value my future prospects of happiness—to please, please keep this conversation to yourself forever."

"Okay, Dad," Sam said, looking right at him, nodding slightly.

"Thank you," he replied curtly. "And here our open question-and-answer session comes to a lovely conclusion," Dad said, turning up the radio. I didn't know the song, but I knew the singer was Mick Jagger. Dad, predictably, had very strong opinions on Mick Jagger.

"This is back when he was good," Dad said to Sam, as though they had been conversing on the history of pop culture rather than the deep mysteries of adulthood and marriage. "Long time ago."

"What about Mom?" Sam asked.

My father turned his head, not looking at Sam, still focusing on the road but seeming to peer into some acutely unpleasant space of ideas. For a second he actually bared his teeth, then started raking his hair with one hand. When he stopped, the whole mane was standing straight up in the air, even brushing against the roof of the car.

"Can you imagine playing pretty much the same, let's say, six or seven songs over and over for *forty fucking years?*" Dad said to no one. "Jitterbugging around onstage, looking over as Keith Richards dies and doesn't know it yet, he just keeps cranking out those same half-dozen riffs while his face rots right off his skull. Mick smiles for the camera, all those thousands of flashbulbs over the years, he goes from king of the world to total hack to old-timer, never really showing a hint of embarrassment. I wonder, does he ever get embarrassed?"

"Dad, no one cares about Mick Jagger except people your age," Sam informed him. "You're probably the only person left in America who even notices when they put out a new CD."

"True," Dad allowed.

"What about Mom, Dad?" Sam asked. "She's been having lunch with that business guy. Elliot."

"You'll see," my father interrupted. "You'll have your turn. You'll listen to all those songs, you'll have all these experiences, and they'll be so wonderful, Sam. Everything is going to mean so much to you the next few years. There are going to be times when you really will feel as

though you're walking on clouds. There's a reason someone invented that cliché, Sam. There are times when you
feel that way."

"Dad, who—"

"But then it stops, Sam," Dad continued. "I don't
want to be the one to tell you this, but you need to at least
try to understand me. It stops. You don't walk on clouds
anymore. You walk on the ground. And your feet hurt
all the time. And when people look at you, they don't
see possibility. They just see this person who has become
pretty much all he's ever going to be. And sadly enough,
it ain't much."

"All right, Dad, don't answer me," Sam said, turning
to look out the windshield. The rain was really pelting
us now, the sky was as dark as night, and the windshield
wipers were slapping in their Sisyphean toil.

"And then someday you'll listen to that same song
that used to move you to tears, the one that perfectly
captured all you wanted to be, all the perfect things you
desired and thought you could have," Dad said, apparently to himself. "And that song really won't mean much
anymore. It'll sound trite and clichéd. And what's worse,
you'll try to remember exactly what it was that made that
song so important. But you won't be able to. It just sounds
like some idiot singing about something that doesn't
really matter."

"All right, Dad, I *get* it," Sam said, trying to shut him
up now.

"And if you're fortunate enough to have children,"
he went on, "and I really sincerely do mean *fortunate*, in
the most profoundest sense, but then your children will
be with you someday when that song comes on, and you

know what they'll say?"

"I don't know, Dad," Sam said.

"They'll say: *turn that down, please.*"

Dad reached out and turned down the radio, shifting in his seat. I looked over at Daniel with my one good eye. He was rapt with attention. He had been listening to the whole thing.

5

I JUST WISH SOMEONE, SOMEWHERE...

WE MADE A COUPLE OF QUICK STOPS THAT DAY IN DEFERENCE to the size of our childhood bladders—Dad, I was thankful to see, twice sidled up to a urinal and let fly, thus assuring me of his mortal status—but we pretty much kept booming along. The rain showers of the morning lifted, or else we simply outdistanced them, and we skirted the edge of Kansas City under a murky pall. I felt sick, although not in an entirely disagreeable way, and Sam in the front seat had fallen into one of her prolonged sulks. Daniel had wrung all the fascination he could out of his Pokémon cards and stared slack-jawed out the window at the flat, unchanging landscape.

I had found a pretty comfortable position, wedged against the car door with my head pressed against the window. My good eye took in things passing by without the benefit of a wider view: rather than the particulars of the farms and oases of settlement, I simply saw shapes and blotches of indistinct color. It was a superior way of taking in the world, I thought, though I was unsettled by the dampness of my clothes against my skin.

Dad had put a CD into the car stereo and was singing

along with a man's voice accompanied by spare drums and keyboards.

"Yeah, that was a long, long time ago," he sang in his sonorous baritone. I secretly loved the sound of my father's voice, though I knew I should never encourage his singing. With a little encouragement, his renditions of Doors tunes in the shower would have turned into an unstoppable all-day vocal marathon.

And as soon as I thought that, he stopped singing and looked at me in the rearview mirror. I started to say something to him, to stop the force of that stare, but he glanced back at something beyond me and flipped on the turn signal to pass a creaky-looking Ford. We had been passing people all day, Dad moving just a bit faster than the flow of traffic.

When we were back in the right lane, his shoulders slumped and he leaned back in the driver's seat. A long silence passed, in which the four of us rocked gently to the road's rhythm, our heads bobbling and slightly lolling as one.

"God damn it," Dad said softly. "I am such an asshole. Why did you have to make me such an asshole?"

No one said anything. I never knew to whom Dad was talking at times such as this. I was almost certain that it wasn't God; while not exactly an unbeliever, my father's understanding of the metaphysical, at least as much as he shared it with me and my siblings, was so amorphous and nonlinear as to preclude any direct contact with anything as specific as a deity. But there were times when he would address *something*, some reality beyond himself, as though it was listening. It made me feel sort of lonely, and I wished he would talk to me instead.

"I wanted to quit," he was saying. Sam had her arms folded around herself and made no sign of having heard him. "But no. Glenn can't quit. Have to see the game through to the end. She's making damn sure of that."

"Right *next to me*," Dad sang along to the stereo as a bass rumbled and drums tattooed a sullen beat.

"You are my friend," Dad sang, his head moving from side to side. "This is not what I intended to do."

My father used to tell me that no man is an island. We're more like atolls, he would add. I never knew what the hell he meant, except that it had to do with that private space he was into now as he drove, looking at things from across a distance that precluded any normal means of communication. Even then I wished that I didn't understand him so well, because it made me conscious of how little I truly knew myself.

"Here's the proposal before the committee," my father said. He waited for a moment. None of us stirred.

"Guys? Are you listening?" he asked.

Sam sat up and stretched her arms as much as she could; though we had all done a pretty good job of not mentioning it so far, the Subaru was becoming increasingly claustrophobic and smelly.

"What did you say, Dad?" Sam asked in a listless voice. "I thought you were just continuing your charming monologue-slash-karaoke performance."

"Nice," my father said to her. "A guy provides entertainment for free, and all he gets is criticism. You'll be sorry after you leave home and have to do without my steady stream of illuminating patter."

Sam gave Dad a warm smile. "I guess it's one of those things I'll have to discover on my own," she said.

"Life's little tragedies." Dad turned and glanced back at Daniel and me. "Anyway, I was saying. I have a proposal. I saw a sign that there's someplace to eat a few miles up the road. What say we take a body break, hit the can and refuel, then we can get a few more hours behind us before we bunk for the night?"

My father's voice sounded hoarse and strange, and I was reminded that he hadn't slept the night before.

"Maybe we should call it a day," I said. "I haven't said anything, but I don't feel so hot."

Dad made a little cluck of sympathy that instantly let me know that my suggestion had been filed away like an unread letter to the editor.

"You've just got a little bug," he told me. "Best thing for you is food and rest. And what better place to take one's repose than a steel projectile moving across America at seventy miles per hour? I tell you, son, it's positively restorative!"

"I'm feeling better by the minute," I said.

"I'm hungry," Daniel moaned. "I want to stop."

"The smallest among us offers the greatest wisdom," Dad said. "Let's stop and eat some good ol' fashioned deep-fried American bullshit."

Dad's mood elevated as soon as we took the off-ramp; we were someplace just past Topeka on Interstate 70, and habitation was rapidly dwindling. My father ostensibly hated eating at chain joints when we were on the road, decrying the homogeneity they fostered and the general dumbing down of our world (though he could scarf Taco Bell and Mickey D's like a competitive eating champion when he saw fit). Here was just the kind of place he was always trying to find: a little one-story diner with a pair of gas pumps in front.

"Now, here we go," he muttered with satisfaction as we pulled across the gravel parking lot. "A clean, well-lit place. Pump a little money into the local economy, blow a few minds. Don't hide your natural brilliance, kids, they'll be talking about you guys as the stuff of legends for decades to come."

I wasn't sure how ironic Dad was being, given the sight that met my one working eye in the reflection off the one-story diner's big glass window. Sam's hair hung lank and stringy over her puffy features, I was a picture of walking illness, and Daniel was bent over at the waist like a wizened old man. Not that Dad looked any better: his shirt was wrinkled and creased with road sweat, and his hair had moved past disheveled into another category entirely. We looked like a contingent of prisoners about to be put away into a cell and forgotten.

"Dad, your fly's undone," Sam said, taking in the same picture as me.

"Jesus," Dad said, jerking and reaching for his crotch. "Flashing Kansas for the last two hundred miles. It's a wonder they still let me roam free."

"I'm hungry," said Daniel, his posture one of profound defeat. He squinted into the window glass. I made out a couple of faces inside checking us out.

"Well, I think you're in the right place," Dad said, patting my brother on the shoulder. "I don't know about you guys, but I am filled with the most profound sense of *optimism* right now. I have a premonition. Mark it down. A week from now, this will be one of the colorful stories we recount as we revel in our restored domestic bliss. Someday all of this will be so *funny*."

"Ha ha," Sam said over her shoulder as she opened the door to go inside. I had no idea what time it was; though the rains were gone, the sun was invisible behind monolithic clouds. It could have been early afternoon, or it could have been dinnertime. It really didn't matter.

Inside it was half-full. Booths lined the walls on two sides, and there were dark wooden tables arranged in a grid in the middle of the floor. The sign read, "Seat yourself," and Sam led the way to a booth in the back. I slid in beside her, leaving Daniel to sit beside Dad.

Our waitress was young, and improbably pretty. She was wearing an old-fashioned white-and-blue-striped dress and an apron tied around her waist. Dad beamed at her, transparently falling in love the way he always did with pretty young girls. To his credit, there was nothing malignant or lecherous about it.

"Afternoon," she said in an incongruent, husky voice. "Can I get you all something to drink?"

"Iced tea would be a small miracle," Dad said, not taking his eyes off hers. She returned his smile and gave him a little turn of her head by way of silent reproof, as though deflecting his attention was part of a fun game the two of them would be playing as long as we were there.

"And you kids?" she asked, speaking to Dad, the gatekeeper of all things treat-oriented.

"Get whatever you guys want," he said to us, still looking at her. "We're on the road. Order something you wouldn't normally have."

"I'll take a coffee," Sam said.

"*Except* caffeine," Dad hastily corrected himself. "We've got some time yet to spend in the car today. Can't have you bouncing out the window on the interstate or composing an opera or anything."

Our waitress gave Dad a funny look, still amused with him but obviously unsure how long a leash to give him.

"Chocolate milk," Daniel pronounced as though it pained him to do so.

"Sprite," Sam said.

"Can I have some orange juice?" I asked. Whenever I was sick, Mom always pushed the orange juice and its virtuous vitamin C. Now that I was out of the car, it was apparent to me that not all was right in the neighborhood of my body. The joints in my knees ached, and my breath passed through a gauzy clog somewhere high up between my eyes. As for my affected eye, the less said the better: it felt like an open sore, and the thought of it was enough to diminish my appetite.

"You all right, honey?" the waitress asked. She had curly dark hair pulled back from her face and dark eyes that flashed with concern and an evident sense of intelligence. I wondered how she found herself at such a remote outpost. Had she been born there? Was she running away from something or, like us, trying to run *to* something?

"I think I'm okay," I said, for some reason feeling that it was very important I put her at her ease.

"What's your name?" Dad asked her.

She pondered his request for a moment, transparently unsure how deep she wanted to wade into our family waters. Sam had yet to even look at her, pretending instead to be engrossed in a laminated menu that she pulled from a little steel ring. Daniel had retreated entirely into some pre-verbal zone of little-boy misery, staring at the table with his bottom lip protruding and slack.

"Jan," she finally said.

"I'm Glenn," my father said, then proceeded to introduce each of us children. Jan listened politely, a little intrigued by us all, surely curious where our mother was. If I had been older I would have checked to see if she was wearing a ring, or whether she glanced while pretending not to at my father's hand to see if he was. He was, of course, wearing a plain silvery band. The question flashed across my mind: would he take it off if Mom didn't come back?

"Nice to meet you all," Jan said. "You ready to order now, or should I bring you drinks and give you time to look at the menu?"

"We'll need a minute." Dad stiffened at Jan's slight hint of distancing herself from us. I caught her staring at my face for just a moment too long, unable to tear herself away from the disgusting picture I presented to the world.

"I love this place," my father said as he examined the single-sided menu. "I'll have to *thank* your mother for leaving me, when I see her. If she hadn't, I'd never have discovered . . ."

Dad flipped the menu over, saw a blank page, turned it back to the front. He widened his eyes theatrically and read aloud: "Heaven's Hideaway. Where the burgers are hot and the pop is ice cold."

My father let out a little laugh that indicated this was either the most brilliant sentiment he had ever encountered, or else the stupidest.

"So what'll you guys have?" Dad tapped the menu on the table. "I'm paying with a credit card, so order whatever you want."

"Chicken salad," Sam said, staring at the wall. I flashed

back, quite horribly, on having told her she was fat.

"Chicken strips," Daniel said in a monotone. He always ordered chicken strips, and probably could have subsisted solely upon them well into adulthood.

I glanced around at random on the menu, not really hungry but not in the mood to sit and watch the others eat without having something of my own to do.

"Spaghetti and meatballs," I read, the first thing I saw.

"Italian," my father said with approval. "Very provocative. *Daring*, even. You have always been the culinary outlaw of my three children."

I knew he wanted me to try to say something funny in reply, but I wasn't feeling remotely amused, or amusing. It occurred to me that an entire school day had gone by without me, which wasn't the most painful thought in the world, but it also meant that I had missed my favorite time of the day: after school, when I was allowed to eat snacks and watch TV, even if it meant hanging out with Daniel. Mom would get home from work, Dad would more often than not be holed up in his office working on something. Sam would come back from hanging out with her friends just in time for dinner. All the interwoven textures, even of things that I had thought at the time I didn't like, or didn't care about, now seemed infinitely precious and impossibly lost.

There was no way Dad was getting Mom back. Things like that never happened in our family. It was just that none of us had the courage, or the cruelty, to tell him so.

Dad ordered our food for us and tapped on the table, his fatigue having passed over into nervous energy. He cast his glance this way and that, taking in an elderly couple, a trucker eating alone (I had seen his customized cab in the parking lot, with airbrushed letters on the side reading, "All For Willa"), a couple of middle-aged women absorbed deep in conversation.

"This place is a dump," Sam pronounced.

"Hey hey!" Dad said, looking in the direction of the kitchen. "Don't let anyone hear you say that. They'll probably put rat poison in our food."

"Rat poison!" Daniel said in alarm.

Dad clamped a hand over Daniel's mouth. "Just a joke, son," he said. "Nothing to worry about. I'll bet they have the yummiest chicken strips in Kansas."

"I can't even describe how much this sucks," Sam said, not looking at any of us. "You said you were going to call and get our homework assignments for us. Do you *remember* that, Dad? I haven't seen you on the phone today. Are you going to get our homework from your psychic powers or something?"

"Don't knock the psychic powers," Dad said. "But no, you're right. I'll call your schools in the morning."

"Did you even bring your cell phone, Dad?" Sam said, more pleading than scolding now.

My father was notorious for under-use of his phone. He owned one, but almost never used it. It was hopeless to think of ever reaching him on it, or him answering a text. Mom was constantly complaining that her life would have been so much easier if Dad would make the most basic accommodation to being reachable.

"It's . . . I'm pretty sure it's in my briefcase somewhere," Dad stammered. "I'll try to fish it out when we stop for the night."

"*God,* Dad," Sam said with bottomless disgust.

"Look, don't give me any *shit*," Dad growled, his voice quiet but unmistakably tinged with spitfire menace. "I'm not going to tolerate any fucking *attitude*. Not right now. Is that clear?"

"Yes, *Donald Trump*," Sam whispered back in an identical tone of seething rage.

The two of them together were *really* something sometimes.

Jan brought us our drinks. My orange juice was clearly from concentrate though, to be fair, we were a long way from any orange grove. Outside the front window the sky was resiliently sullen, and on the other side of the freeway entrance I saw the ruin of a one-room shack with a big sign out in front: *FIREWORKS*.

"I want to go home," Daniel said quietly.

"Well, then!" Dad pronounced. "Soon enough, my boy. Let's stay on mission here. Pick up Mom, take her home. This weekend I'll take us all out to dinner at one of those Mexican joints on Lake Street."

Sam gave my father a pitying look.

"Anyway," he said, turning away from her, "Wednesday in Kansas. What could be finer? It's like an advertisement for bliss."

"Don't be so nervous," Sam told him.

Dad gave her a nod of acknowledgment; he had been working his chin back and forth, and his shining eyes glared with even more force than usual. At home when he got like this, he was prone to explosions of irritation. I always had the sense that he was locked into some signal that burned him up with its intensity, a flow of information tenuous to grasp and which left him drained and on the verge of snapping whenever the mundane world intruded and blocked the signal. My father tended to give the impression of a man with a lot on his mind.

"I want to talk to Mom," Daniel said. "Daddy, can we call Mom on the phone? I miss her."

"Listen, Danny—" Dad began.

"Daniel, cut it out," Sam broke in. "It's too expensive to call long distance while we're traveling. Right, Dad?"

My father looked on his oldest child with a mix of suspicion and profound respect. "Listen to your sister, Danny."

"Hang tough," I told Daniel. "We'll be in California before you know it."

It would take more than this to dissuade Daniel from his little-boy bout of depression, but he had done enough time in our family to recognize that this was about as much indulgence as he was going to receive. He went ahead and lapsed into silence, thinking whatever he needed to get him by.

Dad had a little grin on his face, and his attention was focused somewhere over my shoulder. I figured Jan was lingering someplace in her heartland sumptuousness, but when I turned to look I was surprised to spot a stocky couple with two children in a double stroller. They were immersed in the fussy process of transferring the kids from their mobile perch into booster seats in a booth down the way. They took no notice of us at all.

"Come on," Dad said to me, for no reason I could discern. "Let's go say hi."

"I don't want to," I instantly replied.

"Don't be a wet blanket," Dad said. "We're *here*. Let's not just sit and pretend otherwise."

"Dad, those people don't need us bothering them," I said.

But he was up and out of his seat. He tugged on the arm of my shirt, and by the force of his will I was up and moving past a few open booths to where the young family was still immersed in trying to set up camp.

The mother seemed impossibly stolid, though she was probably only about twenty-five, thick in the middle in a denim jumper with straight blond hair parted halfway. She spotted us coming first, and gave a wary smile.

"Howdy," Dad said. "You guys need any help? I'm an old hand with the little ones."

The father of the family offered up an expression that would have served equally well had Dad walked up and, say, announced that he was the Pope and wished to convert them to the Church of Rome. He was chunky but big in the chest, in jean shorts, a plain golf shirt, and a baseball cap advertising Branson, Missouri (a cultural signifier I would come to understand only much later). He had a thick brown goatee that only partly sharpened his big broad features.

"I think we have it under control, Mister," said the dad. To my mind, it was a pretty clear signal to fuck off, but my father was having none of it.

"Beautiful children," Dad said. "So, how far apart are they?"

"Pardon?" the man said, half-standing still, unwilling to sit down all the way and cede the fighting edge to this lunatic who had accosted them in this roadside diner.

"In age," said Dad. "They seem to be close in age."

Well, Dad was right. The little girl, the older one, was about three or so. The little brother, all sandy blond curls and spittle, stood up in his booster seat like a new walker.

"Two years almost exactly," the dad said tersely.

"I have three myself." Dad leaned onto the edge of

the booth, an intimacy that clearly unnerved both parents. "Thirteen, ten, and six. This here's my boy, Kevin."

The dad stared for a little while at my eye, then
glanced nervously at his children.

"It's just pink eye," I said. "It's contagious, but I won't
touch anyone."

Precisely how it had come to this, with me in the middle of Kansas pledging not to spread my leprous touch,
was not a question beyond my asking. But Dad was right
back on the train, leaving me to catch up.

"Where are you folks from?" he asked the couple.

"Just outside of St. Louis," the mother said brightly.
She had pretty green eyes and an open, kind way about
her that sprang forth probably without her even knowing
it. I sensed her husband stiffen, as though he feared that
we were a band of family murderers who would come for
them now that we knew what city they called home.

"We're from Minneapolis," Dad told her. "Heading
out to California."

"How neat!" the mom said. "Family vacation?"

She peered over to where Sam and Daniel sat, scan-
ning for her equivalent and giving a look of concern
when she found none.

"Afraid not," Dad said. "A little family trouble. Some
things to work out."

"Oh," she said. "Nothing too serious, I hope."

The father shot her a pained look to indicate that she
shouldn't encourage this interaction to go much further;
he pulled out menus from the steel ring and passed one
across the table to her.

"We'll see," Dad said. "We'll see. So where are you
folks headed?"

"Tucson," the father said, looking at us with a pained expression. He slid all the way into the booth, visibly discomfited by having my father leaning over him.

"Visiting family?" Dad asked.

"Her mother," the other man said.

"Super." Dad grinned at them all as though they were a paradigm of some perfection that only he could properly appreciate.

"She's been sick," the woman said, leaning over her son to stop him from grabbing the place setting in front of him.

"I'm sorry to hear that," Dad said.

"Well, the kids really cheer her up," the mom offered optimistically.

"They do that," Dad agreed.

The father passed his daughter a baggie containing a passel of chewed-up crayons, then flipped over the paper placemat so that she could doodle on it. She showed no interest at all in my father or me, instead nicely lodged in her own private reality.

"Mister, is there something I can help you with?" the father asked suddenly, adjusting his ball cap and chewing his lower lip with surprising nervousness. His wife shot him a look of reproach and embarrassment. I sensed that Dad, tall, wiry, oozing with an inexplicable need for engagement, was a figure somewhere between amusement and trepidation in their estimation; whatever their own narrative of the day, his entrance into it was unscripted and not particularly welcome.

"Well, you see, it's like this," Dad began.

"We just want to have lunch," the dad explained. "I don't know what you—"

"Oh, God, listen, I don't mean to *bother* you," Dad said hastily, straightening up, suddenly aware of how much he was invading their space.

"It's no bother," the mom said brightly.

"It's just that I looked over and saw you, all four of you," Dad said. He glanced up at the arrival of Jan, who had her waitress ordering pad in one hand and a slightly disturbed look on her face. "And I just had this feeling like, like, you know, we're all in this together."

"Come again?" the father asked.

"Parents. Families." Dad was starting to stumble now, and I felt a deep ache as a look of self-realization came over him. Jan was staring, not entirely unsympathetic, but now both she and the parents were waiting for him to explain himself.

"You see, your children get older on you," Dad said haltingly. "One day you feel as though all they do is take, but then all of a sudden you realize how much they're giving you. The balance turns, you see."

"That's sweet," the mother said. The father gave a sigh.

"But the *point* is," Dad clapped his hands together; the pair of middle-aged ladies across the room stopped talking and looked at us. Dad gave an embarrassed laugh. "Look, I'll tell you the truth. I was sitting over there with my children when I watched you all come in. And I felt this tremendous *love* for you."

"Mister, I don't—" the father tried to interrupt, in visible agony now.

"Nothing creepy," Dad tried to assure them, semi-successfully. "It's just that I was your age once, and my kids were the same age as your kids, and I spent a lot of my time worrying, and obsessing, and thinking that everything was just so goddamned *difficult*, you know?"

Now the mother was staring at my father with her mouth slightly open. She gave an almost imperceptible nod.

"And I just wish someone, somewhere, would have come up to me like I'm doing now." Dad was speaking quickly now, obviously wanting this to be done with as much as anyone else. Jan was giving him a sad-eyed look. "And told me that everything's *all right*, you know? This is a time of your life that you'll ache to have back someday. Don't ever think your life is anything but beautiful and miraculous. Don't feel bad about anything."

I had gone from my usual level of discomfort with my father to vivid and searing levels of mortification. I truly and genuinely wondered if this was it, if the authorities were going to intervene, if Mom was going to have to travel to rural Kansas to take us home, with Dad locked away and medicated forever.

"I know how much you love your children," Dad added, as though this thought would solve a thorny puzzle they had all been working on together. "Try to love each other, too. Try to *remember* what you are. Don't let it . . . I don't know, don't let it slip away on you. You can see beauty or you can see pain. That's pretty much it. It's all a matter of what you decide to focus on."

"Dad," I said.

Dad was leaning on the back of the booth again. The family father was staring at his wife, his expression entirely unreadable.

"That feeling of being in love, of being young," Dad said, not looking at anyone, relaxed and dreamy. "Your children can keep that alive in you. Even when everything else seems like it's turning to shit."

"Hey," Jan said, putting a hand on my father's shoulder. Pretty much everyone was looking at us now. A mustachioed man stuck his head out between the swinging doors that presumably led to the kitchen, a wary look on his face.

"And don't worry about them." Dad nodded at the two little children; the boy looked up, unsure what to think. "They're old, older than us. We're young; we don't know anything. We forgot everything they know. All you can do is try to cushion the blow when they become more like us."

It was all too much. The man slid out of the booth, holding up a hand to silence his wife, who began to offer a word of protest, or caution.

"Mister," the man began. He stood several inches shorter than my father, though he was probably about fifty pounds heavier.

"I'm sorry about all this," Dad was saying. "It's just that I feel very *sincere*. I really do wish someone had come up to me years ago. Told me not to be such a schmuck. To see the beauty right in front of my face."

"Jesus, man," the father said. And, to my utter shock and astonishment, I saw that his eyes were moist and red-dened.

"I'm going to stop bothering you now," Dad said, trying to laugh.

I stood there, vivid with social pain, as the most awful and lamentable thing possible occurred: the dad opened up his arms and took my dad in his.

"I'm really sorry for whatever's happening to you," the man said. His wife put her hand over her mouth. "Be strong, brother. You can make it all right."

"I'm going to try," my father said in a breathy voice, as his counterpart squeezed him tight. Then the guy released him.

"Now we need to order our food," the man said, clapping my father on the shoulder.

Nothing much else happened until we left. My spaghetti was watery. Daniel barely touched his chicken strips. Dad stared down pretty much the entire time, thinking thoughts that were profoundly unknowable to me.

6

SO YOU THINK YOU'RE FINE FOR A WHILE

THE REMAINDER OF THE DAY UNFOLDED WITH EACH NEW moment like a fresh disappointment. Kansas was crushing. The interstate bisected the landscape like a ribbon around a shabby and unwanted present. The sky was an upended bowl glazed by a jaded and indifferent potter who couldn't be bothered to add any interesting features. The mood in the car, in other words, was less than entirely optimistic.

Anyone living out family life is familiar with how difficult it is at times to come up with anything to say to one another. Take five humans and place them together for years on end, their mutual isolation broken only by frenetic and charged experiences they can't really properly process, much less share. Place them together, say, at a table, or in the cramped confines of a short station wagon, and what can they really come up with? The truth is that they (especially siblings, at the time I couldn't speak for a husband and wife) spend so much of their time selfishly carving away at the marble block of reality, sculpting a private reality away from the judgments and ridicule of those with whom fate placed them in the same boat.

The unspoken goal of course—for me and Sam, at least, I could never be sure about Daniel—was to one day *no longer be a child*. I was hazy on the details, but transcending childhood meant putting together a team of one's own choosing, serving one's sentence with a cast assembled by virtue of their attributes rather than by chance. It was a nice incentive for sticking around and playing the game— though of course there wasn't much choice, at ten years old, which was both deeply comforting and profoundly frustrating. Though looking up at Dad's weary head in the driver's seat, it was disturbingly clear how wrong the entire project of adulthood could go.

I played out the last several weeks of our family's life in my mind as the miles went numbingly past. I scoured through my recent memories like a detective, thinking there must have been cracks in the foundation somewhere that I had previously overlooked. I was getting pretty feverish by that point, and increasingly prone to retreat into fantasy because of the chronic burn in my eye and, to a lesser degree, my sinuses and my ear.

Pictures: Dad and Mom in the kitchen. Him chopping up cilantro, her in her skirt and buttoned-up shirt from work. They talk, he looks up and smiles. She has her arms folded, preoccupied. Dad is talking in that way of his, as though he's angry at the person he's talking to. It takes a connoisseur of Dad to know that he's looking for commiseration, someone to share in his outrage at the stupidity of the world. Dad was always looking for co-conspirators. Now that I thought about it, Mom didn't really play the part all that often. She looked as though she was waiting for him to stop talking, so that she could move on to something in which she was really interested.

Mom watering the garden. A weekend. She is dressed in jeans and a long-sleeved knit shirt. Her long straight brown hair is tied up behind her neck. She has a smallish nose and narrow lips that are frequently pursed in an impatient expression: impatient with us children, impatient with Glenn. Daniel is asking her something. She listens patiently, says something kind that only they can hear.

I hadn't seen my mother in about twenty-four hours, and I unequivocally missed her. I missed the way she tied things together, the kindness in her eyes, the way she would always take an extra moment before replying to my questions, as though really thinking, as though I was valuable enough to merit more than a flip response. I missed the way she would put her hand on the back of my neck when we were standing side by side, her touch warm and assuring, her devotion absolute.

It wasn't lost on me (I don't know about the others) that being a child in a family entailed some portion of the responsibility for my parents continuing to live their lives together. I'm not sure when the realization hit, but I knew there were times when my parents were holding back around each other, one eye cast on us children, knowing we were watching. But I had always assumed something else was going on behind the scenes—and this was such an enormous part of childhood, all the things taking place offstage, all the deleted scenes that would have made the greater narrative make sense if we were only permitted to watch them—that also held it all together in its imperfect entirety. I assumed that my parents would always love each other, no matter what, and that by the time they got old and died I would have my life sorted out, a forged solidity all my own that would enable me to bear the unthinkable end.

Dad was no longer even listening to the radio. Sam was reading some magazine we picked up the last time we stopped for gas. Daniel was staring out the window, looking vaguely traumatized, and the relentless landscape went past like the unchanging backdrop of a cheap cartoon.

"I think *The Day After* was set someplace out here," Dad said, shattering the silence as though we had been talking the whole time.

Sam and Daniel ignored him, so his eyes sought out mine in the rearview mirror; he had an expectant look on his face that was somewhere between a grimace and a friendly entreaty.

"What?" I asked.

"*The Day After*," Dad repeated. "Do you know *The Day After?*"

"The day after what?" I asked.

"Yeah, you're too young," Dad replied.

"How about the day after you take us back home?" Sam said brightly, without looking up from her magazine.

My father appraised her with an expression of wary respect. Then he looked back at me in the mirror.

"It was a TV show," he explained. "Not a series, but a one-shot movie. It took place out here in Kansas, in some small city. I don't remember which one."

"What was it about?" I asked, suddenly quite relieved to be out of the maze of my thoughts.

"A nuclear strike," Dad said cheerily. "Someone, probably the Russians, but I don't really remember, dropped a nuclear bomb on some city. Naturally everyone in the immediate blast was incinerated, but the movie depicted the people who were far enough away to survive but were completely riddled with radiation."

"What's radiation?" Daniel asked, sitting up.

"From atoms," I said. Daniel looked at me blankly.

"When you detonate an atomic bomb, it destroys everything within a certain radius," Dad explained. He slowed slightly as another car pulled into the right lane just ahead of us. "But it spreads this stuff you can't see. Stuff that makes you sick. And it doesn't happen right away, so you think you're fine for a while. But then your hair starts falling out, and you start losing weight. After a while, you die."

Daniel's cupid lips were parted with confusion. "This is happening here?" he asked. "So why did we come here?"

"It's just a movie," Sam said, shooting Dad a look.

"Yeah, yeah. Just a movie," Dad hastily added.

"So a bomb got dropped, and people got sick?" I asked, with reflexive cruelty. I didn't want Daniel's fears to be allayed so easily; it was one of those unconscious big brother things. A weakened Daniel made me stronger somehow. I wouldn't have done it if I had ever stopped to think about it.

"It was really terrifying at the time," Dad said. "They used to tell us we could get bombed at any moment. I've never been able to figure out whether it was real or not. But it was the kind of thing that made you a lot more likely to put your trust in the government. You know: *protect me.*"

Dad broke off, glancing around at each of us with a nervous, flustered manner.

"That's not to say there aren't real dangers in life," he went on. "But one of the biggest dangers is fear. Fear keeps you from really living your life."

"What are you afraid of?" Daniel asked, leaning forward and bracing his arm against the back of Dad's headrest.

"I don't know, being *ordinary*, maybe," Dad offered.

Sam gave a sarcastic laugh in response. "Come *on*," she said. "Daniel asked you a good question. What are you *really* afraid of?"

My father stared out at the road for what seemed like a long time. "It's not that I'm being dishonest, or evasive," he said to my sister. "I've spent a long time trying hard not to be scared, Sam. It's one of the major things you have to work on when you're a parent."

"I always thought you and Mom were trying hard not to *look* like you weren't scared," Sam said. "But I thought adults were just as scared as anyone else."

"What are *you* scared of, then?" Dad asked her.

"Where do I start?" Sam said, trying to laugh and not really succeeding. "I'm scared that I won't fit in. I'm scared of not having any friends."

I really admired my sister's candor. I had been watching from the sidelines as she tried to navigate a complicated friendship triangle with Carrie, a terrifyingly gorgeous and imposingly sophisticated Amazon in my eyes, and Simone, a brainy, caustic girl with a penchant for jealousy and calling my sister on the phone several times on any given day. Two of the three would form alliances against the other, concocting all manner of slights and failings for which the odd one out would have to display sufficient penitence until the power balance shifted anew. It looked like sheer hell to me.

"Oh. That," Dad said. "You know——"

"I *know*," Sam interrupted. "Don't worry about what people think. Be myself, and people will come to me. Don't play other people's games. I got the memo, Dad."

My father laughed. "I'm glad you read it."

Sam smiled at him. "You did your job," she told him.

"Doesn't mean shit, does it?" he asked her. "You still live and die on whether someone smiles back at you when you say hello."

"Pretty much," my sister said.

"If it's any consolation, the whole thing gets a lot more subtle," my father told her. "And you really do get to the point where you pretty much don't give a shit anymore."

"*Great*," Sam said. "I can't *wait*."

"I'm scared of dying," I said, the words popping out before I could think.

"Everyone is scared of dying," Sam said, not without a certain delicacy.

"You don't have to be," Dad offered. It had been raining again but stopped; with a flick, he turned off the wipers.

"I don't understand you when you say that," I told him. "You're always saying not to be afraid of dying. But I can't imagine not being here anymore. And thinking about the world going on without me makes me really sad."

I thought about my double back in Minneapolis, having his innocent dinner with my duplicate family. Maybe he wasn't afraid of death, since he had come into being in a flash of my imagination. All he had to be scared of was *my* death.

"All time exists at once—" Dad began.

"Don't say that!" Daniel shouted. "I don't understand that, and it makes me mad because you always say it."

Dad was quiet for about a minute. We were all waiting for what came next.

"There is no such thing as death," he finally said. "It's the great scam of all of our lives, throughout history. It's one of the ways that they control us."

"*They*," Sam repeated, snapping into insolent mode. "The great *them*."

"You're right, you're right," Dad allowed. "There's no *them*. It's only *us*. We do it to ourselves. All I'm saying is that life becomes a lot more interesting when you get rid of clunky ideas like your own death. You already died, I already died. Now, it doesn't feel so bad, does it?"

"You're *morbid*," Sam pronounced.

"I'm just here," Dad said. "I didn't write this book. I just say my lines."

"I'm hungry," Daniel said.

"You just had a hot dog back at the gas station," Dad replied.

"You know, most fathers don't starve their children like you do," Sam said.

"What do you mean?" Dad asked in real or put-on indignation.

"You always do this," said Sam. "We tell you we're hungry, and you tell us to wait. There's always one more thing we need to do before we can get fed. It's a wonder any of us has grown to normal size."

"I like it that way," Dad said. "I want a tribe of Pygmy children skittering around my yard, talking in clicks and building little miniature dwellings out of the undergrowth."

"I'm small!" Daniel exclaimed, somehow combining triumph with accusation.

"That you are," Dad said.

"I'm hungry, too," I broke in. "And I really want to get out of this car. This fucking car is pissing me off."

"Kevin," Dad said. "People with Tourette's have to take drugs for it to keep them from swearing uncontrollably. At least, I think they do. Is that what you want?"

"You take drugs," Sam said quietly.

A hush went over the car. It had been about a year when my mother and father had a huge argument (by their admittedly reserved standards) about something that he had apparently done. The fight had ended with Dad going to the doctor the next week and coming home with what he brightly described as "brain pills." He took two different ones every day, and sometimes joked with Mom about it:

DAD: Look how together I am, my dear. I'm cured!

MOM: That's not funny.

DAD: I'm serious, though. All is right in my world. I am a walking testament to the powers of the contemporary pharmacy.

MOM: You're going to be a testament to the nuthouse.

DAD: That's why I love you. I can never attain perfection in your eyes.

MOM: And I love you, too. Even if you'll never be cured.

DAD: All alone on the road to perfection, baby.

Like I said earlier, it's not as though they fought all the time. Far from it.

"Well, all right," Dad was saying. "I must admit to feeling a bit peckish myself. Which is not as much fun as feeling puckish, I'll tell you that right now."

"*Stop it,*" Sam said.

"Here's what I'm thinking," Dad continued. "We need to get out of Kansas."

"Why?" I asked.

"I should believe that the answer to that is self-evident, Kevin," Dad told me. "This place is filling me to the brim with bad vibes. The juju is all wrong in Kansas. I don't want to spend a minute longer in this state than I have to."

"I agree," Sam said wearily.

"There's not that much more to go," Dad added. "Maybe an hour and a half. Then we dine like royalty and sleep on the pristine sheets of the best hostelry the interstate has to offer."

"An hour and a half?" Daniel said, from an apparently bottomless pit of despair.

"It'll pass like nothing," my father assured him. "Then we'll be in Colorado. The Fresh Start state."

"You're making that up," Sam said. "Isn't it the Rocky Mountain State or something like that?"

"Colorado will be what we say it is," Dad replied. "It will be a most pliant and obedient state, existing only to serve our needs and put our heads right. And cure Kevin's goop-eye."

He looked in the mirror and winked at me.

"Let's all say a prayer and an amen for Kevin's disgusting goopy eye," Dad said in his best preacher voice. "Heavenly father, Kevin is a *good boy*——"

"No he isn't," Daniel said.

"Who doesn't *deserve* this affliction with which he awoke this morning on the open roads of your most very favorite country in the entire world."

"Dad, you're just doing Reverend Lovejoy," Sam said.

"Let him finish," I told her, caught up in Dad's moment.

"So cure that goopy eye," he said, somber and sonorous. "Let him be *a-healed*. And let this road lead us to greater happiness. And let us all be together again."

I flinched at that last, unexpected part.

"Amen," I said.

And then we all said it, one by one, the Subaru suddenly, and in all seriousness, a chapel rolling toward the mountains, toward a simple and humble prayer for something approaching the normality we had all so unforgivably taken for granted.

7

WHAT A GIFT . . . THANK YOU. THANK YOU.

WE EVENTUALLY DID MAKE IT OUT OF KANSAS AND INTO Colorado. Dad must have been extravagantly exhausted; he kept making little moaning sounds and big pre-verbal exhalations of which he didn't even seem to be aware. The sun went down, and although the landscape didn't change from its relentless lack of dimension, our communal mood brightened a little when we crossed the state line.

It felt as though we were deep in the eternal night by the time we stopped, even though it wasn't even our usual bedtime yet. We got some take-out burgers and fries and waited in the car while my father went into a motel office and got us checked in.

"Who's going to sleep with Dad?" I asked.

"Not me," Sam replied. "I want my own bed."

"I doubt he's going to get more than one room," I told her.

She let out a petulant sigh. It was apparently just one more indignity she had to suffer, here in this all-male new order in which she found herself.

Beneath the surface of this exchange was the

unspoken subject that was rarely discussed in our house: my father was, at best, a restless sleeper. At worst, he suffered some kind of neurological malady that had gone undiagnosed for decades and which probably could have earned someone a doctorate if they took the time and effort to study it and publish the results.

My grandmother, his mother, died when I was five after a long period of mental instability that, even in my limited perception at the time, obviously put my father through an inordinate degree of anguish and frustration. Still, I liked her, the few times we met, and knowing her certainly explained a thing or two about my father. She was quick, warm, and very funny. Like Dad. She also had several screws permanently loose and, while I wouldn't necessarily say the same thing about my dad, he occupied at least a point on the same continuum.

The few times we were alone with a chance to chat, she loved telling me humorous stories in which my young father was the central protagonist. I remember feeling uncomfortable with this, not sure what she was getting at. She had a way of talking, particularly to me, as though there was some conspiratorial point she was making that I was certain to understand because of our unspoken affinity. It felt as though she was trying to explain something to me about my father, to make some greater point about his behavior and his attitudes, as though she knew something about him that presumably I would understand if no one else would.

He was an inveterate sleepwalker as a child. He would try, in his slumber, to open a door and attempt to disembark from a moving car on family road trips. He would rouse the family in the middle of the night and insist that they were all late for work and school. One time, she told me, she heard rustling sounds in the middle of the night and woke to see the bathroom light switched on at the end of the hall. She went there, and found him stirring a jar of Drano with his finger.

"What are you doing?" she asked him.

He looked up, seemingly awake, totally relaxed. "I'm making chocolate milk," he said.

So Dad got an early start on being sometimes unnervingly difficult to deal with. I started to piece things together, over the years, from conversations between him and my mother in the morning, especially on the weekends, when the pace was slower and they had time to converse like two people rather than harried functionaries.

"Do you remember last night?" she would ask him, and his head would hang. I felt sorry for him, listening to how he'd gotten up and banged his head on a shelf, or acted out some elaborate dream without the slightest bit of input from his waking consciousness. Dad always listened to what he had done, looking abashed and pained, and I used to wonder what it was like for him. It seemed like getting a morning report on some transgression one had made in the world of sleep, which I suppose pretty much describes it, though it doesn't account for the way Dad's dreams bled over into reality, and how he had to take ownership for things the rest of us manage to keep tamped down. And Mom was generally a good sport about it all, given that being a good sport was pretty much part of the territory. But there were times when she bore a grudge in the morning over being awakened by a delusional and sometimes hostile maniac in thrall to aspects of the mind that we generally put to one side and don't discuss with one another.

None of this was a tremendously big deal, mind. It wasn't as though Dad would ever hurt any of us; to his credit, even when he was most out of his mind, the most vicious weapon he could muster was an unkind word (or several). But no one really wanted to sleep in the same bed as him, what with the prospect of being conscripted into some weird Freudian—or, worse still, Lacanian—drama in the middle of the night. I mean, life was tough enough. Mom at least had some authority over him.

"You should sleep with him," I told Sam. "If he wakes up and starts acting weird, he'll listen to you if you tell him to stop."

"I'm not going to," she said in a tone that precluded any argument. "I'm too old to sleep in the same bed as my father."

I really had no earthly idea what she meant by that, and since she trumped me in years, there wasn't much I could say in response.

"I don't want to!" Daniel exclaimed in alarm. "I'm scared of him."

"Daniel, don't say that," Sam said seriously. "We're talking about Dad. There's nothing to be scared of."

Daniel's lower lip went out in a stubborn pout. We all knew what he was talking about, though Daniel as the youngest had the license to come right out and say it. It was in fact no easy prospect, being out there in the wider world alone with Dad. I supposed the notion that we were traveling to see our mother at least gave the prospect some shred of logic.

I could see him in there, through the motel's front window, leaning on the counter and saying something to some old guy who was nodding in response. Dad's shirt hung wrinkled over his big bony shoulders, and he bent forward, unconsciously minimizing his height as he often did when talking to someone shorter than him. His hair sprouted in great waves from his forehead and around his ears and, looking at him now from a distance, I could begin to see that the gray had made real inroads against the blackish predominant strands. Weirdly, I could see the first glimmer of what Dad would look like when (if) he got old: wiry, pulled down by gravity, bones jutting out everywhere.

I looked away for a moment, trying to stay out of some renewed conflict between Sam and Daniel that had something to do with whether we should go ahead and dig into the sumptuously fragrant fast food that perfumed the car's interior like some dreamy abattoir—I must have been very hungry—when he came out of nowhere. Dad threw open the car door and leaped inside with what must have been the last reserves of his energy.

"Okay, I made peace with the locals," he said, starting up the car. "They'll let us stay the night as long as we clear up their little outlaw problem in the morning. I told them we had guns and ammo. No worries."

"*Dad*," Sam said.

"We're gonna shoot people?" Daniel asked excitedly.

"Now, son," Dad said, throwing the car into gear. "I've told you a thousand times. We don't go around shooting people. Unless they're dangerous bandits and we've been hired as badass mercenaries to deal with them. Then it's perfectly okay. *Commendable*, in fact."

"You're going to be sorry when he grows up and shoots up a post office," Sam said.

"A postal carrier is a perfectly dignified and necessary profession," Dad said, driving slow through the parking lot. "And sometimes you just have to let the bastards have it, you know what I mean? You can only be pushed so far before you have to push back. Blammo!"

"Yeah! Blammo!" Daniel yelled beside me. Sam looked over the seat at me, as though looking for some sign of rationality.

We grabbed our various bags and tromped up a flight of stairs to our room. It was the kind of place where the door opened up to an open-air corridor; the moon was out, and the sky was clear, with a cool breeze that sneaked its fingers through the neck of my hooded sweatshirt.

Inside there were two beds, a dresser, a TV, and a painting of mountains affixed to the wall. Dad turned on all the lights and dropped his heavy case on a small table around which there were two chairs. We promptly dispensed with the burgers and fries with the zeal of a wolf pack after a long hunt, then sprawled across the furniture in various states of satiation and exhaustion.

"That was good," Dad said, mopping a bit of mayonnaise with his finger from a crumpled piece of foil. "*Damned* good."

Sam had disappeared behind the bathroom door, which she loudly locked. I hadn't had a chance to pee yet, a fact of which I was suddenly quite acutely aware.

"We made good time today," Dad said, looking approvingly at his worn USA Adventure Atlas. "We'll try to get an early start tomorrow."

He started fiddling with the clock radio on the nightstand between the beds.

"I don't suppose any of you kids thought to pack

pajamas," he said, looking up at Daniel and me. We stared at him blankly. "Me either. Oh well."

Dad stripped off his shirt and tossed it in the corner. He rummaged around in his gym bag until he found a T-shirt with the logo of a bookstore and put it on. "I don't know about you guys," he said. "But I'm fucking exhausted."

Dad turned off all the lights save for the one in the entryway. Daniel and I looked at each other. There was no sound from the bathroom save for the sound of the fan; light seeped out from inside.

"You guys can stay up if you want," Dad told us, climbing under the blanket of the bed nearest the door. "But don't make too much noise. And I'd really prefer it if you didn't watch TV. Your mother would disapprove."

True enough. Without a word, Daniel climbed into the open bed, clothes and all, and turned his face toward the wall. I went over to the bathroom and knocked on the door.

"Go away," Sam said from inside.

"I have to *go*," I told her.

"Wait."

"Sam, *really*."

After about thirty seconds I heard the lock click, and the door opened a miniscule crack. I snaked in and, without a word to Sam, took a long and infinitely pleasant leak.

"Flush that when you're done," Sam said disapprovingly. "It stinks. You aren't drinking enough water."

"Well, I'm not exactly getting a lot of chances to," I told her.

I zipped up and finally looked at her. She had changed into sleeping pants and the Beatles T-shirt Dad had bought her at Target the year before (it was made to look decades old, all faded and worn-looking). Her pale features were blotchy, her eyes ringed with red.

"Have you been crying?" I asked her.

"What if I was?" she said defiantly.

With a sudden wave of horror I saw a box of tampons sitting next to a puddle of water on the sink ledge. Sam grabbed it and tossed it into her case.

"Don't," she said, looking away from me. "Just don't say anything."

"You got your *period*?" I said, awestruck.

"Like two months ago, idiot," she said. She blew out sharply to clear the hair from her eyes.

"Do you . . ." I trailed off. "Do you feel all right?"

"Jesus," she muttered. The door was closed, yet she still cast a glance in the direction of my brother and Dad in the next room. "Just don't make a big deal about it. I didn't even want you to know."

"It's kind of amazing," I said.

"Yeah, life's just one wonder after another." Sam turned on the sink and ran water over her face. I held out a towel for her when she was done.

"Dad doesn't know," I said.

"Dad doesn't *need* to know," she said. "He'd probably want to throw me a party or something. You know how he gets."

"Yeah."

"It's funny, you know," she said, suddenly intimate with me in a way she hadn't been in ages. "In a story like this, I should be getting my first period now, not my third."

"What do you mean?"

"You know, like I would start bleeding in the car and not know why," she continued. "Dad could freak right on out, some woman in a drugstore could take me into the restroom and show me how to jam it in."

"*Sam*," I said, totally scandalized.

"It's not a big deal, Kevin," she said, smiling at my shock. "It just means that I can make babies now. Imagine that. A little niece or nephew for you."

I had read the children's book about reproduction that my mother brought home from the bookstore last year; none of this was news to me. But it was distinctly disturbing to apprehend that Sam had crossed over the great divide between childhood and at least biological adulthood. She was a sufficiently awesome figure for me without adding this to her repertoire.

"Well," I said.

"Yeah. *Well.*"

"You have fun with that," I told her.

"I guess," she said, ignoring my joking tone. "It hasn't been much fun so far. It's just been scary and weird."

Her eyes met mine and, without thinking, I reached up and wrapped my arms around her shoulders. She squeezed me back, hard, then pushed me away.

"You're bunking with Dad," she said.

"I know."

Things were very quiet back in the room when I left Sam to whatever else she had to contend with. Daniel was a truncated lump in the darkness, and Dad was on his back, his mouth open, and seemingly beyond stirring. I took off my sweatshirt and let my pants slip down to the floor. I slid into the bed beside Dad.

"Kevin," he murmured.

"It's just me, Dad," I whispered.

"You're with me? I'm glad." He softly held out his hand, and I slipped in next to him with his arm around me. I couldn't remember the last time we had been like this, the way we used to nap sometimes when I was little, a circumstance that was surely my own doing as much as anything else. Now, though, it felt calming to be close to him, in the glow of his acceptance and undeniable love. He breathed softly in the semidarkness and didn't say another word.

I never heard Sam come out of the bathroom. I was so exhausted that I had no memory even of running through one of my bedtime anxiety checklists replete with school fears and general worries. Instead I slipped right into a sleep unusually luxurious with otherworldly bliss.

At first when I woke up I had no idea what was going on. I looked around, trying to get my eye to adjust. The other had obligingly sealed itself shut again. I finally made out the form of Dad sitting bolt upright next to me.

"Dad?" I asked.

"Just what did you mean by that?" he asked, looking at me strangely. I could barely make out his face, but he was staring at me with an entirely disturbing intensity.

"By what?"

"A game of me," he said, with sudden resentment. "You told me I was playing a game of me. You can't just say something like that, you know. Your words have consequences."

"Dad, I think you're dreaming." I started to reach out to touch him, then thought better of it.

"This room," he said, turning his face in profile, his eyes blazing and his mouth in a wondrous smile. "Is this why you brought me here? Is this what you wanted to show me?"

"Dad."

"What a *gift*," he said. "Thank you. *Thank* you. That light . . . it's *shimmering*. It's shimmering because it can move forward and backward in time. It's all the same."

The clock radio read: 2:18. I looked over at Sam and Daniel, who were silent and unmoving.

"A game of me," Dad repeated, looking at me again, still smiling. "You're funny. That light is so *funny*. You brought me here to make me laugh, didn't you?"

I just looked at him. With a final chuckle, he lay back, turned over, and immediately started to breathe deeply in peaceful slumber.

It took me more than an hour to go to sleep again.

8

AND EVERYONE ELSE HAS IT SO EASY?

I THOUGHT I WOKE UP BEFORE EVERYONE ELSE, UNTIL I heard the hum of the bathroom fan and, after executing a quick head check, realized that Sam was in there. She might as well have spent the entire night in there, though I remembered the sound of her breathing during that long sleepless spell I had endured following Dad's dream.

My father was in one of his typical comas next to me—it was all or nothing with Glenn unconscious, either restless delusion or unreachable oblivion—and Daniel was curled semi-fetal in the bed across from us with just the top of his head poking out from the covers.

I lay there in the not uncomfortable hotel bed and thought about everything that was going on that day that I was going to miss. School, my friends, my teacher: it was surprising how little I cared about it all. I would be perfectly content to rejoin the current of everyday things when the time came, and I knew that the sooner it happened, the better, for self-interested reasons of not wanting to expend more effort than I had to. But, just a day removed, I marveled how little anything I had left behind moved me, or excited me to passion. I wondered if my father had felt this way when he was a boy, and if it had developed into his Manichean love and hate for all things real.

Morning sun trickled through the worn-out drapes, and the bathroom door opened. Sam was up and ready, in tights, a skirt, and a black sweater. She had her hair tied back, and her pretty features were drawn in, tied up by some inner anxiety. I wanted to tell her how beautiful she was, but she wouldn't take it the right way, and it wouldn't make anything better.

"Morning," I whispered.

"Morning yourself." She stuffed her sleeping clothes into her bag. She seemed to be waiting for something to transpire that would grant her the proper venue for expressing her anger.

"Did you hear Dad last night?" I asked.

"What?"

"Oh. Nothing."

I hauled myself out of bed and made my way to the bathroom. Along the way I made a welcome discovery: I had regained binocular vision. Now *this* was encouraging. I shut the door behind me and sidled up to the mirror for a better look.

At least part of our prayers of the night before had been answered. My eye was ringed with the expected crud, but with a raspy washcloth I was able to wipe the lion's share of it away and, blinking, I was able to see out of it. I still looked terrible, and the white of my infected orb was crimson and sore. But I could see again. And my ear and sinuses hurt, but it was a lingering kind of pain, not the flowering of yesterday. I relieved myself and rinsed out my mouth with water (no toothbrush, no toothpaste), confirmed in the belief that this day would be better than the one before.

"Oh, *Christ*," I heard Dad saying from the next room.

"Dad, *chill*," Sam rebuked him. "He can't help it. Put yourself in his place."

"You're right, of course," Dad replied. "It's just that—*Jesus*."

I came out and saw Dad holding a big wad of bedding in his hands, a look of futility and anguish on his face. The smell hit me immediately, pungent and enveloping, and my eyes tracked to Daniel, who was trying to take off his pants amid a big mess of runny shit.

"Wow," I said.

I supposed I hadn't smelled it before because it had been trapped in Daniel's little jeans. Now that he unleashed it, the odor was astonishing. He seemed to be only half-awake, with his short hair sticking out in spikes. The three of us were just standing there looking at him in amazement; after a moment, I caught a glimpse of his face and saw that he was in tears.

"Daniel," I said.

Sam and I got him in the bathroom, neither of us really expecting much help from Dad. We stripped off his clothes and tossed them in the trashcan, then started running warm water.

"I'm sorry," Daniel said, his face clenched up with sleep and humiliation. "I don't know why this happens."

"Don't worry about it," Sam said, in the process of soiling a towel on his backside. "We're here to help you. That's all that matters."

"But Mom's not here!" Daniel said, his skinny naked body shivering with a burst of frustration. "She said she would always be here for me, and she's not!"

"Stop it," I said. I picked up a fresh towel from the stack over the toilet and handed it to Sam.

"I want Mom!" Daniel said.

Sam's mouth formed a horizontal line of irritation. "Stop saying that," she said. "Yeah, okay, Mom's not here. But she must have a really good reason. Everything will make sense later."

"No it won't!" Daniel shouted. "People always say that, but nothing ever makes sense! I want Mom!"

His face had turned an alarming rosy red, but Sam had done quick work cleaning him up. She tossed the towels in the trash along with his clothes, then straightened up and pinched her nose. The room smelled terrible.

"Well, then," she said, sounding very much like our mother. "You think you can give yourself a little rinse while I go get you some fresh clothes?"

"Whatever," Daniel said, sullenly daubing himself with the still-running water.

I looked up. Dad was standing in the doorway, watching us, expressionless.

"Do you think you could actually help out?" Sam said to him, her voice taut and acid with disdain.

"Come on, Sam," Dad said. "I—"

"You *what?*" she snarled back, then elbowed past him.

My eyes met his; Daniel had finished washing and stood there with his narrow arms folded across his chest. He looked like a pink bug folded up on itself. I shut off the water and pulled down another towel to start drying my little brother.

"Whose genius idea was it to let a six-year-old pack his own bag for this trip?" Sam was saying in the next room. "He doesn't have any *underwear.*"

"I have some," Dad said.

"Fantastic," Sam shot back. "We can wrap him up in your briefs and send him out in the world dressed like little baby *Gandhi*."

"Come on, Sam," Dad said.

Daniel muttered something too quiet to hear. Dad and I both leaned in close while he composed himself to repeat what he had said.

"What, Daniel?" Dad asked.

"I don't need to wear underwear," Daniel said, his head bowed so we couldn't see his eyes. "I don't really care about underwear."

Sam appeared in the doorway and handed me a pair of Daniel's sweatpants and a long-sleeved T-shirt with a silhouette of a baseball player on it. In block letters it read: "HOME RUN HERO."

"We're going to need an *army* of shrinks by the time you get through with us, Dad," Sam said. "They're going to have to ship them in by the busload."

"Cool," he said, looking at her with a little grin. "I'll make iced tea and sell it to them in the sun. I'll finally be rich."

Sam stared at him. "Very funny. Just hilarious."

Daniel was toweling himself off. He looked at my sister and Dad for a long time, then said, "Maybe their buses would be dirty from driving all the way to our house. We could wash them and make money that way."

"*That's* my boy!" Dad exclaimed. "All those hungry shrinks, we can sell them *hamburgers*! I'm telling you kids, your old Dad is going to be the salvation of us all."

"It's really not at all funny," Sam said.

Dad put his hand on her shoulder. She flashed a grin at him, then recomposed herself.

"I know it's not," he said. "Just bear with me, all right? These things come out all right by the end."

"You have no idea what you're doing, do you?" she asked, reaching up to cover his hand with her own.

He breathed in and out loudly, then motioned to my brother and me. "Watch it," he said. "Someone might hear you and get the wrong idea."

● ■ ●

We ate breakfast in the car (fast-food French toast dipped in syrup for me and Sam, stinky egg sandwiches for Dad and Daniel) and crossed an eastern Colorado landscape that didn't, in my opinion, look much different than the Kansas of yesterday.

"You're looking better," Dad said to me from the rearview mirror. "Your eye, I mean."

"I can see out of it," I said cheerfully. Working as a team, we had managed to get all the smelly food wrappers into a single paper bag that I tucked away in the back. It was amazing how the smell of fast food was so mouthwatering before one ate it, then so thoroughly repugnant once it had gone down.

Daniel had wrapped himself up in a jacket and wedged himself into a slumping vegetative state in his neighborhood of the backseat. Sam was immersed in a magazine, and Dad was humming along to the radio. The sun had come out, which was vaguely disappointing—there had been something comforting about traveling under cloud cover, as though the unblinking eye in the sky couldn't track our movements.

I leaned back and closed my eyes, and it came over me all at once, this feeling I had been experiencing and,

I thought, sharing with the others since the moment that Dad awoke us with that note from Mom: it was *shame.* I was embarrassed to be in this situation, and I didn't want anyone to know about it.

I had always thought that our family occupied a fairly unique position in the social gallery of our world. I was biased, but I knew that Mom was beautiful and brilliant, and she was so outgoing that she left psychic traces of herself on everyone she came across. Dad was Glenn, of course, and even if everyone at large didn't particularly embrace him, he was at least unlike anyone else. Sam was pretty much on a genius track in middle school, and I got my own share of strokes and approval (we were casually referred to as record-setters, based on standardized test scores).

Now that I thought about it, I figured that we all had a pretty high opinion of ourselves, one that was tempered by our family talent for holding up one another's faults for examination and sometimes ridicule. Dad was always good for comic relief, even if it was tinged with existential panic, and Mom was . . . she was . . . *gone.*

It wasn't so much that I felt ashamed of suddenly being a part of a broken family. That was commonplace enough. And it wasn't as though I couldn't bear the idea of facing my peers, or my teachers, when they were armed with the knowledge that my parents were giving up. If anything, part of me reveled in the idea that people would have to treat me differently, perhaps even make allowances for my state of mind as I went through tough times.

No, the source of my shame was the crux of this unsolvable puzzle: *why* had she gone? By folding up and

abandoning her place at the table, my mother had managed to negate all the unspoken accommodations that
kept everything in place. Sam's moods, Daniel's fragil-
ity, my deep and pervasive unease with things, and Dad
being Dad: my mother, keeping so many mysteries to
herself, had always without ever saying so insisted that
we were *all right.* I had never entertained the idea that
my mother had any deep struggles of her own, or that
the churning mental ecology of our family could ever
become overwhelming for her. My father infected everything he touched with his particular brand of electricity,
both empowering and burning, including us, but Mom
had always seemed above it all.

She had always been the part of us that made it possible to *be* in the world. Dad was sporadic help with that.

I wondered how I was ever going to find the words to
ask her what really happened.

"—swoop right in, and everything is going to be
hunky-dory again?" Sam was saying up in front. I
realized that I had been dozing. Daniel was entirely inert
next to me.

"Well, it's not like I have a ton of experience with this
kind of thing," Dad said apologetically.

They clearly both assumed, yet again, that I was
asleep. I closed my eyes and nestled against the car door,
in no mood to disabuse them of the notion.

"I know I can't talk you into turning around and going back home," Sam was saying. "Even though it would
be the best thing to do."

"I'm glad you have a clear picture of your limitations
in the persuasion department," Dad told her.

"But did it occur to you that this little trip we're taking

might make things *worse*, Dad?" she asked him.

The car whooshed and hummed.

"How so?" Dad asked.

"Think about it," Sam said. "You pulled us out of school. You haven't even called our schools to let them know where we are, have you?"

"Shit," Dad said. "I'll do it first thing when we stop."

"Do you have the phone numbers?"

"Someplace." Dad paused. "I guess I can call information if I can't find them."

"Did you look for your cell phone?"

"It's in my bag somewhere." Dad sighed. "Sam, honey. Don't be a nag. I don't do well with nagging. I have enough on my plate just being me."

"Why do you always think you're so *different?*" Sam asked. "*I have enough on my plate just being me.* And everyone else has it so easy?"

Dad tapped on the steering wheel. "I can't really presume to speak for other people," he said.

"Well, how is it nagging when I'm just trying to get you to do some of the things that normal people do?" she said.

Dad didn't have a reply for that.

"Parents call the school when they keep their kids home," Sam said. "People are going to wonder where we are. They might call the police or something."

"I don't think I can be accused of *kidnapping* my own children," Dad said.

"I'm not here by choice," Sam said.

Dad let out a weary sigh. "Honey, I'm trying very hard to keep this family together," he said. "I think that much at least should be clear to you."

Daniel was watching all of this with a sort of subdued

horror. He had slipped out of his seat belt, then his shirt, and was contorted so that his head was perpendicular to the seat, and he looked up at an angle at the side of Sam's face. Recently I'd been fascinated, a little horrified, by the sight of his naked form. His ribs jutted out alarmingly, and his arms were long insectoid stalks covered by papery, impossibly delicate-looking skin. In his current position, blood was filling one side of his face, giving him a two-tone look that was quite ghastly despite his commonly accepted reputation as a precocious beauty.

"I'm just filling in the blanks for you, Dad," Sam said.

"Which is usually your mother's job," Dad said wearily.

"What do you mean by that?" Sam said, flashing back into her angry mode. I thought about the box of tampons I'd spotted back in the motel, and thought that Dad didn't know what he was dealing with. I wasn't thinking anything so vulgar as women being fearsome during their periods—men must have their own equivalent, I always thought, it just wasn't marked by blood—but simply that Dad thought he was talking to a girl. He wasn't. He was talking to a woman.

"I just mean that I am quite routinely made aware of my shortcomings in the reality department, Sam," Dad told her.

Sam was staring him down; Dad stared glumly out at the road. Despite the recent appearance of the sun, it was still a rather cloudy day, though it wasn't raining.

"It sounded to me like you were criticizing Mom," she said. "Do you really think that's a good idea right now?"

"Criticizing . . . " My father trailed off and pondered this. Finally he gave the steering wheel a thwack. "I wasn't criticizing your mother, Sam. If anything, I was criticizing myself."

"Yeah, but you can say one thing and mean another, can't you?" she parried back. That was one of Dad's favorite expressions, and he was always uncorking it on us when he wanted to expose one of our childhood hypocrisies.

"Of course I can," he responded wearily. He started to curse under his breath, and I sat up straighter in the backseat and saw why: up ahead the traffic was slowing, our two westbound lanes merging into one. I spotted the dreaded sign: "ROAD WORK NEXT 22 MILES."

"You always do that," Sam said, continuing on, her eyes still locked on Dad's profile. "You make a mistake, or you let something slide, and then you act like Mom is being a drag for pointing it out."

"Your point being?" Dad said in a tense, tinny voice.

"I've just spent the last half-hour pointing out that you might be making a big mistake," Sam said. "So you show up at Aunt Alayne's house. Big deal. Mom's going to ask about school, and whether you remembered to ask the neighbors to bring in the mail. She's going to ask if you've been feeding us nothing but fast food for the last couple of days."

"No, she's not," Dad said brightly. "She's going to *thank* me for coming to get her, and for negating what she immediately realized was an enormous mistake. We're going to rest and have a nice meal, and then we're going to drive straight back to Minnesota."

"Has it occurred to you that she might just think you've gone crazy?" Sam asked.

Dad slowed the car as we entered the work zone: "FINES DOUBLED." The pavement was striated at regular intervals, and when our tires passed over them it sounded as though they were executing a low bass Spanish rolling "r."

"It's not crazy to want things to return to the way they were," he told her.

"Dad, Mom's the last person I would ever expect to do something like this," Sam said, glancing back at me. I must have looked suitably impressed with her bravado, because she went on. "What happened? Something must have happened."

"Sam, I don't respond to interrogation," Dad said.

"What are you hiding?" Sam asked, her voice rising. Next to me, Daniel shifted his twisted posture so that his face was pressed down against the fabric of the seat. "What aren't you telling us?"

"*Stop*," Daniel moaned.

"Sam," I said by way of warning.

"Why are we in this car?" she said, far past the point of hemming herself in. "It's nothing *we* did. It must be because of you."

"Because your mother's perfect," Dad retorted.

"No." Sam gripped the edge of her seat as she moved closer to Dad, her seat belt straining. "She is not perfect. But even if she got fed up with it all and needed to escape, she wouldn't have just vanished and left us alone. There's something here that doesn't add up."

"Your mother has simply had an irrational reaction," Dad said.

"But to *what*?" Sam boomed. "What did you do to make her feel she had to get away from you like this?"

"Sam, go easy on Dad," I said.

My father looked into the mirror at me with an expression of boundless gratitude.

"I don't *have to*," she snarled. "Because Mister Fucking Rescue Mission over here has forced me to be in a car in the middle of nowhere. He blew up his marriage, and our entire family, and I can't even get a straight answer about why any of this *shit* is happening."

"Sam," I said.

"And don't take his side, Kevin," she said, turning to me. "You're always making *excuses* for him! That's part of the problem—everyone in this fucked-up family is always making *excuses* for him!"

"Sam," Dad barked. "You stop it right now. I'm still your father, and I won't have you talking to me this way."

"I have to pee," Daniel said, his words somewhat muffled by the seat.

"*Still* my father?" Sam said. "Congratulations! Nice work! You have three kids and look at you now! Who knows, Dad, maybe Mom will meet someone else. Maybe she *already has*. Don't you think it's going to be confusing for us, having to call someone else *Dad*?"

By now tears were streaming impressively down Sam's face, which instantly turned blotchy red, and puffy. As soon as the last word was out of her mouth, Dad let out a nasty primate howl and, just for a second, clenched his fist and coiled it in Sam's direction. The car swerved, and someone behind us honked.

"I'm sorry, I'm sorry," Sam was saying, her face turned to the side window, her slim, tall frame seeming to shrink and collapse.

I looked out my window as well, thinking thoughts of escape and flight. A lone bird soared overhead, possibly looking down at the vast rising vista and the parade of single-file ant-like vehicles moving across the country. It was as though we had never begun, and would never end. I reached over and took my brother's hand, watching the fleeting forms of the highway workers re-texturing the road for the use of future travelers.

9

I'D LIVE ON TOP OF A MOUNTAIN. ALL BY MYSELF.

THERE WAS VERY LITTLE TALK, ASIDE FROM THAT OF THE strictly functional variety, for quite some time after Sam and my father's meeting of the minds. I was crushed with pity for my sister, who stared out at the ascending Colorado landscape with a worrisome lack of animation, though I was still stung by her comment about my always taking Dad's side. I didn't think it was true, or fair, for her to say that.

And then I went right ahead and took Dad's side. Evaluating his plan of cross-country salvation was pretty much beyond my powers of strategy; it seemed mildly ill-conceived, and it was beyond a doubt inconvenient for all concerned. But I could understand his desperation. After all, I was beginning to share it.

As for invoking some future stepfather we would all call Dad, well, that one entered the Low Blow Hall of Fame on a unanimous vote. It truly worried me, what sort of tormented frame of mind Sam must be enduring to compel her to say something so insanely hurtful and mutually destructive.

The terrain started to turn mountainous as we neared

Denver. There were apparently two Colorados: one flat and featureless as the rest of the plains, the other a place of mountains and rare air. The irritation in my ear staged a rally as my eardrums popped with the rising altitude.

Dad tried to rally us with some talk of being Mile High as we skirted the sprawling city, but none of us were having it. Daniel had long since retreated into whatever district of himself he needed to visit in order to deal with all he had seen and heard. Hell, *I* could barely deal with it, and I considered myself pretty sober-eyed and square-shouldered when it came to facing up to things.

For starters, Sam obviously felt that this trip was going to lead to ruin. Which meant that Mom probably wasn't going to come back. I knew how these things worked, and that we'd probably end up spending most of our time with her and visiting Dad in some new and materially reduced living arrangement. Though the fact that Mom walked out was troubling—my friend Benjy's parents had gone though a prolonged and rancorous divorce proceeding the year before, one that had unearthed all sorts of unsavory accusations and revelations about each parent's proclivities and transgressions—I *didn't* know how *those* things worked. But I had a vague idea that Dad could conceivably try to drag up matters against Mom in an effort to force us to live with him instead of her.

Which I most definitely did *not* want to happen. Dad was fine in the doses with which he was usually administered, but the prospect of living with him in some apartment somewhere, without the mitigating influence of Mom, sounded about as attractive as moving my things into the Horror House at the State Fair—it would have its moments, but it was an unsound choice given the other possible options.

We were stopping more often now, at Sam's insistence. We'd pull off the interstate and, without a word, she would pop inside the convenience store attached to the gas station, grab the ladies' room key inevitably attached to some big plastic thing, and disappear inside for up to fifteen minutes. I enjoyed looking at the mountains and the sensation that we were closer to the clouds than in watery, icy, earthbound Minnesota. The altitude seemed to inflame my eye again, but no one was staring at me, and I was still seeing in three dimensions. An unexpected side effect of whatever was ailing me was a ravenous increase in my appetite; every time we stopped I loaded up on whatever processed cuisine was available. Dad paid the bill at the checkout with increasing bemusement, watching me approach with handfuls of Slim Jims, hot dogs loaded up with mustard, ice cream pops, sandwiches wrapped in transparent plastic.

Daniel had gone the other direction. He hadn't eaten much at breakfast, and I hadn't seen a bite of food pass his lips since. He cravenly lobbied for soda pop at every available opportunity, but Dad was maintaining enough of a semblance of our family routine that he had to settle for bottled water and, twice, fruit juice.

The three of us stood outside by the gas pumps, a real chill in the clear mountain air. A gentle vista of tall trees unfolded to the north, and in the midday it was quiet save for the sound of the cars and trucks pulling in to the filling station.

"I can see why people choose to live here," Dad said. He had his hands in the pockets of his chinos, and his shirt was untucked. He rocked on his heels and exhaled loudly, inspecting the space in front of him to see if his breath turned to vapor.

"I'd get bored," I said. "I need to live in the city."

"I could live in the mountains," Daniel said with as much animation as he'd produced in hours. "I'd live on *top* of a mountain. All by myself. Maybe I'd have some dogs."

"Sounds lonely, son," Dad said.

Daniel shot him a look, as though Dad's comment had somehow tipped the balance of his patience and that he wouldn't be able to bear much more of such foolishness.

"Jumping Jesus," Dad said suddenly, going around the back of the car.

"What's the matter?" I asked.

My father had gotten the hatchback open—it had a tendency to jam, and would yield its treasures typically only after a good deal of cajoling, if not outright violence—and started digging around inside.

"I'm actually going to do something right for once," he called out triumphantly. The entire top half of his body had disappeared, and his feet were off the ground. "God, you kids certainly packed a lot of shit," he said to no one in particular.

When he emerged, it was with the dreaded valise. He propped it up on the ledge over the bumper and started to search through its contents. This entailed dumping out a bunch of stuff: a couple of notebooks, several shiny review-copy books, folders jam-packed with papers in varying stages of distress. I glanced around to see if anyone was watching him. I always felt acutely protective of my father at times such as these, assuming that anyone looking on would see him as a picture of well-intentioned failure and come-to-nothing brilliance. Of course I know

now he was just a guy with his sons, looking through a messy briefcase, but at that moment it felt as though all our inadequacies were laid painfully bare.

Dad had actually found his cell phone and, miracle of miracles, it was charged and let out a little three-note melody when he switched it on.

"Ah, your mother must have charged this thing for me," he said wistfully. "I don't even know where the goddamned charger is."

"Who are you calling?" I asked. "Aunt Alayne?"

"She'd tell me not to come," Dad said, looking at the phone's screen. "That would be awkward all around, seeing as how we're halfway there."

"Then who?" Daniel asked.

Dad was pressing buttons on the phone with a look of befuddlement. "I think your mother . . . how do I find the . . . here it is. The phone book. Cross your fingers, boys. I *believe* your mother programmed important numbers for me in here at one point. And high on the list of important numbers is . . . *here it is!* Bless her sweet heart."

"Whose? Mom's?" Daniel asked.

"No one else." Dad pressed a couple more buttons. "I'm going to call your school, boys, and inform them of your whereabouts. You see? I'm going to be responsible."

I looked at the pallid sun. "Dad, isn't it late in the afternoon?" I asked. "School is probably closed by now."

Dad waved away my doubts and turned to face partway from us. He dropped his head close to his chest and sealed off his free ear with one hand.

"It's ringing," he said, and then unnecessarily, and quite vehemently, shushed us. Neither Daniel nor I had said a word.

"No one's picking up," Dad said with an edge of panic. "I don't really care," Daniel said. "I don't care if anyone knows where I am."

"Your mother cares," Dad hissed, pressing the phone tighter to his ear.

"Yeah, she really cares," Daniel said to me. "That's why she left us all alone with you."

Dad looked stunned, but the majority of his attention was focused on the ringing phone affixed to his ear. "Sarcasm is unbecoming in a six-year-old," he said, turning away.

Daniel said something under his breath. He, too, turned away to take in the view, looking for all the world like a tragic hero in his own first-grader drama.

It appeared, for some reason not quite understandable to me, that I was to be the only one of us not to turn on Dad. My deficit of comprehension didn't extend to why Sam and Daniel were being so hard on him; no, that was extremely easy to conceive. But I couldn't see why I still wanted to protect him, to see him through all of this. In some secret corner of my soul, viewable only for a few horrible moments at a time, I had harbored fantasies of being rid of him. Now it was quite possible that I would be, and soon, at least on a daily basis. The prospect gave me a nauseous lurch. I wanted him close, for my own protection as well as his.

Dad turned around with a quick, warm grin. He reached out and mussed my hair.

"Got the machine," he said conspiratorially.

"Tell them I went away," Daniel said, too quietly for Dad to hear. "Tell them that I went to Jupiter."

"You can't stand on Jupiter," I told him. "It's all gas. You'd sink right in."

"I already know that," Daniel said, giving me a smile of triumphant superiority. I doubted he really did.

"Yes, okay, so Daniel is in first grade, and Kevin's in fourth grade," Dad was saying into the phone. "We've had a family emergency of a very personal nature, and I've had to pull the boys out of school for a few days. We're in Colorado now, and after we reach Southern California I expect we'll be returning right away. So I'll just call back when I have a definite idea when the boys will be back in school, but I'm shooting for . . . let's see now. Monday?"

He pulled this deadline out of his ass and phrased it as a question rather than a statement, which would probably earn deserved skepticism from the hawk-eyed women at the Attendance Desk.

But then Dad repeated his feat, finding the number for Sam's middle school and leaving a quite coherent message with the attendance line. When he shut off the phone and looked at us, it was with humble satisfaction. He had enough of a sense of our collective mood not to crow too much about his meager achievement, but he had just pulled off the sort of minor logistical act that he normally left almost completely to Mom's sphere of things. He glanced around, and I imagined he hoped to see his wife appear out of nowhere, perhaps offering congratulations and blurting out that she had him wrong all along—that is to say, throughout the fifteen-year term of their marriage.

"Well, then," he muttered, his glimmer of excitement visibly cooling. He looked inside the gas station, where there was no sign of Sam. "Say. Has it occurred to either of you that Sam might be sabotaging our little mission here with these increasingly protracted and mysterious disappearances of hers?"

"How should I know?" Daniel said darkly.

"I'm just saying," Dad replied with exaggerated mock-innocence, his eyes puppy-wide and mouth pursed. He looked at me, expecting me to contribute.

"I don't think so, Dad," I said.

"Perhaps subconsciously," said Dad, making more an open speculative statement than any continuation of conversation. "Not that I would blame her. She clearly has arrived at the strong opinion that this is all a poor idea. God knows I respect her opinions, but I have to bank on her being wrong in this instance."

Again he looked at me.

"I have no idea, Dad," I told him. "It's pretty much beyond me to put myself in your place, to tell you the truth."

Put myself in your place. Imagine the confusion, I thought, when the secretary at my school listened to the message line and learned of my absence: *But he's here! He's been here all week.* My doppelgänger would be called into the office. Perhaps they would look in his mouth, his ears, for some sign of his inauthenticity. But none would be found: the simulation would be that good. They might dismiss Dad's call as coming from a crank, or the product of confusion in a disordered family. My double would be sent back to class, perhaps slightly shaken in the conviction of his own essential realness, but it was a feeling that would fade as the day went on, as the reassuring array of routine enveloped him and informed him who was real and who wasn't.

"I don't like that look on your face," Dad was saying.

"Sorry. What?"

"I was just explaining that it's sacred ground, the
things women do in the bathroom," Dad went on, tilting
his head at me slightly as though looking for an answer
to an unvoiced question. "You can't ask them what goes
on in there. You can't even suggest that they hurry it up.
Even when you live with one of them for years and years,
sometimes they *close the door and . . .*"

"Dad, knock it off. Please." Sam had appeared out of
nowhere and was now standing next to us, looking at the
same mountainous landscape, her hair hanging lank and
her soft face slightly puffed out in a way that inexplicably
made me think of cake.

"I'm hungry again," I said.

"*Gross*," Daniel moaned.

Dad peeled off several ones from the wad of cash in
his pocket. "Go on," he said motioning to the gas station.
"And see if you can find something Daniel likes, while
you're at it."

"I don't like *anything*," Daniel said in a whine that was
both alarming and extremely unattractive. For a second
I entertained the notion of giving him a brisk slap across
the face. Of course, that would serve to improve nothing.

I went inside and loaded up on meat sticks, bags
of assorted chips, a candy bar, and the most artificial-
looking processed-snack-cake product I could find. It was
as though I wanted to fill myself with the synthetic, to
taste flavors that weren't real, to map out the chart of a
new land on my tongue that bore no relation to anything
that grew on the ground or bleated on an airy plain.
While at the time I would have been hard pressed to put
any of this into words, what I wanted then was to forge a
red-hot open channel, coming out of myself like a gastric

aberration, between everything that I had been taught was good and this lousy situation that I wanted desperately to be rid of.

Well, that's the more elevated way of putting it. By afternoon I had to make Dad stop the car three times so I could deal with my protracted, vehement, and regretful diarrhea. The experience was enough to make me lose my taste for metaphor, and by the time it was over I had made all sorts of healthy-eating pledges to myself, some of which lasted quite a while before temptation eroded their banks and they were forgotten like so many other things.

● ■ ●

We burned up the miles across Colorado, the four of us sinking into spells of silence that felt more amiable than the charged post-explosion periods that had roiled my guts and left me fantasizing about opening my car door, unlatching my seat belt and, to cries of "Kevin! No!" allowing myself to gently roll out onto the asphalt ribbon, welcoming the abrasions, becoming one with the pain in blissful escape.

Dad had dug around in his pants pocket and, wordlessly, produced a worn and folded piece of notebook paper. He smoothed it out meticulously on his lap with one hand, the other on the wheel, then placed it next to the cup holder by the gearshift. Sam pretended not to notice.

I recognized what it was. It had been taped to a kitchen cabinet for months, a gift from Daniel to Dad, from some kindergarten handwriting exercise Daniel did last year. In his labored caveman scrawl it read:

Dear Dad!
I love you! I love you!
You're the best! You're the best!

There was little evidence at that point to connect
the cherubic lovebug who had scrawled that sentiment
to the taciturn, long-suffering, and increasingly malign
little spider-boy curled up into a resentful ball in the seat
next to me. I looked over at the blue veins crisscrossing
his beautiful brow, the big artery in his neck pulsing beneath his membranous skin. If he was an angel, a charge
leveled against him more than once in his time, he looked
like a fallen one, nursing his resentments in the fiery pit
after being cast down for a rebellion for which he never
knowingly signed up.

More often than I would have liked, Dad used to
dredge up a routine from some old movie he liked—
apparently it starred Bill Murray, whom I largely knew as
a somewhat catatonically depressed actor in artsy movies
my parents inexplicably enjoyed. He'd slap his heels together in a mockery of military precision, stare into the
near distance, and proclaim, "There's something *wrong*
with us! There's something very, very *wrong* with us!"

The joke, of course, was that he was referring to our
family, and in a crude bit of voodoo, apparently voicing
our communal apprehension was a way of banishing it,
mocking it, rendering it powerless if not entirely untrue.

I never found it all that funny. For one thing, some
event would necessitate his breaking out the routine, usually something that had happened to us that didn't happen to other families: Daniel would have to sit out a field
trip because Dad spaced out on packing his permission

slip; my mother would mutter darkly about a bank over-
draft while Dad haunted the mailman for some check
that was inevitably weeks late in arriving. Dad's sense of
humor was one of his primary defenses, and none of
us really wanted to take that away from him, but there
really was no shaking the definite sense that something
indeed was *really* wrong with us.

Now I had always figured Mom was more or less exempt from this classification; she had a job in the real
world, and she nicely juggled a majority of our family's
real-world concerns. Of course, she had signed up for
the ride, which by extension suggested that maybe she
deserved to be lumped in with the rest of us. But that was
a territory too rocky and shadow-filled to be traversed,
especially now that Mom had apparently, finally, opted
out of the enterprise or at least showed a definite desire
to reshape it all into a future that she could bear.

All of this came to me in the backseat because it occurred to me that Dad hadn't done his Bill Murray routine even once since we left Minneapolis, and if there
was ever a time for it . . .

But no, it simply wouldn't be funny in the slightest.
Yet when I imagined him doing it, cocking his eyes as
he spoke, his voice breaking with shameful admission, I
realized there was a deeper dimension to his proclaiming
us damaged: if it was true, none of us really cared. Sure,
Sam was over-serious, a bit brittle, prone to sullen injury
from her preteen set, but she would be fine, we all knew
it without having to say it. Sam was her own person apart
from the family; in that moment, I had an overwhelming
insight that Sam had entered into a period of biding her
time until she could get away from all of us. That was

probably what galled her so about this car trip: it was a vivid demonstration of her current powerlessness to be free of all the craziness, a last foray into a period of her life she would spend the rest of it trying to exorcise.

As was my custom, I had no inclination to turn the eye of scrutiny upon myself. If there was something *wrong* with me, I chose to deal with it by ignoring it entirely. I frightened myself with the thoughts of oblivion that crept into the periphery of my consciousness, but as long as they stayed at the periphery, I figured, I would be fine. It wasn't as though I was tangibly suicidal or anything.

Daniel was another matter altogether. In the last couple of days I had been shocked by how deeply and essentially *unappealing* he could be. If it were possible for a child to coast on his looks, he had, yet somehow in the midst of all the easy adoration the world bestowed upon him he had been brewing up something fairly dark. Perhaps it was exaggeration borne from extremity, but I seriously wondered then whether or not Daniel truly cared about us, or about anything, so deep was his shell of self-pity and the strange aggression inherent in his bowel disruptions.

I remembered a time about six weeks before, when he had been in first grade for less than a month. I had been assigned with the task of bringing an armful of paperwork from my teacher down to the office (working hard already on teacher's pet status, for which I wouldn't apologize or be ashamed: I craved allies) when I stopped on the way back to glance inside the vertical window in the door to Daniel's room. I saw all the little five-year-olds sitting cross-legged on the floor, receiving some kind of instruction from their teacher. (She had been my teacher years before, and the sound of her droning voice mixed memories of succor with raw stretches of boredom.)

It took me a moment to spot him, my skinny little towheaded brother, and when I finally did, I gave a start of surprise. Instead of looking up at the teacher, as all the other children did, Daniel stared down at a spot on the floor in front of him. He was clearly spacing out, and disengaged from what was going on around him—which was of course not all that unusual for his age, but what gave me pause was the expression on his face.

Daniel was smiling. But for no reason. And it was the same smile he gave my mother, his aunts, all of the adoring adults who absorbed his beauty and transmitted their unconditional approval to him. Here in this context, though, it seemed like an expression of utter self-regard, contained and entire, and bearing no relation to anything around him. On the one hand it looked like a rictus, an agreeable social mask that his facial muscles produced without thought. But on the other, it seemed genuine. It looked as though my brother was so pleased with himself, with what he was, that it didn't really matter what anyone else was doing or thinking.

At the time I simply shook my head and went back upstairs. I loved my brother, but I also knew better than anyone else what an asshole he could be, and if the little fucker wanted to be so high on himself, then I could certainly find ways to derail *that* train.

That was my thinking at the time. But now, with the car rocking gently on the currents in the air, with the silence over all of us as though we were all waiting for the next bad thing to happen, I really looked at my brother.

He had his knees up to his chin, his arms wrapped around them. There was a crust of dried snot on his upper lip that he hadn't bothered to deal with. He was staring with apparent hatred at the back of Dad's head, his eyes unblinking and his mouth curled into a chilling S-curve of seething resentment.

ME: Psst. Hey, Daniel.

DANIEL: (Says nothing. Stares ahead.)

ME: (Speaking low, not wanting the others to hear.) Daniel. Hey, listen.

DANIEL: What?

ME: I don't know. It's just that—are you all right?

DANIEL: (Still staring ahead.) I'm fine. Just shut up. Leave me alone.

ME: It's going to be all right, you know. Everything's going to work out fine. For all we know, Dad's plan is going to work.

DANIEL: Don't say that. You're talking to me like I'm an idiot because I'm littler than you. You should just shut up. I don't need you to make me feel better.

ME: I didn't say that. Don't be so difficult.

DANIEL: Don't tell me what to do. You can't tell me what to do. No one can tell me what to do anymore.

ME: Well, technically that's not really true. Mom can tell you what to do. Dad can tell you what to do.

DANIEL: (Inaudible.)

ME: What's that?

DANIEL: (Inaudible.)

ME: Come again?

DANIEL: (Clear, quiet.) I said fuck you, Kevin.

ME: (Slapping Daniel, hard, on the side of the head.)

DANIEL: Dad! Kevin's hitting! He's hitting and he won't leave me alone!

DAD: (Sighs.) Come on, guys, break it up back there. We'll sign you up for pugilistic after-school activities once we're back home.

SAM: Dad, Daniel doesn't know what that means.

DAD: Sure he does. (To Daniel.) Pugilism, son! Boxing, right? Marquis of Queensbury? We'll find a way to channel all that aggression into something constructive.

DANIEL: (Inaudible.)

DAD: Huh? What's that, Danny?

DANIEL: (Inaudible.)

ME: Forget it. Just forget it.

Daniel was telling my Dad to fuck off, which it was better Dad didn't hear, and the consequences of which, if he did, I really didn't want to deal with at the moment.

So instead I watched Colorado pass by outside the window, and thought morbid thoughts such as whether I would ever see this state again, or whether it would be lost forever, one memory among many as life whittled down its options into a familiar diet of regret, confusion, and the lost illusion of control that I would have moved mountains to get back.

10

SOME BAROQUE ARRANGEMENT COULD BE MADE

By nighttime it was awfully apparent that my brief spell of relative decent health was little more than an intermission in the unfolding drama of whatever bug I'd managed to contract. At first I experienced my condition as little more than strong sleepiness, which was no great problem since slipping out of consciousness suited me just fine. No one was really talking, I was increasingly frightened of my little brother, and my ears continually popped with shifts in our elevation—one feature of which was prolonged periods in which I could hear nothing much at all.

Again, no great problem. I hadn't liked much of what I had heard lately, anyway. But by sundown, after a perfunctory fast-food dinner that featured mostly monosyllabic conversation and a pronounced lack of eye contact, I was back in the car with a sense that something was going wrong with me.

The eye was all right, a little tender, but working in concert with its twin to provide me with vision in three dimensions. But there was a little tendril of pain that had started to snake from the back of my throat, up my ear canal and, with a sadism that I had to objectively admire, around the back of my head to a tender spot on my scalp that stabbed whenever I rested my head against the curvature of the car door—which was frequently, because I was having a hard time keeping my head upright.

"You guys all right back there?" Dad was asking. Daniel was semi-fetal, and talking to no one. I tried to say something, recognizing the need to restore some façade of comity among our troops, but the air between us had taken on a strange viscosity. My cranium, propped up onto the wadded Mexican blanket, felt as though it was floating in space. I let my eyes close.

"They're both out of it," I heard Sam saying.

We had pretty much traversed the Rockies, descending in great parabolas as the road traced the path down. Big semitrucks roared past us in the passing lane, taking advantage of gravity's pull to make up for time lost on the ascent.

"We'll make it there tomorrow," my father said, an understandable note of apprehension in his voice.

"Dad, I'm sorry for everything I said," Sam told him. I opened my eyes into slits and saw her reach out and grab hold of his hand on the steering wheel. He turned his over, and squeezed.

"You don't have to be," Dad said. "I love you the way you are, Sugarnut. If that means you have to tell me off from time to time, that's part of the package. A guy like me needs to be put in his place once in a while, anyway."

"That's not true," Sam said. "Dad, I was wrong."

"You weren't. And you know it."

Sam laughed a little, which cheered me immeasurably. I tried to relax the muscles in my neck, which for

some reason had begun to feel hot and abraded. I listened to the ambient hum of the road and wondered
how I was going to stand it when it stopped.

"—too late to turn back now, anyway," Sam was
saying on the other end of a gulf that had opened up
without my being aware of it. "So let's hope for the best,
Dad. For all I know, you were right all along. I really,
really hope so."

"Me too, darling," Dad replied, letting go of her
hand. "That's for goddamned sure."

"Too much swearing," Sam added.

"Sorry," Dad said, apparently genuinely chastened.
"It happens in times of stress. I think I'm fucking Touret-
tic or—oops. Sorry. Sorry."

Dad turned on the radio. The reception wasn't very
good, due either to the hills blocking the signal or the
paucity of towns now that we were heading toward the
desert. I closed my eyes again and listened to the news,
much of which seemed to comprise people going on
shooting sprees.

"You guys good for another hour or two?" Dad was
asking, in a manner that suggested we were indeed going to keep going. I was fine either way, because despite
the localized zones of discomfort that were taking root
throughout my body—my knees had begun to ache, I had
a strange sensation of fullness between my ears, and it was
now difficult for me to swallow—my consciousness was
rising above it all. I felt comfortable, even mildly blissful.

I was going to see my mother, after all, if things
worked out. Whether she accepted or rejected my father,
I missed her voice, and the gentle way in which she told
me what to do and lent form to me. It would have been

an oversimplification to say that I yearned for her to take me away from the crazy man behind the wheel of the Subaru, albeit one that contained a grain of truth. I hated it when Dad was making all the decisions; of course, I don't think it was a position in which he particularly reveled, or sought out. More than once in heated moments I had heard Dad tell Mom not to "mother" him, but he would probably always be a man who sought out guidance in one form or another. I recognized beneath his semi-manic state a need for someone to take care of him, and the horror of being left in charge.

None of which mattered too much to me. Dad was grown-up enough to drive the car and keep us out of immediate calamity, and I was in charge of nothing. Daniel was asleep next to me, or else in a state that was an adequate substitute, and I felt enveloped in warmth and ease.

My twin back home would be wrapping up the night's homework, tossing the family's dinner napkins in the clothes hamper upstairs, maybe settling in with a *Sports Illustrated* in bed before changing into his pajamas. Dad's double would be down in his office, ostensibly working on something but more likely reading blogs and listening to opera on his antiquated boom box. Mom would make a pot of tea and offer him some; he'd grunt, run his hands through his hair, and deliberate as though she had asked him to solve the Palestinian question.

Thinking idly, I flashed upon the notion that the four of us were extraneous to the larger equation. Mom had made her statement, like it or not. Maybe she really desired a new life, away from us all. Our doubles could carry on, fill our daily roles, live out the lives we had known until a couple of days before. The four of us could pull over somewhere, change our names, rent a little house. Life was probably cheap in a small town. Dad could get a job, something menial, and we could live out this fractured tangent while the mainstream of things carried on without us. We could simply disappear.

It might be discomfiting to Mom, of course, once she finally called home and learned that she was indeed still living there, and that Dad and the rest of us had no idea she had ever gone. But it could turn out to be a liberating scenario for her, a free pass, the get-out-of-jail card about which we all secretly fantasize about and yet still fear. Some baroque arrangement could be made, come to think of it, in which Mom could slip into the house from time to time, with her double graciously making herself scarce. Mom could dip her toe into the waters of her old life, then leave again. She would, of course, want to make sure that we were all right without her. Or with her. However you wanted to look at it.

"I should have bought more CDs," Dad said from up front, fiddling with the radio dial and producing all sorts of unpleasant static.

I was alternating between feeling very hot and very cold, although neither state troubled me much. I got it into my mind to tap Dad on the shoulder and tell him about my proposal—he'd always talked about getting a relatively simple and mindless job, driving a bus or working in a shop—maybe the idea would appeal. We could pick the town on the road ahead that had the most humorous name. Spittle, Bottom Bend, Panic: there had to be one like that, one that made you laugh every time you wrote your return address on a letter or filled out a form.

To my frustration, though, I found that I couldn't

summon the will to sit up and get Dad's attention. Someone seemed to have glued me to the seat when I wasn't
looking. That idea struck me as pretty funny, and I
laughed in my mind without the impulse extending to my
body. I had sufficient self-awareness to realize that what I
was laughing at—or rather, *not* laughing at—wasn't really
all that funny, and that I was in a very strange frame of
mind indeed.

We couldn't disappear without finding my mother,
that was borderline mad—not to mention, it would be a
form of abandonment eclipsing even her own. She had
never said, or written, that she didn't want to see any of
us again, or that she no longer wanted to be our mother.
This was between her and Dad, and I needed to let them
sort it all out. Moving to a tarantula outpost in Arizona
wouldn't solve anything.

Then I had the unwelcome realization that dinner
wasn't sitting well in my gut, and that the country music
coming from the car stereo was the most irritating and
intolerable sound I had ever heard. I turned a little in
my seat and felt as though I was still spinning long after I
settled into a facsimile of comfort.

Everyone was oblivious to my torment. My throat felt
as though I had swallowed a razor blade, and it seemed
entirely feasible that I might vomit. The pleasant fullness
in my head turned on me, shifting into a sickly pain that
made me breathe with jagged pulse.

This wasn't the way things were supposed to be. I
considered trying to rally to get Dad's attention, but it
seemed like too much effort. Instead I closed my eyes,
tried to blot out the fact of my own existence and, hap-
pily, succeeded for a time.

• ■ •

I never told anyone about it, for obvious reasons, but since the school year began, I had harbored a suspicion that my classroom was haunted. Back when I was in first grade, one of the older kids had corralled me and a group of my friends and spun a story about a child dying in our school decades before. I was sufficiently sophisticated to know that not everything I heard was true, but still.

You see, my school was big and old. It had a giant brick smokestack inexplicably located away from the main building, like a vent for some vast underground oven whose purpose was kept hidden from us kids. Inside, the halls were vast, with big fluorescent lights hanging from the high ceilings like perched birds, the floors kept gleaming by the janitorial staff, who for the most part stayed hidden in their basement lair next to the cafeteria. I had passed by there once when the door was open, and seen a stack of old newspapers and an oversized chess board; ever since, I had imagined the room as a den of stranded intellectuals, perhaps the hoarders of the real knowledge fastidiously hidden from us by our outwardly benign teachers.

While I took pains to avoid it, there were times when I would find myself alone in the halls—sent to the principal's office to pick up a form, for instance, or compelled out there by the insistence of my bladder. Every step echoed in the cavernous corridor, and the silences in between were charged and fearful. In the wintertime, sickly light from the low sun would press against the windows, too weak to come inside. I would look into the far distance of the hall's other end and my vision would blur with the vastness, as though there were a cave down there where some bone-rending creature waited for me.

But those were pedestrian fears, and in truth I enjoyed the thrill and the sense that I somehow understood a fierce and unwelcoming quality beneath the mundane spaces in which my friends and I spent our days. Since the onset of the new school year, though, I had felt a panicky dread far more often than I would have liked, and in the presence of my teacher and my classmates. Much of it centered around the way in which the classroom was constructed, with a narrow chamber just inside the door through which the children had to pass before entering the main classroom. My teacher had made the most of this architectural oddity, setting up a couple of computers on a long table and making it the main station for our individual cubbyholes, which we emptied every afternoon of our various graded tests and notes from the school administration.

A couple of times, during the mundane course of math, or our ongoing course on human anatomy, I had seen the shadows shifting in that ostensibly empty next room. I fully understood that light and shadows shifted for entirely neutral or innocent reasons, but I would also note that the light in our main room didn't shift at the same time, or with the same quality.

Like I said, this wasn't the sort of thing one mentioned to anyone. I got frightened sometimes when I was alone in the upstairs of our house. That was more or less out in the open, though, because my father had once seen me hightailing it down the steps to the safety zone of the living room and intuited that I had gotten a case of the creeps up there all alone.

"Kevin," he had said, startling me.

"Oh, Dad. Yeah."

He took me in his arms, another surprise, and leaned in close. I don't remember who else was home at the time, but it was clear that he wanted to say something to me that no one else could hear.

"Ever get scared in the shower?" he asked.

I think I just blinked at him. I hated to shower alone in the bathroom with the door closed. I always thought I heard sounds, and I dreaded what might be on the other side of the plastic curtain.

"When you get that feeling of fear, it's hard to shake," Dad said quietly. "Don't worry, though. I've been around forever, and none of that scary shit I used to worry about has ever happened to me. And after a while you're scared of so many real things that the imaginary ones get crowded out of your mind."

Of course he thought he was being comforting with this nugget of insight, but as usual he had given me a glimpse into the macabre terrain of his own mind that only added to my overall sense of being chilled and un-settled in a way I didn't enjoy.

None of which passed through my mind when I sensed a subtle shift in the air in the middle of the day at school; my classmates were oblivious, of course, but in general I found even my friends to be heedless about the more subtle textures around us.

My neck hurt. My scalp was tender.

So, my nature being what it was, I contrived to find all sorts of excuses to be in that little side room alone. There were hooks for our coats there, so I would arrive almost late for class and slowly doff my jacket while all the other kids were assembling for our morning circle. I would breathe slowly and calmly, as though my serenity would coax out whatever was hiding and make it comfortable enough to reveal itself.

I had a very strong suspicion, to make it explicit, that the room was haunted by the dead kid the older children had planted into our minds. None of my friends had ever brought up the topic again, but I returned to it again and again like a loose tooth I couldn't help but manipulate no matter how much it ached.

Think of dying at school. During the day. With everyone looking.

The older guys hadn't supplied any details regarding how the mysterious student in the past had died. It hadn't been necessary, we were shit-scared enough just with the skeletal details of the story. It could have been an accident, I supposed, something to do with the big boiler downstairs, or maybe a fall down the stairs and a surprise head trauma. Of course I knew that sometimes people simply dropped dead. It had happened to the father of Jackie, a kid in the other fourth-grade class, a year before. Jackie had gone home one day, then the next we all received a note from the principal: Jackie's dad had died in his sleep the night before.

Once I was well along this road, the idea of this dead kid haunting the school possessed its own tidy logic. I had heard that many ghosts were unaware of the realities of their deaths, and wandered the world playing out their routines with little inkling that they had been sidelined from the main game. My school had been around for a long time; the boy (it had to be a boy, it just *had* to be) could have died thirty, forty years ago. Perhaps he looked out the windows with half-awake comprehension, unable to notice the buildings on Hennepin Avenue changing, and the annual procession of new students through his old room.

And maybe that was what made the light shift, and made it difficult for me to concentrate on math class in the afternoon.

We came back to school one night after Mom got home from work, for Family Night, at which the PTA doled out pizza slices and orange pop to foster some vague sense of community (I sound quasi-cynical, but at the time I looked forward to these evenings all month). Once we'd all tucked into our food and sat in the cafeteria being hectored by some teaching aide about some form "less than twenty percent" of the parents had filled out and sent back with their children, I slipped away and climbed up the back stairs to the second floor.

My classroom was in the corner of the building. The lights were out but the door was open. The light from the hall bled in through the doorway just enough for me to make out the familiar coat hooks, computers, and cubbies.

The light switch was just inside, to the right. I didn't turn it on. Instead I went inside, stepping as silently as I could, and sat down on the floor against the far wall, under the windows. All was quiet. My school's floors and walls were so thick, so well built, that sound from downstairs was lost and evaporated before it could reach this elevated perch.

"Are you here?" I asked the silence.

At night everything looked unfamiliar and strange, like a classroom in some foreign country. Even with my line of vision I saw workbooks (*Adventures in Reading*) stacked on the table next to a dormant computer monitor.

"You can come out," I said. "It's okay, I won't hurt you. Aren't you lonely?"

My throat was unaccountably parched. I had my head pressed against the side of the wall. For a moment I thought I heard my father saying something to me, but that was impossible—he was downstairs, with the rest of my family.

"I know you're in here," I said. "I can see you moving sometimes."

It felt as though I was moving, but that didn't make any sense. Why would *I* be moving?

"Kevin?" someone said to me.

I gasped and jerked.

"Kevin can you hear me?"

"I'm right here," I said, but everything was wrong. I felt hot, suffocating. The air around me was unpleasantly stale, and I found myself blinking, unable to see as well as I had a moment before.

"Who's there?" I barked, more frightened than I would have liked to sound.

For the third time in recent days I came to abruptly with everyone staring at me. We were pulled over to a highway rest stop. Dad and Sam were leaning over from the front seats, Dad with one hand on the side of my face. I glanced over at Daniel, who shot me a rather predictable look of disgust.

"You sound like a *pussy*," Daniel muttered.

"Daniel!" Sam yelled.

It was nice of her to rise to my defense, it really was. But the harsh tenor of her angry voice sent a lightning bolt of pain over my scalp, running as though along strung wires into my ear and finally taking root in my throat. I let out a moan that was entirely involuntary.

"You look terrible," Dad said. "I mean, you look sick again. Here, look at this."

My father held up his big, bony index finger and started to track it in front of me. I looked at his face, unable to comprehend what the hell he was up to.

"Dad, he's sick," Sam said. "I don't really think that's helping at all."

Dad put his finger down and looked at my sister.

"So you're a *doctor* now?" he asked.

"Look, guys," I rasped. "I think I'm coming down with something. I was doing better, but I have been feeling really bad for a while now."

"Why didn't you say something?" Dad asked.

Sam snorted in exasperation. I suppose she thought that I had been playing the good soldier, taking one for the team, suffering alone in the backseat while Dad's crazy quest unspooled hour after hour. But then I remembered that I had *tried* to say something, but I hadn't been able to. I shifted in my seat and felt my clothes clinging to my skin. I must have been sweating like a warthog while wandering through that dream, and even then it felt real, as real as anything that had ever happened.

Dad put his hand across my forehead. "You're pretty hot," he said. He looked at Sam. "I don't suppose you packed a thermometer?"

Sam just stared at him.

"Well," Dad pronounced, withdrawing his hand and pulling himself back into his seat. "Rest and liquids. That's all we can do. We'll pull off and hit the road early in the morning. I'm thinking if I put the pedal to the metal we can be in LA by afternoon."

"Goody," Daniel said, still not deigning to look us.

"Tomorrow afternoon?" Sam said, the incredulity in her voice mirroring my own thoughts. The actual prospect of ending this journey was a tantalizing one that hardly seemed possible; at the same time, I dreaded on behalf of my Dad the trial that lay ahead for him.

"I'll try to get better by tomorrow," I told him. "I'm sure I'll be feeling better."

Dad hummed softly to himself. Surely he was thinking of the reception he would receive from Mom if he showed up unannounced with me deathly sick. It would probably confirm all of her doubts and apprehensions about him, whatever terminal qualms about his sanity and capability that had driven her from him in the first place.

"Okay, Kevin," Dad said, looking at me in the mirror. He knew exactly what I had just thought, every single word of it. "You do that. You just see what you can do."

● ■ ●

My double back home in Minneapolis slept under my down comforter, which was covered in representations of baseballs, fielding mitts, bats, and actual bases. It was a comfortable fucker, as I once heard my Dad say about his own king-size bed, probably the possession he treasured most in the world after his ever-present laptop. My double had eaten a Clementine orange while watching the dismal Timberwolves on TV in the living room. He had done his homework and brushed his teeth. He had fallen asleep moments after his head hit the pillow.

I lay in the dark next to Dad. I think we made it some-where inside Arizona before we stopped, but I had been in and out of consciousness and so numbed by physical pain that I scarcely paid any attention at all. There had been the usual fast-food feast at the motel—Dad had called it "The Last Supper" in honor of our arrival in LA the following day, going so far as to break off pieces of hamburger bun and start to deliver the Jesus transub-stantiation speech. He didn't get the reception for which he had hoped; Sam glared at him and sullenly dipped her McNugget in barbeque sauce, while Daniel stared slack-jawed at Nickelodeon flickering on the room's TV. I had shrugged at Dad, unable to muster a more animated response and completely uninterested in eating anything. After a while I slipped off my pants and sweatshirt, then got under the covers. My breath felt hot, and it was hard to fully inhale.

Within an hour Sam and Daniel were sacked out in the next bed, and Dad had turned off all the lights save for one in the bathroom, leaving the door halfway open. His breath was even and calm next to me, though I couldn't tell for sure whether or not he was awake. I really wasn't sure which I preferred, Dad fretting sleeplessly through the night next to me, or Dad falling asleep and having one of his tooth-grinding, sleepwalking episodes.

Sleep, which had come so easily to me in the car, now naturally eluded me. Often when I couldn't sleep I would run through the events of my day in reverse or-der, starting with the act of lying down in bed. But that had little appeal, given that I had essentially spent the day in the car, rounding matters out with the rapid on-set of whatever jungle virus to which I had succumbed.

So I thought about what was going to happen the next day. I pictured us pulling up in the Subaru, bumping over the rise at the end of Aunt Alayne's driveway, slowing down and parking just feet from her front door. I saw the house sitting there in silence for a few minutes, then an unidentifiable face peeking out from between the curtains. The front door would open, then the screen.

Aunt Alayne might come out first. "Glenn," she might say, so serious, perhaps not even hiding now the fact that she had never really liked my father. Us kids would pile out one by one, while Dad still sat in the driver's seat, his window open, too nervous to step out onto the solidity of the driveway.

And then I would see her. My mother, emerging onto the porch, perhaps wearing one of the dresses she always favored when visiting Southern California, strapless in bright colors, cut just above her shapely knees. I would pretend not to be sick, I knew I could maintain the illusion for a while, as I hugged her, smelled her hair, felt the way she wrapped a single arm tight around my shoulder and drew me close.

By then, Dad might have made it out of the car, his clothes wrinkled, his hair all over the place, that sheepish look on his face that always came over him whenever he had messed things up and gotten himself in trouble with my mother.

Their eyes would meet. Years of familiarity and recognition would pass between them, the way it always was, so many things understood without needing to be said.

And then the things that *did* need to be said would finally be given voice.

● ■ ●

I finally did fall asleep, and though Dad's tooth grinding
woke me once, he stayed put in bed and fell prey to no
ambulatory dreams that I could recall. When I woke in
the morning I felt as though I had sustained a decent
blow to the head at some point during the night, but I
was rested, and I was able to get myself together and
walk unsteadily out to the car under my own power.

We skipped breakfast, hitting the westerly highway
with little more than a few words passing between us.
Dad had the radio on low, barely loud enough for us to
hear, and the morning sky was hazy, a color that I would
have been hard pressed to give name to.

It's always the case with long car trips that, after the
first six or eight hours or so, time starts to become elastic
and notions of boredom become almost quaint. The four
of us were now attuned to the road. The car hummed
and hissed, the trucks roared, and Daniel at least took a
renewed interest in the video game Dad had bought for
him way back when we had started on this trip.

When the signs started to appear announcing the
proximity of Los Angeles, albeit still more than two hundred miles away, the dreaded countdown began. I had
no idea what Daniel might have been thinking, but Sam
and I from time to time exchanged nervous glances, our
unitary anxiety directed entirely at Dad, and whether the
culmination of this entire effort would come to nothing.

Dad was sitting up a little straighter in his chair, and
every now and then he raked his hand through his hair in
the mirror in an effort to tame it. Once, when we stopped
for gas, he plunged himself into his bag and found a clean
and relatively unwrinkled shirt.

Hours passed, and empty desert gave way to settled

desert, the mountains, the thickening traffic. A general anticipation settled over all of us, even Daniel, who was watching the road now. He looked for all the world like a wholesome, normal little boy, and for the moment I decided to gull myself into believing it was true.

After a while we pulled off the freeway at a familiar exit. Dad drove on a wide street that was more like a highway, then pulled off. We drove past bungalows, palm trees, convenience stores. In my memory, the day was sunny and bright. The universe's lighting director had chosen optimistic tones for my father's moment of reckoning.

And then everything happened pretty much the way I had visualized the night before. Turning into the driveway, the little bump. The stir at the curtains. Us kids getting out, stretching on the pavement. The front door opening, then the screen. Aunt Alayne. Dad still sitting in the car. Dad getting out. Mom appearing. The greatest hug of my life. Then Dad and Mom face to face.

My father had indeed managed to surprise her. She was distracted for a moment by my appearance, but I would be physically well within days. In what came after, all the shifts and changes, my illness would be forgotten as though it had never happened. The car ride west, the motels and the shock of being woken up back home in the middle of the night—all of it would lose its intensity and take on the soft-focus hue of uncertain memory. My mother, who had of course been absent while we were barreling toward her, had to reconstruct a partial picture from our four perspectives, like four photos taken with different filters taped together into an unruly whole.

Yet it would have strained her imagination, and mine as well, to imagine everything that happened after.

PART II:

TEN YEARS LATER

1

THE LIFE, THE BLOSSOMING, THE SEX, AND SAP

SAM I AM. GREEN EGGS AND HAM. SAM I AM.

I had been home for less than twenty-four hours before the craziness began. It was like everyone in my family had to ramp up the hysteria in honor of my return; because Mom and I held down the unspoken honorary titles of the Stable Ones, my presence threw off the intangible balance between the others. Someone had to go off the reservation from time to time—it seemed to be our way.

Although I had to admit, driving the Hiawatha corridor headed north toward the city lakes, things had been pretty stable lately. Mom had her judgeship and all her financial stability, and Dad had been with the same woman for almost a year (a post-divorce record for him, or close to it). Daniel had been his usual mysterious truant self, or so I gathered from my last trip to town over the holidays; he wasn't engaged in anything felonious, as far as I could tell.

I cranked open the sunroof on the Subaru. The thing was almost twenty years old now (old enough to drive itself, Dad said), but it got me to and from Madison, and represented one of Dad's great symbolic acts of generosity.

"This car represents a lot of memories to me," Dad had said before my sophomore year began. He pretended to wipe away a tear as he handed me the key, though maybe his jokey gesture was a cover for the real thing. "Maybe a few I would prefer to forget, but that's life. You can't pick your damnable fate, you just have to learn to live with it."

Daniel had been standing there, too, in front of Dad's apartment building, a smirk on his boyish face.

"Dad, Jesus," he said. "Does everything have to come with a speech?"

Dad had looked at Daniel in that way of his, as though he couldn't believe he had landed on this planet, surrounded by this set of people. There had lately been a new look in his eye as well, as we had all gotten older, which I took as something held in reserve. He could no longer lavish love on us the way he used to, when we were kids. We wouldn't allow it, the terms had changed.

The warm June air coursed through the car, tinged with a not unpleasing aroma of diesel. Even on this ugly industrial artery, no one in her right mind could have resisted Minnesota this time of year. All the life, the blossoming, the sex, and sap that had been repressed and tamped down the last five months was coming back to life. It was near to an angry feeling, this need to break down the climate's previous demands of denial, to grow, to undress, to fuck someone.

Which reminded me of my own recent troubles, which no one in my family knew about except for Daniel, with whom I could sometimes discuss these things. The bare outline of the situation was that, for the last half of my senior year of college, I had been sleeping with both my boyfriend and my best friend, who was a girl. Or a woman, if one prefers, though she showed little sign of wear from her twenty-two years and could pass for eighteen (to her chagrin, the gargoyle gatekeepers at the campus bars always thought her driver's license was a fake I.D.).

I didn't find this arrangement particularly objectionable, but the complicating factor was that my boyfriend, David, didn't know I was also sleeping with my best friend, Aimee. And when I was alone with Aimee, I may or may not have, depending on your perspective—or, to be more accurate, whether or not you're Aimee—downplayed the intimacy of my relationship with Dave and led Aimee to believe that she and I were developing, if not a long-term relationship, something that might transcend our perfectly serviceable situation and evolve into something more emotion-based than our frequent and immensely enjoyable knocking of boots.

So I had probably conducted myself badly. In my defense, I was in the process of finishing my undergrad dissertation, and Dave and Aimee were wrapping up their degrees as well, so it wasn't as though we all weren't under a lot of pressure (pressure that was nicely relieved, I found, by sexual intercourse with those lovely people, although not at the same time). But then Dave came across undeniable proof of my infidelity to him—walking in while I was kissing Aimee with one hand up her snug little ironic Sbarro T-shirt—and reacted in such a way that Aimee interpreted that I had led Dave to believe (and that *is* arguable), that the terms of our relationship precluded me doing things such as lightly grazing my girlfriend's nipple while chewing on her upper lip.

Inevitably, by the time this encounter was completed, Dave and Aimee had both come to the conclusion that I was a tease (both of them, mind, had loads of evidence to the contrary), a deceiver, a girl who toys with the emotions of innocents.

Sam I am.

So they both plummeted in my estimation that day, and I was pretty much done with both of them—convenient, since neither wanted to speak to me anymore and left me there in my apartment with a mug of cold coffee and a half-pack of cigarettes that I set about demolishing while cursing both of them in silence. Which probably sounds callous, I know, and the reality is that I was anything but.

By the time I was on my fourth or fifth cigarette, I had to admit to myself that part of me had tired of both of them—despite the fact that I paradoxically felt something akin to love for them, I couldn't really see how they fit into post-graduation life. It wasn't anything as cold as calculation, but it was a truth that had been bubbling under the surface of things for some time and it appeared to be time to face these thoughts.

Packing up and leaving town turned out to be so much easier without having to say good-bye to anyone who really cared about me. In the days since David's discovery, he had been going around telling everyone extravagant stories about how I had hurt him, what a sneak I was, and Aimee had already decamped to the Rocky Mountain hideout her rich parents maintained.

They both really pissed me off. David walks in, sees me kissing Aimee, and his first reaction is to get *angry*?

What a *pussy*.

I ended up taking 26th Street all the way across South Minneapolis, because it was an entirely life-affirming sort of day that would surely turn to shit as soon as I returned to the orbit of my family. I sensed something stirring, one of those every-few-years explosions in which all the stress and strain amid the Burns family had to be released like tectonic plates that had been rubbing for far too long.

Crossing over Hennepin into Kenwood represented one solid notch up the class scale; we had lived just on the other side when Dad and Mom were still together, in a funky three-bedroom they had sold for a pile of cash when they split up. Dad, I suspected, had been pretty much living on the proceeds ever since, and the dough had surely been invaluable during his child-support years. I drove past the old place every time I was in town, and the sight of it gave me strange pangs.

Mom had moved up in the world since those semi-Bohemian years. I hated to think of it this way, but jettisoning Dad had been a pretty solid strategic move for her. She threw herself into her work during the separation, rose up at her firm, and started earning an outsized salary, and almost a year ago she had accepted a pay cut for a place on the bench. She seemed happy. Happier than with Dad? I couldn't say. Of course she was a different person, no longer defined in such a large measure by her reactions to him, all the compromises she had had to make when they were together. I do know that Dad challenged her and made her laugh, which she must have missed on some level.

I tensed when I saw her house near the end of the block: big, brick, with a long lawn and a three-car garage behind it. Her Lexus was parked at the end of the drive.

Normally I would have come to her place first thing after arriving back in Minny, but I had gotten a call on the road from my friend Calvin, who had a crisis at his apartment. He knew about my handyman reputation and had heard I was back in town. I went over and fixed some wiring for him—seemed he'd gotten a shock when he used his hair dryer the night before and was convinced that painful death by electrocution awaited.

He was actually right. His wires *were* a mess. It was a good thing I had spent so much time with Dad in all those shitty apartments of his. I could do wiring, basic plumbing, Sheetrock, and could paint a room without needing to tape. The wonders of me.

I had just been finishing the job when my cell went off. It was Mom.

"Where are you, honey?" she asked.

"Here in town, actually," I told her. "I'm over at Calvin's place."

"I think I need you here," she said.

"Of course," I said. "What's the matter? You sound like something's the matter."

"Oh, I don't know." Mom paused. "I got a call from Gle—your father. You know how he sounds the alarm over nothing at all. But it has to do with Daniel. Apparently he didn't show up at your father's place when he was supposed to. I think we need you here."

Of course. Because of my special *rapport* with Daniel, our special fucking *understanding.* Jesus, those psychologists and family therapists really sold me out when they came up with *that* one. There were times when I figured that I *did* have an understanding of Daniel that no one else seemed to be able to grasp: that he was an amoral,

manipulative little shit who had never given a damn
about anyone other than himself since he was in kindergarten and probably before.

Not fair, not at all. Sometimes I thought he had been
done in by his beauty, which had made itself apparent
early and if anything intensified when he hit adoles-
cence, with his big dinner-plate eyes, plush full kissing
lips, and graceful way of moving as though the atmosphere was somehow thicker for him than for the rest
of us, propping him up, buoying him. And the timing
of my parents' divorce had surely hit him hardest of us
three kids—not that the journey to California had been
a morale builder for anyone.

What had it been, about ten years?

I parked at the curb and got out (a fleeting thought
that I didn't park in the driveway because of some
allegiance to Dad; *stay neutral*, said the inner referee).
I saw the backside of a familiar pair of Levi's sticking up
from a bed of roses.

"Hi, Elliot," I said, causing said ass to unfold itself as
my mother's *life partner* hastily got up, adjusting his gar-
dening kneepads and standing with a wince as his various joints popped and slid themselves into place.

"Hi, yourself," he said, his deep voice warm as always, his arms opening up to envelop me in a hug.

I could tell from smelling him that he'd smoked a
cigarette sometime in the past hour, probably lurking
out back behind the garage. It was one of the things I
liked about Elliot, his little furtive smokes when Mom
wasn't looking. He was tall, with a big chest and arms
that he carried apologetically; with his dark beard and
rounded glasses, I always thought he looked like some

Russian intellectual from a bygone century. He used to be a corporate executive, though he had made so much money that he had been able to walk away, and now he did foundation work, served on boards, and occupied himself in various ways that he strenuously insisted were all too boring to talk about.

"It's truly good to see you," I said when he finally let go.

The one uncomfortable thing about Elliot was that Mom had known him when she was still married to Dad. She had kept him pretty much behind the scenes when she and Dad were sorting out the cinders of their marriage, but a little rudimentary math yielded a distinct suspicion that Elliot had been lobbying her for a while, so to speak, or that they at least had an understanding upon which they finally acted once old Glenn was out of the picture.

I never talked to Mom about it, though she probably assumed that I would disapprove. I didn't. Life was complicated. People did their best and then tried to make sense of it after they turned the lights out at bedtime or woke up in the morning. I might not have learned much more about life than your average thirteen-year-old, but I knew better than to judge people.

"You finish your big paper?" Elliot asked. He bent down and gently dropped his clipping shears to the ground.

"*Finito*," I said. "Wrapped up with a bow, with lots of sugar on top."

"How's David? Is he going to come visit?"

"Don't ask," I told him.

Elliot gave an appropriately serious nod of his big brick head and let it go. It was such a luxury that Mom had shacked up with someone I could actually tolerate.

"She inside?" I asked.

Elliot glanced at the big reflective window on the other side of the front porch and gave a sigh.

"Trouble in the blended family?" I asked.

Elliot gave me an appreciative smirk, a mark of our little conspiracy. He had two kids of his own, both grown, who lived in other places and didn't come around much, a fact that didn't visibly bother him.

"Glenn called earlier," he said. "He was kind of worked up."

"You don't say."

"Well, you know your dad." Elliot let that nugget of obviousness hang in the air for a while. "I told Eliza not to worry, but apparently Daniel was supposed to be at Glenn's last night and never showed up. Since it was a Friday, I figured he just stayed at a friend's house and was too thoughtless to call."

Elliot had put in sufficient years with Daniel to earn the privilege of speaking critically about him to me. In fact, I usually beat him to it.

"But look, I don't know." Elliot grabbed a rake propped against the house and leaned on it. "Glenn thinks that Daniel's been troubled lately. Frankly, I haven't been paying close attention, because as usual your brother doesn't want to have much to do with me. So maybe your dad's onto something. I just wish he wouldn't push the panic button the way he does. It always freaks out Eliza."

Yeah, well, if I were Elliot I would also wish that my partner's ex-husband didn't have, and exercise, the power to roil her emotions the way he did ten years since they had last slept under the same roof. It must have sucked.

"I hear you," I said.

Elliot gave one of his slow nods of infinite patience, put his hand softly on my shoulder, and turned back to his garden. He would probably spend most of the day out there, and was probably all the happier for it.

When I went inside I let the screen slam behind me. I heard my mother's voice calling out from the kitchen.

"Kevin?" she said.

I crossed through the dining room.

"Guess again," I said.

Mom met me at the doorway. "Oh, *Sam*," she gushed, taking me in her arms as though we had been separated for years rather than a couple of months.

"Come on, now, Mom," I said. "You're going to break something."

She released me but held onto my shoulders, looking me over like I was something precious, which I didn't mind at all, having spent the last week as the Harlot Bitch of Madison, Wisconsin. Her hair was shorter than the last time I saw her, and its brown strands were streaked through with alarmingly more gray.

"I stopped dyeing it," she said, turning her head to let different light pass over it. "I might take it up again, but Elliot said he finds the gray sexy."

"All I can say is, keep him away from the nursing home, then," I said.

Mom did her little Three Stooges boxing of my ears, making a popping sound with her cheeks and her free hand. I wished the defendants in her courtroom could have seen her acting that way.

"Bad child," she said, and wrapped me up in another big, needy hug. Which I returned. I was a few inches taller than her, and I squeezed tight to her bony shoulders.

"I'm sorry I called you and worried you the way I did," she said, pacing into the kitchen and motioning for me to follow. "Coffee?"

"Please. And don't worry about it. I needed to get out of there before Calvin started asking me to replace the carpet or something."

"People *do* rely on you, don't they?" Mom asked, her voice rising as though this was inspired revelation.

"I guess that's just who I am."

"You look good," Mom said, which was actually a sincere compliment; for most other women I knew, that would have been code for *you've lost some weight. Not enough, but some.* But my mother had read all the books and assiduously labored throughout my childhood to keep me hang-up free about my body, a relative rarity (it seemed like almost every other young woman I knew had some tinge of eating disorder). At the moment I knew I was carrying about fifteen extra pounds, but I didn't care all that much. Anyway, I had genetics on my side. Mom was in her early fifties but had taken care of herself; her lanky, tomboyish way of moving made her seem much younger.

Mom poured coffee and we sat at the sturdy wooden table that looked out on the back garden.

"Elliot's slaving away out in front," I said.

Mom blew on her coffee and her brow wrinkled. "He's avoiding me," she said. "Not that I blame him. If he wanted to get more involved in these little family episodes, I'd probably think something was wrong with him."

"That's because something *would* be wrong with him," I answered.

Mom laughed. "Honestly. Your father."

"He's a real hoot," I said.

Mom turned serious. "Have you talked to him since you got back in town?"

"No, and I haven't checked my voicemail," I said. "He's too *intense* over the phone. I'd rather deal with him in person, where I have a chance of calming him down."

"Standard speech #402 about how much your father cares about you and so on and et cetera," Mom said, looking outside.

"Anyway. So what's the deal with Daniel?"

"Well, here's the thing," Mom said. She curled her lips over her teeth the way she did when she was organizing her thoughts before speaking. "Daniel's been running a bit of a game between your father and me."

"How unusual."

Mom gave a touché nod. "He's been splitting his time between here and Glenn's place, which is fine as far as it goes."

"I assume Dad's powers of discipline have not undergone a revolution since the last time I was here."

"No." Mom paused. "Glenn lets him smoke in the apartment. I *hate* that. Daniel's just a teenager."

"Mom," I said. "If Daniel's going to smoke, then he's going to smoke."

"Stop it. You sound like your father."

"It's hard to help it sometimes. But point taken."

Mom took a long slug on her coffee and I noticed that her hand shook with a noticeable tremor.

"But forget the smoking. For the moment." Mom put down her coffee cup. "At first I thought this split-share thing would be good. Daniel spending more time with Glenn seemed like a positive. I mean, he's a good father. I certainly never disputed that. And maybe Daniel was craving a more masculine influence or something."

"I don't know. Elliot's pretty masculine," I said. "He looks like a New Age linebacker out there in the yard. If he gets over his fetish for old ladies you might have some competition in the neighborhood."

"Smart. Ass." Mom saw that my coffee was running low and got up to fetch the pot. "All I'm saying is that it's good for a son to be with his father. But, Daniel being Daniel, he has to take advantage."

And, Sam being Sam, I was starting to feel pissed off. At least Elliot had asked me if I had actually managed to graduate from college before walking back into this drama. I felt like exploding at her that I was sick of being in the middle all the time, insanely tired of being the one person in this family with whom everyone could parlay. But I have an innate aversion to recycling old material.

"What, is he stealing or doing nasty drugs or something?" I asked.

"Could be. I don't really know." Mom sighed. "You see, recently we started noticing that there were certain *gaps* in our awareness of your brother's whereabouts."

"By *our*, you're talking about you and Dad?"

"And Elliot. And, I suppose, Katrina."

Mom pronounced Dad's girlfriend's name with such an absence of tension, lack of rancor, and little emotion that, all in a flash, I realized that the exact opposite was true. Mom never pulled off that level of a poker face unless she was hiding something positively rancid.

"And how is Katrina?" I asked, regretting my cruelty an instant later.

"Don't know. Ask Glenn." My mother stared me down for a long moment, then turned back to the garden.

"Fair enough," I told her.

"What I'm saying is that we all began to realize recently that Daniel has been playing us," Mom continued. "Telling me he was at Glenn's when he wasn't. Telling Glenn he was with me when I hadn't seen him in almost an entire day. We only found out when Glenn called me up about a week ago to ask me if I had any soy sauce I could send along with Daniel when he came over that afternoon. *I* had thought Daniel had been over there since the night before."

I stared at my mother. "Soy sauce," I repeated.

"*What?* I suppose Glenn was cooking rice or something. I don't know what he eats over there."

"It's not the soy sauce," I said. "It's that it took you and Dad this long to figure out one of the most basic tricks of divorced kids. Daniel's playing you off each other so he can go off and do something without you knowing about it. It's insane that you and Dad weren't more suspicious."

Mom's eyes narrowed in a wary stare. "You mean we should have known? But you and Kevin were never like this."

"News flash, Mom. We hid things from you."

"What things?" Mom immediately demanded, a sly and titillated grin forming at the corners of her mouth despite herself.

"Things," I said. "I overthrew a small Pacific Island country and installed myself as dictator one weekend when I said I was at Andrea's house. I had to come back, though. I had a Health test the next Monday."

"Is that after the times when you were sneaking pot in the basement?" Mom asked.

Despite myself, I blinked. "Before, I think."

"Well," Mom said. "I figured it was better for you to be smoking it in the house rather than in some park where you'd get arrested."

"Well, it's not like you and Dad did such a great job of hiding it, either."

"Hush. Your mother is a judge now. I never had sex before I was married and never let a joint cross my lips. And that's the official story if the newspapers call."

"So you want me to go over to Dad's and see what's going on?" I asked.

Mom didn't mind this abrupt change of gears; she did, however, fold her arms and look at me warily.

"Is it asking too much?" she said. "You're a college graduate now. If you tell me to buzz off, I'll respect it."

"Yeah, and you'll do what?" I asked. "Go over to Dad's? Have the two of you figure out where the hell Daniel is?"

"If necessary."

It wasn't that my parents never communicated, or hated each other. But ever since my mother left a decade ago, and the rest of us tore out to California to find her, there had been some unspoken business between them, something that prevented them from looking each other in the eye. And though they had handled the divorce with as much grace as they could muster, it had never been sufficiently explained to us what had gone on that compelled Mom to leave.

I could give her a hard time, and routinely think my share of ungenerous thoughts about her. I *am* her daughter, after all. But the fact was that my mother had been as lovingly reliable in my life, and that of my brothers, as any mother could have been without smothering. The fact that she had once walked out with only a brief note of explanation had never quite matched up. It was a sole, anomalous episode of apparent selfishness in an otherwise unblemished record.

And the strength of that inexplicable fact, the sheer mystery that underpinned the most momentous series of events in my family's life, made them impossible to speak about. But it certainly lent legitimacy to my mother not wanting to deal with my father on emotional matters for some reason that I couldn't quite pin down.

"No, you shouldn't have to do that," I said, not even sure of the precise meaning of my words. "I can deal with Dad. I'm a regular lion tamer."

"You're kinder than you probably should be, is what you are." Mom brushed a lock of hair off my forehead.

"You can give me a cookie when I'm finished."

"I can do that. Yes." Mom paused. "You're not still smoking pot, are you?"

"Only sometimes," I told her. "But mostly, I just sleep around."

"Oh, good," she said. "Pot is bad for your motivation. Sleeping around probably has the opposite effect."

"Well, it's gotten me in some trouble."

"Really?" Mom cocked her head. "Not—"

"I'm not *pregnant!*" I shouted at her. "I'm just a slut."

"Well, there are worse things." Mom put her arm around my shoulder, and I realized she was subtly leading me to the dining room. "Have your adventures, Sam. Don't let anyone pin you down."

"Dad pinned you down pretty early," I pointed out.

Mom winced. "And that turned out very well in the form of three children whom I happen to like and admire very much," she said. She aimed her luminous brown eyes at me, and I felt a girlish giggle well up inside that I had to suppress. No matter how old I got, part of me worshipped her like she was a pagan idol.

"And a crazy ex-husband who lives a half-mile away," I added.

We were in the living room now. I could make out Elliot's big frame in the front yard, where he had partly taken apart his lawn mower and strewn parts across the grass.

"Not so terribly crazy," Mom said, sounding a little far away. "But he is an ex. An ex-this, an ex-that."

"An X-File?" I offered.

"Well, that would explain some things," Mom said.

We paused at the door and looked at Elliot.

"Is he going to make up things to do all day?" I asked.

"He'll probably stop soon," said my mother. "Now that you're here to fix everything, he'll probably determine that it's safe to come inside."

"Look, he can tell we're talking about him."

Elliot glanced up from his disassembled contraption, gave a confused smile and a tentative wave.

"He looks like a little boy," I observed.

"We're all children," Mom said, more seriously than I thought at first. "We're grown-up children. That's all we are."

"Some of us grow up more than others," I said.

"You think so?" Mom asked, painfully sincere.

"How is Kevin, anyway?" I suddenly realized I hadn't seen much sign of my other brother; last I heard, he was still living with Mom and Elliot.

"That thing I said about marijuana sapping your motivation?" Mom asked.

"Is Kevin your case study?"

Mom laughed. "He's Patient Zero for cannabis ennui."

"Is he going back to school?" I asked.

"I hope so. But you know me. The master manipulator. Everything that comes out of my mouth is laden with a hidden agenda. Or so I'm told."

"Pot makes you paranoid, too."

"Kevin doesn't need pot to be paranoid," my mother said. "He's quiet. You wonder what he's thinking about, and it turns out he's spun out this vast intricate narrative starring you—only it bears a glancing resemblance, at best, to the way you see things."

"He's always been that way," I offered.

"Go, Sam," Mom said, opening the door for me. "Be my emissary. Calm your father, locate your brother, and then come home to me. I bought a couple of expensive bottles of wine at Surdyk's, and we can get shitty together tonight and celebrate your finishing up with school."

She closed the door behind me. When I passed Elliot, for some reason I mimed cocking a shotgun.

"Big-game hunting?" he asked. His hands were completely covered in grease.

I nodded. I suppose it was nice to be the girl they called in when they needed big weapons.

2

THE BONINESS IN HIS BIG SHOULDERS AND SPIDERY ARMS

WHENEVER I WAS AWAY FROM MY MOTHER FOR A WHILE, THE milky warmth I felt from her physical presence would wane, and I would begin to nurse my grievances against her. The shrink I saw on campus told me this was all very normal, that I idolized her and felt unconsciously that I could never measure up to her standard. So I would begin to blame her for all the things that weren't right, implying that she had omnipotent power to shape reality, and that every little thing would be tucked away tight and hunky-dory if she only willed it.

As theories went, it was fine; I did look up to her, and overall I thought she had conducted herself pretty admirably through the sorts of challenges that I planned to avoid entirely—by, for example, never getting married. My campus shrink, or therapist, or whatever she was, picked into my past for a while, and naturally dug up the whole episode with my mother leaving, and Dad's crazy plan to bullet out to California and win her back.

Some of my worst memories revolved around that car trip; the fights with Dad, the way I broke him down with cutting remarks, my resentment over his having put us all in that situation in the first place. It hadn't really occurred to me that Mom could have avoided the whole gruesome mess by simply throwing Dad out on his ass. My final therapy session had ended with my mousy inquisitor quietly asking me to leave. Apparently I had become hostile and threatening. Some people.

● ■ ●

I cruised down Hennepin slowly, a one-girl motorcade, taking in my surroundings. There was the big old school where I spent a vast chunk of my childhood, winter mornings slipping off my snow boots outside my locker, long classes waiting for the slow students to understand what the teacher was saying so that we could move on to the next pointless thing (there, I had to admit, I was conflating with high school. When I was a little girl I was Miss Perfect, always the first to raise her hand, and sincerely thrilled every time I comprehended a new idea before anyone else). I caught sight of the playground out back, where I would hang behind from the gaggle of kids, wanting to be a part of things but never understanding precisely how to go about it.

As Kevin's big sister I always felt the responsibility to blaze a path for him, to make things easier for his sensitive soul. Dad and Mom chipped in with their own pressures on this front. Kevin got placed in classes with the same teachers I had had, teachers he had already gotten to know, and even they contributed to the sense that Kevin was some breakable thing. No one ever mistook me for anything that would shatter, of course. Sam was impenetrable, granite. That was the assumption. Right.

The Burns family. The genius people. Glenn, Eliza, Sam, and Kevin . . . then Daniel. Whom no one took for a genius. They just held him in awe.

East-West and the avenues in alphabetic order in the other: Aldrich, Bryant, Colfax. Here the population density was as great as anywhere in the Upper Midwest. Some old Victorians still stood, but in the sixties zoning had been loosened, and some of the great old houses were torn down and replaced by long, squat apartment buildings that looked to me like malformed kitchen appliances: a broken four-slice toaster here, a stack of convection ovens there. I didn't blame my mother for moving to the other side of the metaphorical tracks once life gave her the option.

Dad's latest place was a six-stacker, three apartments one atop the other arranged around a central staircase. It was brick, which I knew he liked, and had two bedrooms, which was a step up from his last hideout. He had a fairly steady gig those days, copy editing for a weekly paper and writing for an arts funding group downtown. He was able to work out of the house like in the old days; the jury was still out on whether that was good or bad.

I managed to find a parking space halfway down the block—decent luck—and I checked to make sure the car was locked. I had some possessions from Madison still in the hatchback, stuff that wasn't even particularly valuable, but I'd had crappier cargo stolen in the past. I tugged on the big wooden door in front of Dad's building; the lock was broken, just like the last time I visited. No need for the buzzer, then.

By the time I reached the top floor I was feeling the effect of the nonstop smoking marathon I'd indulged in while driving back from Madison (no, actually, it had been going on since that mess with David and Aimee). I heard the sound of loud voices coming from the other side of his door. As usual, he had public radio blaring.

I banged on the door. Nothing. I banged some more. Still nothing. I stood there for a minute, contemplating leaving. But there was nowhere to go, so I raised up my foot (clad in a fetching, if slightly butch, mid-calf black leather boot) and started kicking the shit out of the door. I had to admit it was fun, all that kicking, and pretty soon I was kicking for the sheer fun of it—even after Dad turned the radio down and I heard his footsteps running for the door.

"Jesus!" he exclaimed as he opened it, because I was in mid-kick and would have planted one in his crotch had he not swerved back to one side.

"I was knocking for a long time," I explained.

"Were you planning on kicking my fucking door down?" he erupted. "You could have just used the buzzer downstairs, you know."

"Yeah, right," I said. "Like you'd have heard that. I could hear your radio blasting as soon as I crossed the Wisconsin border."

Dad scratched his head and smiled. "I like to listen to it whenever I'm alone in the apartment. I guess I'm still not used to living in such a big place."

Having apologized, in his way, my father took me in his arms and squeezed me tight. No matter how old I became, I was always surprised in that first moment by his height, then by the boniness in his big shoulders and spidery arms. With his head next to mine, I saw that wiry gray had edged out the bushy black in his hair, the balance having tipped since I last saw him.

"I'm proud of you for graduating from college," he said, still holding me.

"And I saved you the trouble of driving out to Madison and standing in the sun with all the other parents," I told him. "Don't forget that."

"My considerate daughter."

Dad was wearing wool slacks too heavy for the weather, along with a gray rumpled button-up that he had tucked in at an angle, so that it formed a tent at his side. His sleeves were rolled up tight, over the elbow, and he had his reading glasses stuffed into the front pocket.

He closed the door behind us and we made our way to the living room. His secondhand furniture and voluminous stacks of books and papers were familiar enough, though there were a couple of plants in pots and a general sense that some hand had made an attempt to rescue the place from utter entropy.

"Um, Katrina's been spending a lot of time over here," Dad said. "You know her, right?"

"*Dad*, I've met her about fifteen times. We even had *dinner* together."

"Of course." He was standing in a sunbeam between the living room and the dining room, unaccountably embarrassed. "Well, she's kind of taken it upon herself to civilize me. At least on the surface level."

Katrina was a few years younger than Dad, a redhead who worked downtown at Target's corporate octopus. She was kind of a hippie chick in her downtime, burning incense and teaching yoga classes. She was an odd match for Dad, though a mental canvas of the succession of women he had dated since the divorce yielded no real pattern. It was kind of hard to picture a female equivalent of my father, or even someone with whom he would be ideally compatible. Other than my mother, of course.

"You want coffee?" he asked.

"I had some at Mom's."

"Oh." As usual, the very mention of his ex-wife sent my father into a moment of befuddlement.

"What are you thinking?" I asked him. "I mean, right this second?"

He looked up and blinked as though he had been caught at something he shouldn't be doing. "Well, I suppose I was thinking about your mother," he said. "I was . . . I was wondering about her."

"Is it weird?" I asked him.

He opened his mouth, shut it again, clapped his hands together. "I suppose the thing is, it's continually odd, once you've been such an integral part of someone's life, to imagine them carrying on just fine without you. And that's leaving aside the bitter notion that they might even be doing *better*. I suppose it's no different, in a way, than how she and I feel about you children."

It went both ways: it was difficult, painful sometimes, to think of either of my parents carrying themselves through the day without me. Sometimes I tortured myself by wondering how long after getting out of bed did either of them think about what kind of shape I was in, or about me at all.

But I didn't tell any of this to my father.

"I guess weirdness abounds," I said instead.

"Forsooth," he replied.

Then followed an awkward period of silence in which, for my part, the spiraling dynamic between us overwhelmed me, and I fought off the urge to maybe strangle him or fall into his arms weeping. He must have been feeling something similar because, without a word, he burst off into the kitchen. I heard the sound of pouring coffee, and I went into the dining room and sat at the chipped wooden table. (I had been with him when he bought it, at the downtown Salvation Army; he had pledged to rehabilitate it and learn woodwork in the process, which hadn't happened.)

Dad came back with a steaming mug and a look of relief on his face, as though some storm had passed.

"How's What's His Face?" he asked. "Dave?"

This was a little game we played. My father had a running gag: he lavished elaborate scorn upon whatever boy I was dating. The subtext was that none of them were good enough for me. I played along, not having much choice, though it was irritating when he would pal around with my boyfriends and then trash them behind their backs afterward. Hilarious.

"David," I said. "He prefers to be called David. Most of the time. *As you know.*"

Dad grinned. "*David,*" he said solemnly. "Perish the thought that I would offend his delicate sensibilities."

"You don't have to worry about it," I said. "I really doubt you'll ever see him again."

Dad immediately dropped his act. "He didn't hurt you, did he?"

"No. I hurt *him.*"

"Oh." Dad sat down in the chair next to mine.

"He caught me cheating."

"Heavens." Dad plunked down his mug. "That sounds dramatic."

"With my best friend."

"Who would be—"

"A girl," I said. "Aimee. You remember her."

He chewed on this for a while, staring down uncomfortably at the edge of the table. I let him agonize over what to say next for longer than I probably should have.

"I'm not coming out or anything," I finally said. "It was just one of those things. I prefer men, generally speaking."

"Generally speaking," he repeated.

"It's a different thing for girls, there's more flexibility," I added. "In my experience."

"I have heard. For some, at least," he said.

We stared at each other for a full thirty seconds, then we both broke into uncomfortable laughter.

"Goddamn," he muttered, getting up. "Here I was going to try to make it until nightfall before I lit a cigarette. So much for that."

He pulled out a drawer in the buffet and produced a pack of Marlboros and an ashtray. When he pulled out a smoke, I motioned for him to give me one.

"Not you, too?" he said with exaggerated pain.

"It's the hip thing to do," I said. "Even Elliot does it."

Dad's eyes widened. "Mister Perfect?" he said. "Mister millionaire lumberjack sullies his lungs with smoke?"

"Come off it," I said. "I know you like him. He's a good guy."

"I know," Dad admitted. "And that's precisely the worst thing about it. Why couldn't your mother have had the decency to shack up with some turd I could look down my nose at?"

We both lit up. Dad positioned the ashtray halfway

between us.

"Because she wouldn't," I said. "Because she's so basically good."

Dad nodded, exhaling a big cloud. It wasn't often that I could shut him up, so I savored the moment.

"Anyway, to the business at hand," he said after a pause. "Daniel."

"Away without leave."

"Precisely." Dad rolled his ash-end around the brim of the ashtray, an oddly delicate ritual I had never seen him perform. He had developed new patterns in my absence.

"You seem pretty calm," I told him.

"I've decided that I need to be philosophical about your brother."

"That's not what Mom said."

Dad chewed his lip; the sunlight through the window revealed that he hadn't shaved yet that day (he was a late-afternoon bather and shaver, a luxury of his longtime freelance lifestyle); the stubble on his chin was flecked with silver. It made me think of an aging Labrador retriever gone gray in the muzzle.

"You think I'm a crazy old dog," my father told me.

I once would have been shocked, but I was used to him reading my mind.

"In any case," I said.

"Well, sure, I was freaked out at first," Dad said. "I mean, he's in high school. Technically, I suppose, I'm obligated to know his whereabouts. But Daniel has been seeking his independence for a while now."

"Mom is pissed off that you let him smoke when he's staying over here."

"I know," Dad answered.

"Which is part of the reason you let him," I added.

Dad gave me a look, a grimace as though he had bit into something gone bad. "Let me tell you something," he said. "Annoying your mother is not something I do on a premeditated basis. It's something that comes as naturally to me as breathing, I'll admit it, but I have no need to pile on. If anything, I try to be as placating as I can toward her, because she's put up with enough shit from me over the years."

"Dad—"

"You started it," he pronounced. "If you're interested, I'll tell you precisely *why* I allow your little brother to smoke cigarettes in this apartment."

"You mean there's a reason."

Dad let out a big dragon cloud and looked at me with satisfaction. "Common ground," he said.

"Come again."

"I haven't been able to understand Daniel since as long as I can remember," Dad said. "But I let him smoke in my resplendent little bachelor pad here, and he softens toward me. A fraction. An *iota*. It causes him to let down his guard and occasionally deign to talk to me as a legitimate human being."

Dad had changed a lot. He still kept the world at arm's length with his spew of verbiage and his weird, intimate quasi-aggression. But in recent years he had been subtly advocating for an abstract quietude, not far beneath his instinctual idea labyrinths. When I was younger, he was fanatical in his need to know, to have, to experience. Time seemed to have stripped away much of that desire, and if I could distill what he now conveyed to me, it was: Life is going to disappoint you.

Best know that going in, and settle for the small pleasure of irony, rather than expecting the clouds to part
and meaning to reveal itself. And don't expect too much
from people, especially the ones you love. They simply
aren't capable of shouldering the burden.

Not that he had ever actually *said* anything of the
kind, but it was implicit. Dad's wanton impatience
had given way to bittersweet disappointment, a sense
that no matter how he tried, things would never turn
out the way he wanted. The problem, I could tell, was
that he had reached the far shore on the other side of
need, and expectation, maybe even passion itself. It was
as though he was waiting for a ship that would never
come in, and knowledge of his own predicament was
all he had left.

"Come on," I said. "It's not that bad between you
and Daniel. In his own way, he still idolizes you."

"We're very different people," Dad said, flicking the
fingers of one hand as though deflecting what I had
said. "I know he looks up to me, in the sense that I have
traits he lacks. I certainly wouldn't mind if some of his
certitude would rub off on me. Or his skill with people."

"You do all right," I said.

Dad pursed his full lips and looked at me as though I
might be putting him on.

"Does it really seem that way?" he asked.

I weighed several different responses, factoring
how each might be filtered through Dad's massive
self-absorption and abundant willingness to beat the
metaphorical shit out of himself over all his faults, imagined and otherwise.

"Let's just deal with Daniel for now," I said. "Then

we'll sort your life out."

"Oh, goodie," Dad said, putting out his cigarette with a flourish. "Because I sure as hell could use some sorting out. You got here just in time."

3

REALITY TOOK A FORK

WHENEVER ANYTHING BAD HAPPENED WHEN WE WERE children—bruised feelings, a setback at school, existential panic—my father would tell us that time was an illusion. Every moment exists at once, each a mini-eternity, and if we wished, we could cast our minds back to a happy one and take comfort knowing it was still there, shining, humming, ever unfolding.

Other fathers would have tried to placate with a trip to Dairy Queen (Dad availed himself of humble fatherly options as well from time to time), but this was Glenn, and so it was metaphysics over soft-serve. I took this too much to heart, though, and with a sinking feeling realized that the opposite had to be true as well: all the awful moments, the hurts and humiliations, were also hanging on the laundry line of time like stained sheets. Pain and shame suspended in the fabric of eternity, vibrating like a malicious chord on an out-of-tune piano.

I never brought this up to my father. He would have countered with some Zen, the-bad-and-the-good-make-up-the-whole, you-need-shit-to-make-the-garden-grow platitude. Maybe he would have been right.

The aggressively homely concrete pedestal outside

the Hennepin Avenue SuperAmerica was a handy place to set my blueberry slushie while I finagled with the wrapper on my fresh pack of smokes and hunted for my phone. I glanced through the glass at the grim cashier inside; his every motion seemed a stage in some larger and operatic defeat. He stared back at me. Gray, stout, stoic: he had been working there since I was in high school. I lit my smoke and nodded at him. He stared for a while longer, then nodded back.

I snagged a quick sip of my slushie while I waited for the phone to ring. In the heat of the day (early summer still, pleasantly so), blue ice condensed on the cup's plastic peekaboo lid.

"Sam." A nice and husky voice, sounding surprisingly happy to hear from me. "Are you back in town? What's going on?"

"Hey, Katrina." I liked Katrina for some of the same reasons I was fond of Elliot. She treated me like my own person, rather than an extension of Glenn, and my dad's life seemed generally improved by her presence.

"So did you graduate and all that?" Katrina asked.

"And all that," I told her. "I skipped the cap and gown, though. Dad's pretty glad."

"He talks a big talk," Katrina dropped into conspiratorial-girl mode. "But he's so proud of you. Just so you know, he told me that if you changed your mind and wanted to go through with the ceremony and everything, he would have been there."

My father was proud of me.

"Well, anyway," I said. I cleared my throat. A big cement mixer roared past, forcing me to take refuge in the little alcove by the side of the building.

"When can I see you?" Katrina pressed. "Do you want to come over for dinner tonight at Glenn's place? Or do you have plans?"

I hadn't realized we were so close. In Katrina's new-found intimacy I picked up on a distinct poison splinter of need. Was Dad putting her through one of his wringers, making her epically insecure? Was she trying to pull me close as an ally, in some probably unplanned and ill-thought-out campaign to solidify her place in his life?

She clearly hadn't known my father long enough. Glenn was experienced and adept at acting as though he didn't need anyone, when he probably needed those around him even more than they needed him, a truth too awful ever to voice.

So I didn't.

"That's the thing," I said. "Something's come up. When's the last time you talked to Dad?"

"A couple of days ago," she said, then added quickly, "It's because of me, this project that I'm on. I'm at work right now actually, at my desk. I think they're going to start chaining me to this thing. Literally, I mean. Meta-phorically, I'm already there."

Katrina's laugh was too quick, unsettling. *Don't take Glenn so seriously*, I felt like telling her. *Or he'll drive you to insanity. Humor him, enjoy him, just don't start wandering through the maze with him. That way madness lies—for you.*

"Then you probably haven't heard," I told her. "No one can find Daniel."

She let this sink in. I put out a hand to ward off a skate punk who had all the indication of asking me for a handout—a cigarette at the very least. I knew I was getting older, because an internal voice noted that he had

enough money to cover his hide in tattoos, so times must
not be terribly rough.

Okay, that was definitely Glenn's voice. In my head.
That happened far too much lately.

"Daniel's gone AWOL?" Katrina said, wariness entering her voice. I could well imagine the dots she was
connecting in her mind. She had, sensibly enough, maintained a policy of dealing with Dad as an individual,
shunting to one side as much as possible his reality as a
father and ex-husband, though her dinner invitation indicated that she might be considering a change in tactics.

"Yeah." I paused. "Look, Katrina, I don't want to
draw you into the family drama. But I kind of have the
idea that Daniel, I don't know, sort of opens up to you a
little. Sometimes."

Over the holiday break I had seen Katrina and Daniel
sitting next to each other by Dad's arch and ironic Charlie
Brown Christmas tree festooned with appropriately pa-
thetic tinsel and a single strand of lights, while Dad and
I commiserated at the dining room table. There seemed
to be something between them, some alliance formed no
doubt in solidarity against Dad. I hadn't thought much of
it. Dad often unwittingly encouraged that kind of thing,
but now I thought she might actually have some insight
into my brother's comings and goings (the ones he hid
from public consumption, as I assumed he did).

"Well, I was the youngest in my family, as you know,"
she said.

I didn't know, actually.

"And, well, it's hard for him being the youngest. In
your family." She paused, checking the depths of the
waters. "I mean, you're all so *imposing*. I mean it as a

compliment. But he's the youngest member of this genius family, you know. It's a lot to live up to."

Genius family. I had just got done imploding what was potentially a lasting and fulfilling relationship. Dad eked out a living on his laptop, but I'd lost count of the number of times I'd seen bills on his desk with ominous red lettering. Kevin was a stoner, apparently, in addition to being increasingly anodyne. And Mom . . . well, I could concede that one. She, miracle of miracles, seemed to be making life work.

"You're not saying anything. I said something wrong."

"No, no," I told Katrina. "I was just thinking."

"I don't mean to be insulting," she laughed. "What I'm trying to say is that you all have these big personalities, these strong points of view. Sometimes I think Daniel feels a little overshadowed."

"I think you have the wrong—"

"Anyway, you're trying to find him. Is everyone really worried? I mean, is there some problem you're not telling me about?"

"I hope not," I said. "Mom and Dad are trying to stay cool for the moment. Small-scale teenage rebellion. No one wants to be the one to lose their shit."

There was a pause at the other end. I heard the phone being muffled, and Katrina saying something in a serious tone. I took the opportunity to light a fresh cigarette and scan the people on Hennepin. With any luck, I'd see Daniel ambling by, send him to Mom's, then settle in to the serious business of my post-college drift.

"Sorry about that," Katrina said. Her manner shifted, and I sensed the old familiar distance between us. It was comforting, in its way.

"I shouldn't have called," I said.

"No, it's all right." Katrina went silent for a moment, fending off someone else at her desk. I did not envy her life.

"I should let you go."

"Look for him where he hangs out," Katrina offered.

"That's the thing. Neither of my parents has much insight into—"

"Try the New Age place over on Harriett," she said.

"Come again?"

"Daniel has been getting into that stuff," Katrina informed me. "*I'm* into that stuff. It's something we have in common. We're both seekers, even though your father rolls his eyes whenever I use that word. And Daniel has also been hanging out after school at a theater on the West Bank. The Abyss."

"Daniel's hanging out at the Abyss?" I'd been there once myself, on a date during a college break. His name was Kurt or Kirk, the show had been a parody of a Greek classic, the sex afterward remained in my memory only because it took place in a car, and Kurt/Kirk's performance was hindered by the possibility of us being arrested for public indecency.

"Yeah. He's helped out painting sets and things like that," Katrina said. "You know, it's a tight little community over there. It's good for him."

A tight little community. The reality of living in a fractured family, in my experience, was mainly manageable, understandable, and coherent. The problem was that you were reminded, daily, sometimes hourly, that your family did indeed fracture, that reality took a fork and everything afterward was different, fundamentally changed. Daniel seeking out a tight little community, for instance, reminded me that my family had once been just that. Tight. A little society of its own, wagons duly circled. Then my mother absconded for Los Angeles, and that society splintered.

"Sam? You there?"

"Sorry. Just—"

"Sam, look, I have to go." Katrina paused. "I don't want to overstep my *role* here. I know I'm just your dad's girlfriend, and no one needs me getting overly involved."

I said nothing, but I gained respect for her.

"But have you asked yourself *why*?"

"Why what?" I said, knocked off balance. Across the street, a massive semi was trying to make an illegal left turn into the Kowalski's parking lot. It seemed quixotic, ridiculous. "Why has Daniel gone? I don't know. I'm not his shrink. He probably has some deep—"

"No, Sam," Katrina said. "Why do your parents have *you* looking for him?"

Because I was always the internal police in matters of the children. Because I was the oldest. Because I always looked after him. Because my parents couldn't really deal with each other, not anymore, and so neither was able to take the lead because that would have entailed communicating with the other.

Because we once shared a life that had seemed unbreakable, an ever-ascending curve upward that instead veered sideways into a life that none of us could fully come to terms with. We were all ashamed, and none of us could see straight.

"Because," I told her. "Just because."

4

I WANTED TO PICK HIM UP AND SHAKE HIM

BACK IN THE SUBARU I FOUND MYSELF SMOKING AGAIN; whenever sense-memory catapulted me back to the drive to California when I was thirteen, which was pretty often, sometimes accompanied by a queasy sense of my girl-self taking stock of what I had since become, I remember smelling the coffee, but not the smoke. I couldn't remember at what point on the line of nicotine addiction Dad was perched in those days, but it must have taken considerable will not to light up even once when we were all in the car together. All bets were off, after all, but Glenn managed not to smoke around us even as his life was violently crumbling. As a smoker now, an anachronism myself, that memory inspires a certain respect.

I rubbed some moisture out of my eye, flicked ash out the window, and cursed the traffic. In Minneapolis, a half-dozen passive fuckwits behind the wheel can create a mini–traffic jam, while just beyond them, open pastures extended to the mocking horizon. Then traffic would suddenly open up, and I'd get to drive a block or two until another mini-jam, and then another. I noticed

that a formerly boarded-up apartment building on 28th
Street had been given a coat of paint and, for some inexplicable reason, a pair of columns (Doric? Ionic? Ironic?)
on each side of the front door, like some disheveled college dropout donning toga and laurel for a last-minute
revel. Across the street, what had once been a Mexican
grocery was now a diner, apartment for lease, real-estate
agency, and employment service all under the same roof:
eat, work, sleep, fuck—maybe, hopefully.

I wondered if the last couple of hours signaled the
beginning of a long gravitational pull back home, to family, to familiarity. This was in no small way terrifying. I
mean, I couldn't think of *anyone* inside the city limits, in
that moment, who I wanted to shag.

Well, that wasn't *entirely* true. I wouldn't want to open
myself to accusations of lacking imagination.

My cell phone went off the same instant the light
turned green, and I started tacking to the right side of
the road until I found a parking space behind a moving
van ("MOVE U," painted on the back). I managed to
pick up before the voicemail kicked in.

"Sam," said a thick, deep voice.

"Kevin, Jesus," I said. "What in the world do you
have to be so depressed about? Hearing you say my
name is enough to make me want to find the nearest
bridge and jump."

"Yeah. It's nice to talk to you, too."

Dead air. I shouldn't have jumped down his throat
like that. But I wanted to pick him up and shake him, until all the stupidity and bloody-mindedness came rattling
out like so much loose change.

"Sorry," I said.

"No problem." Kevin paused. "I'm at Mom's. In my room. So I can talk."

"I don't think Mom is really very interested in listening to your conversations, Kevin."

"You'd be surprised." A pause, an ambiguous noise.

"Are you puffing on a joint?" I asked him, with more accusation in my tone than I intended.

"No. I am not at the moment." Kevin gave a laugh suggesting that, if he wasn't puffing on a joint currently, he had been recently. "What, do you think I just sit around and get stoned all day?"

"It crossed my mind," I said.

Kevin released a groan of disappointment. I knew that I was supposed to be the *cool* one in his life, the one who *understood*. But maybe I didn't. I had managed to do my share of fucking around and imbibing recreational substances—while also working a part-time job and *graduating from college*. Kevin had been the one whose institutional test scores had eclipsed my own (until him, I had been at the upper echelon in our school's history); we had made mockery of the PSAT. While I hated to be the one chiming in with the conventional majority, it was appalling that he had dropped out. And it was maddening to hear the torpor in his voice. He was better than this.

Deep breath, Sam. I looked into my sunglasses in the mirror. Now wasn't the time. Kevin wasn't a problem for me to solve alone.

"Little brother," I said, trying to beam a much-needed light into the chasm.

"Big sister," Kevin said, surprising me with his affectionate tone. "I love you, you know. It's so nice to have you back in town."

I had to turn my head, as though something was shining at me, too bright to look at directly.

"I know," I said. "Me, too."

"So where are you, anyway?"

"I am surrounded on all sides by what appears to be the southern districts of the city of Minneapolis," I said.

"Are you going to be staying here at Mom's?" Kevin asked.

"Why? Do you mind?"

"Why would I mind?" Kevin asked. "You always make enough for me when you cook omelets for breakfast. Maybe it'll give me motivation to get out of bed earlier in the morning. In fact, now that I think about it, it actually *will*."

"Make sure there're mushrooms in the fridge," I said. "And plenty of cheddar."

"Sam," Kevin said, serious now. "I really am terribly glad you're back. I think that maybe not having you around has contributed to this . . . *thing*."

"Thing?" I repeated.

"Come on," he said, sounding more like the brother I wished I had. "I've been in a thing. I'm *aware* of it. I shouldn't have dropped out of school. Probably. I could have had my *thing* and at least gotten a degree at the same time."

"That's kind of what I did," I said.

"I figured as much. Damn." A pause. "So, Sam, I should at least tell you that I'm going to get out of this *thing*. Maybe that means just getting into another *thing*, we'll see. But for whatever reason, I just don't want to give Mom or Dad the satisfaction of admitting that I haven't exactly been wowing myself with the way things are going. Perverse, huh?"

"As always," I said.

He chuckled. "Yeah. Yeah, I guess that describes it."

"So what do you think about this Daniel situation?" I asked. The moving van was now occupied by a couple of hefty guys carrying take-out trays from the Mexican place across the street. I remembered that I had forgotten to eat anything all day.

"We'll need lots of eggs, of course."

"For what?" I asked.

"Breakfast, remember?" Kevin said. "Most important meal of the day. Even little children know *that*."

"Well, that's appropriate," I said. "Because right now it feels like I'm talking to one."

A quiet sigh. When, exactly, had my little brother developed this attitude of *resignation?* I supposed we could have seen it coming in high school, when he gradually receded from his circle of friends, allying himself with a couple of quasi-outcasts and sitting back in the comfortable perch of mockery while his peers acted in plays, wrote for the newspaper, played sports, got laid. Kevin had had a total of one girlfriend in those four years, during his junior year. Her name was Glenda, of all things, which set off all sorts of squishy associations in my mind, hopefully not Kevin's. She wore her dyed red hair in a bob and generally gave the impression that she regarded my brother as attractively easy to manage. She eventually cut ties with him at the end of the school year, citing irreconcilable differences. More than once she had hinted to me that their sex life was a disappointment (I didn't inquire further), and the whole campaign visibly deflated Kevin for months after. I wasn't even sure if he'd been with a girl since, although like all three of us siblings, he managed to fit all sorts of high jinks into the periphery of what others knew about him.

Kevin was still brilliant, still funny, still reasonably good looking. He was young and there was plenty of time. It was the pressure of this family that had gotten to him; I understood that better than anyone.

"Look, I don't really know much about Daniel other than the public image," said Kevin. "We don't hang out much. He's been drifting between Mom and Dad's for a while now. It's hard to say exactly who he even lives with."

"And how has he been getting away with that?" I asked.

"Because he's *Daniel*."

No further elaboration was required. It wasn't that Daniel actively resisted scrutiny, or judgment; it was that he effortlessly bypassed it, gave it a toreador's sidestep, glided on to the next thing. His grades were always in the B range, with some fluctuation here and there, and he always performed a bit better than average on the standardized tests. He wasn't particularly curious about the world, except when he needed something from it, which could range from a burst of intimacy (a conversation, usually a private sit-down, after which he would pretend it never occurred—I, like everyone else, always let him get away with it) to a sum of cash or a concert ticket. He took more than he gave, in every relationship and interaction in his life, although no one ever seemed to hold it against him.

There was no question of his having girlfriends, of course. The topic never came up. But he quietly, to my mind stubbornly, had never come out to the family (like I just had, sort of, to my father). My parents sailed along without raising the subject, and Eliza in particular seemed entrenched in abstract denial. This was a topic about which Elliot and I had shared a long, non-verbal dialogue, usually in the form of widened eyes, pursed lips, and sidelong glances. If there had been a boyfriend, Daniel had kept it hidden from me.

"Well, *speculate*," I said. "I haven't been home in months. I'm trying to get the lay of the land around here."

Kevin uncorked a put-upon exhalation. I watched an elderly woman and a small child crossing the street together, holding onto each other. The sun was beginning to heat up the Subaru's interior.

"He's probably doing the usual teenage things," Kevin said. "Sex, drugs, heartbreak, I don't know. He's more the heartbreaker type than the heartbroken type, but who can say? He's probably hanging with friends and being passive-aggressive by not calling and letting anyone know where he is."

"But he's never done that before," I said.

"Sam, first time for everything. You know. Whenever he actually does decide to have a conversation with me, it's about whether I think he can get into First Avenue for a show, or one time he had this idea about going to Central America and wanted to know how much I thought it would cost. I told him to check the airfares online, but he kind of laughed at me. I think he expected me to do it for him."

The moving van was long gone, replaced now by a two-seater convertible, out of which came a young couple (him in glasses and customized facial hair, her in a mini-dress and the kind of artful makeup job that had always eluded me). The two converged on the sidewalk and proceeded to engage in a very intense conversation, a confab that looked to become flamingly contentious in no time.

"Do you think he's in trouble?" I asked. "Because neither Mom or Dad will come out and say it, but they're both worried. You know—"

"Maybe it's a gay thing," Kevin said quietly.

We let that one hang in the air for a while. Kevin and I had previously had a couple of short, clandestine talks on the subject.

"In what sense?" I asked.

"How should I know?" Kevin exploded. I knew he had developed an unexpected, uncharacteristic degree of discomfort with all things homosexual—excepting the typical lesbian fetish, of course, evidence of which I found in abundance once while using the computer in his room—a closed-down conventional streak.

"*You* brought it up," I said.

"I don't know," Kevin said quietly. "It's not like he's exactly *closeted* or anything. But if he sees guys, he doesn't let Mom or Dad know about it. Or me. Not that I'm fixated on the topic."

"Of course not," I said.

"But I can tell he's frustrated," Kevin plowed on, oblivious to any irony. "He brought up the parade during Pride weekend a couple of months ago. Mom was like, 'Uh-huh. That's nice, honey.' Maybe Daniel's just off, you know, *exploring.*"

Part of me certainly hoped so. But despite Daniel's massive self-absorption, he was always considerate of our parents. Meticulous, almost, as though he regarded

them as fallen creatures who needed to be granted ritual-
istic respect and little else. It was, in a somewhat modified
form, the same attitude he took toward Kevin and me.

"I suppose I'm worried that he's gotten in over his
head," I said. "But come to think of it: That's the thing
about Daniel. He *doesn't* get in over his head."

"That would require coming out of his defensive-
reflexive shell," Kevin stated. "As well as allowing himself a moment's vulnerability."

"Nice one, *Dad*," I laughed.

Kevin allowed himself to laugh. "That's the thing.
You think I don't know that I'm eventually going to turn
into him? At least you're a *girl*. That mitigates fate *somewhat*, you have to figure. And Daniel's Daniel, that'll
never change. But for me, it's a long slippery slope right
into Glennville. I'll start *pontificating*, and going on about
spacetime, and all the while my fly will be unzipped and
there'll be a roaring grease fire on the stovetop that I
won't even notice."

A cruel part of me thought Kevin was wrong. If he
wasn't careful, he wouldn't turn into Glenn. Glenn, for
all his admitted ridiculousness, was sharp and seeking,
alive. It was what I loved about him most. Kevin was in
danger of turning into something else. He needed to *try*.

"Mom's worried about you," I said.

"You know, we almost got through *this* conversation
without having *that* conversation," Kevin said.

And what was I going to say? That I agreed with her?
That we weren't harpies bent on his persecution, but that
we had eyes and ears, and that Kevin had been indulging
unattractive personality traits that had been brewing for
years? That if he kept going in this fashion he was going

to turn into the sort of man people didn't much like?

"Well," I said. "You know Mom."

"Yeah, I do." Kevin let out a humorless chuckle. "Oh, well. I'll turn things around. I have some things simmering. And then you know what I'll tell her?"

"What?"

"Top of the world, Ma," Kevin said. "Top of the world."

5

MORE SENSATION AND ACTION

THE WHITE FLAME WAS TUCKED AWAY A COUPLE OF DOORS from a corner of Harriett Avenue, next to the office of someone who offered "unconventional therapies" and a bakery that specialized in gluten-free chow and whose austere window display seemed designed to attract those who enjoyed denying themselves pleasure. Chimes jingled as I went through the doorway. I caught a smell of incense, the stinky kind, and complex, restless electronic music playing at a level just above subliminal.

Not my kind of ambience. When I wanted to alter my consciousness I tended to gravitate toward bars.

The place was inundated with all manner of shit: one whole back wall packed to the ceiling with books, shelves with stones and crystals, racks of clothes made presumably without animal contribution, and behind the counter a galaxy of glass jars stuffed with what I took to be herbs, ground-up leaves, perhaps the odd tincture in a long array of vials. The place had been there for as long as I could remember, and I'd driven past countless times. Not once could I recall any curiosity about what was going on inside.

David had told me, shortly before discovering my extracurricular behavior, that he felt me pulling back.

Shutting down. I hadn't granted him much by way of reply, but my first, unkind thought was that if I was shutting down it was because of him. Now I wondered. I had no idea Daniel hung out in a place like this. I never thought about places like this. People who came to this place *believed* things; it was all hokum, I assumed, but I didn't have anything to counter hokum. I didn't believe in much of anything. My entire existence was a long, elaborate process of reacting to whatever was going on around me.

"I hope you don't mind my saying this," said a voice from behind the counter. "But you look like you're going through something heavy."

She was about five years older than me, her long dark hair pulled back from her face. Countering all my hippie stereotypes, she was equine in big, chunky heels and a sleek dress that emphasized . . .

Perhaps I was getting confused. I was just noticing too much.

"Nice boots," she said.

"Thanks," I replied, suddenly very self-conscious. I was one of about a half-dozen customers in the place; most had the absorbed air of regulars.

"Been here before?" she asked, her smile sweet, disarming, and chill. A ways down the counter a scowling man with facial tattoos was fussing with a batch of what looked like lawn detritus on a big sheet of brown paper.

"No, never," I said.

"Are you from out of town?"

She seemed so static, so *still*, so sure of her place in things. I wondered if it was an affect that would come to me when I was her age. Because I liked it.

"No, I'm from here," I said. "I just came back. From college. I just graduated."

She took in the nervous edge in my voice and smiled again. "Are you going to stay?"

"Beats me," I said. "I don't have any other plans. I thought maybe I would have something going on, but a couple of situations kind of fell through for me at the last minute."

"Oh," she said with sympathy. She put her elbows on the glass countertop; it was spotless, and reflected her chin and slightly asymmetrical nose from underneath. "Well, then. Is there anything I can help you with?"

"I'm actually not here as a customer," I said.

Her eyebrows rose a couple of millimeters. "But you're here."

"That I am." I paused. "You see. Here's the thing. I'm looking for my brother."

"What's your name?" she asked.

"Sam. My name is Sam."

"I'm Lida," she told me in a way that suggested, to me, that this was an introduction to something that would go on forever. "It's nice to meet you."

We shook hands. Mine was a good deal larger than hers, and hers was very soft. I think she lightly ran her fingertips over my palm as we disengaged. This was not the ideal time for the feelings I was having.

"Anyway." I coughed, and tasted Marlboro. "His name is Daniel. Daniel Burns. He's a teenager. A high-school student."

"And why would I know him, Sam?" asked Lida.

"My dad's girlfriend told me he hangs out here," I explained, though it sounded silly as soon as I said it.

"Katrina? Big red hair?"

I couldn't think of Katrina's last name. Damn it. I was sounding like a nutcase, and what made things worse was that I was suddenly aware of being massively worried about what Lida thought of me.

Wonder of wonders, Lida's expression opened up. "*Katrina*," she said. "I've known her for ages. I think my mother went to high school with her."

I decided that I would not relay that information to Katrina. I had a solid sense that she didn't want to be bracketed in age with Lida's mother.

"Well, anyway," I said. "My brother Daniel hasn't come home in a couple of days, and I'm trying to track him down."

"And he hangs out here?" Lida asked.

"So I'm told. Look, it's probably—"

"What does he look like?" asked the guy at the other end of the counter, still regarding his leaves and branches and bark. His fascination with the stuff was convincingly organic, in line with the black tribal tattoos that ran up his neck. He wore a black leather vest over a black turtleneck, and his clothes strained against muscles that looked as though they could pulverize stone. His head was shaved, and stubble traced the borderlines of his hair's recession.

"Well, he's skinny and kind of short," I said. "He has straight brown hair. Delicate features, pretty striking, really."

He looked up at me, finally.

"Looks kind of like you," he pronounced.

"Well, yeah, people say that sometimes."

"Only, and don't take this the wrong way—"

"No worries."

"*Prettier.*"

I wasn't sure exactly what was the *right* way to take that. Yet I knew exactly what he meant, and it was true.

"Fair enough, I suppose," I told him. Lida was looking at me with something like concern, a sisterly expression, protective of my feelings. It was nice, although some other part of my brain immediately kicked in and inquired whether I might play on her empathy for future contact.

"Yeah, I know him," the guy said. "I didn't know his name. But I see him around. Never buys much of anything. Always has other kids with him."

"I only work here part-time," Lida said. "That's probably why I never see him. I also do therapeutic massage."

I let that bit of information slide past for the moment. I had an ache in my back from all the driving I'd recently endured. It took a supreme act of will not to tell Lida about it in great detail.

"I saw him about a week ago." My tattooed comrade took a second to reflect. "You say you can't find him?"

"That's right."

"Can't say I'm surprised." He looked back down at his handiwork; he was sorting out his floral debris into piles: stems, leaves, buds. He had a little scale and a hand grinder.

"What do you mean, Gary?" asked Lida. "That's kind of judgmental."

"Is what it is." Gary shrugged. His mammoth shoulders rippled. "I'm just saying. If he's the kid I'm thinking of, he has a weird vibe."

"Oh, that must be him," I instantly chimed in.

I shifted closer to Gary when a customer—male,

middle-aged, white beard, soft-spoken—chatted up Lida over a display of jewelry. I burned with irrational jealousy, and sidled up to the counter. Gary fixed his jaw, clearly annoyed that I was interrupting his plant communion in order to chat about something as trivial as my missing brother.

Gary stared at me; his eyes were black and nicely devilish. He looked to be in his mid-forties, maybe older. "What, are you like some kind of detective?"

"Not really," I said. "But assuming he hasn't gotten into any real trouble, it would be nice to save him the embarrassment of having his parents scour the city for him."

"Maybe you just need to call the cops, you know. Why is your family making you find him, anyway?"

I sensed something other than disdain and annoyance from Gary. It was enough to warm a girl's heart.

"Nobody's *making* me," I said. "It's . . . it's just the way it works out. We give each other a lot of room to operate. Disappearing for two days is stretching the elasticity of the system, though. That's a problem."

Gary looked at me as though I had just started speaking ancient Aramaic.

"What is this stuff?" I motioned at his paper, which looked as though a forest fairy had vomited all over it.

"This is sage," he said.

It looked different than in a spice jar, which I supposed was the point of Gary's labors. The music shifted now, warbling from hidden speakers, a slow cascading piano. It wasn't bad, actually, sort of calming and meditative. Although in recent years I'd gone out of my way *not* to feel calm and meditative, I could see the appeal.   Whenever I tried to relax, such as with a

guided meditation tape the university mental health office had given me free of charge during my sophomore
year (when I had slid into a routine involving two boys,
not at the same time, and whatever I could get my hands
on to drink, smoke, or snort), I got this panicky feeling,
as though if I unclenched I would cease to exist. It made
me want to move, grab something, do something, do
someone to get more and more sensation and action.

"—if it's just me, or if there's been a real genera-
tional *shift*," Gary was saying. "The kids today seem *older*
or something. More sophisticated. In some ways it's good.
Free of all the racist bullshit baggage that was in the air
when I was growing up. But they also seem *bored*. They
carry themselves like nothing matters. Like, where's the
fucking *passion*, you know?"

I must have looked confused. I couldn't be sure
whether Gary was talking about Daniel in particular, or
maybe me or someone else. Lida was standing with her
hands clasped behind her back, one hip cocked to the
side as she rattled on to her customer about necklaces
and rings. She glanced over, caught me looking at her,
and looked down, still talking.

"I mean, I don't know your brother," Gary continued. "I'm pretty sure I know who he is, but I don't know
much of anything about him. I don't *presume*, you know."

"Of course not."

The sinews of Gary's great muscled neck pulsed
with the rhythm of his speech, undulating the black
bands of his ink. He was at least a foot taller than me. I
couldn't tell if he was handsome or not, beneath all the
ink and body mass. He could have hired himself out on
the side to an agency crafting nightmares—the sight of

him standing at the foot of my bed in the middle of the night would be enough to turn me Christian.

"But when kids come in here," Gary said. "And they're *kids*, I don't care what they think or what anyone says. When they come in here, they wear that smirk. Like they're checking out the whole spiritual seeker thing, it *interests* them, but they don't want to let on that they're looking for real *meaning*, or that they have a big black void at the center of their lives. Because, you know, to admit *that* is to admit we don't know what the hell we're doing. We're not *cool*. We don't have everything figured out."

"I guess—"

"Mediation, that's what's killing them," Gary went on, as I looked pointedly at my watch. "Everything in their life is a stand-in for what really matters, what they might allow themselves to *feel*. They act like nothing matters, but it's a *pose*."

We all have our strategies for getting through it all. Gary had found solace, apparently, in massive amounts of weightlifting, body art, and herbs. Come to think of it, he hadn't found all that much solace. The big ropy vein in his neck was pulsing as he spoke, and a deep red hue accented the black tattoo tributaries.

"Look," I interrupted. "I'd better get back to looking for my brother. You know, bringing him home."

"Maybe he *is* home," Gary said gnomically, getting back to his sage business, dismissing me. Apparently I was part of the problem rather than the solution.

"No, I just—"

"In the bigger sense," Gary said tersely. "Some people live their whole lives as part of a family, but it's more a cell than a home."

Yes. A decent point. Roaming the city to find Daniel *did* have an aspect of arrest and incarceration to it. But the possibility that he might live apart from my parents before turning eighteen was never on the table (we had some impermeable strains of middle-class conventionality). There was definitely an unspoken assumption between all of us that Daniel would hightail it from our close orbital proximity as soon as he gathered the years and the means. As a child he had been ethereal, otherworldly, somehow apart from us even when he was most dependent. The man he was growing into, I had known for a long time, wasn't going to come visiting much. He was like a cold star in space, content with his powers of attraction but caring little about where he had come from or the constitution of his flame.

The older man had bought two woven bracelets from Lida, taken his bag, lingered for as long as was socially acceptable, then left. There were no other customers in the store, save for a couple in the back having an animated discussion by the book section on astrology's efficacy. (Him: it's symbolic of the transcendent mind, the universe sending information to us. Her: it's unconscionable bullshit, you're stupid.) Lida turned away from me, tidying up the incense display.

"Well, thanks anyway," I said.

She smiled. "No worries. It's not like we actually *helped* or anything."

"That's all right," I said. "It was . . . really nice to meet you, anyway."

"Gary wasn't giving you a hard time, was he?" Lida asked. "He tends to go off on tangents. He's actually a pretty good guy. He's been a little tightly wound since his Shih Tzu died a couple of months ago."

For the life of me, I couldn't tell whether she was teasing me. Gary worked on, apparently oblivious.

"I hope you find your brother," Lida said. She had an extraordinarily high, pale, and lovely forehead. I was filled with an overwhelming desire to kiss it.

"I will," I said instead. "He's probably playing video games at a buddy's house or something."

I had no idea why I said that. Daniel didn't play video games, and some great male-bonding session was the polar opposite of any way he would spend his time.

Lida's eyes widened a little, as though with a realization. Then the expression passed.

"Video games," she said. "Sure."

I turned to go; I was suddenly on shifting and uncertain ground, and fleeing the place was the most sensible option I could come up with.

"Hey, wait a second," Lida said. "When you get things all sorted out, why don't you . . . stop by and say hi? I work Tuesdays, Fridays, and Saturdays."

"Stop by," I repeated.

"Yeah." Her eyes met mine, then skippered off. "Definitely."

"I will," I said, one hand on the door. "I'll do that. I will. *Definitely*."

When I got back inside the car it was stifling; I'd forgotten to leave the windows cracked. So I sweated, and lit a heater anyway, and started the car, and fumbled for my cell phone, and tried to figure out what the hell had just happened.

Because I had just made the most outrageous,

embarrassing dork out of myself in there. And because I truly could make no sense of anything I was feeling. I put the car in gear and drove, needing motion, needing to get outside myself.

6

DESCRIBING A VOID

THE CITY WAS DOGGED AND DETERMINED TO DENY ME THE satisfaction of spatial flow; I pointed the Subaru toward the freeway and encountered a thwarting galaxy of red lights, lane-clogging delivery trucks, and constipated ineffectuality all around.

Mom picked up her phone on the second ring—a surprise, since she rarely had the thing turned on. She said my name in an unfamiliar, clipped way.

"Tell me something good," she pleaded.

"A meteor the size of Mt. Everest isn't about to hit the Earth," I told her. "As far as I know."

"Smart ass."

I maneuvered through *sloooow*-moving traffic and got myself onto the freeway without rear-ending anyone. I was adrenalized, amped, and raw-nerved. The endless barrage of nicotine on my central nervous system probably wasn't helping. But it *was* helping otherwise.

"I went to this New Age bookshop gift-store place."

"The White Flame."

A surprise. The White Flame wasn't the sort of place I associated with my mother. Eliza always banished notions of the spiritual firmly into the category of things enjoyed by those soft in the head. Decades of dealing with the law, with offenders, with the guilty, had given her an accrued disdain for the faulty thought loops in which people lived and designed their lives. She regarded some traits as weaknesses if not fatal flaws: emotionality, pliability, religiosity. I didn't know to what extent she understood this about herself.

"You've heard of it," I said.

"Well, I've seen Daniel come home once or twice with bags from that place," Mom said. "About six months ago, he broke out some dried sage and burnt it in his room. He said it was a ritual to cleanse the vibrations. Or something."

"Did it work?" I asked. "Were the vibrations cleansed?"

Mom gave a chuckle. "Ask him. I mean it. Right now. Ask him. Tell me he's with you."

It wasn't doing much for my state of mind, having Eliza demand reassurance. It felt as though we were in the dawn of the coming parent-child role reversal I had heard about, and which filled me with vivid dread. I blended into traffic and pointed my nose north.

"He's not with me," I told her. "And from the sound of it, he hasn't been by your place, either."

"No, and I just talked to Glenn."

"And?"

My mother sighed, long and deep. "He tried to calm me down," she said.

"So he hasn't heard anything."

Mom paused. "Now, on top of everything, Elliot is pissed at me. He's out sulking in the backyard, probably smoking behind that tree of his. He won't talk to me."

"Why?"

"He's angry with me for sending you to look for Daniel." Mom paused. "He's probably right."

"It's not like I'm in harm's way," I said.

At the time, of course, I had no way of knowing about the gun, or what would happen before the sun went down.

"You know, Elliot is not very critical toward me," Mom said. "It's one of the ways in which he's very good and kind. Your father was the same way, when he wasn't all excited and making impossible emotional demands."

I shifted lanes. I was trying not to think about Lida. It wasn't working. So I thought about Lida, her eyes and her voice. What an awkward and adolescent ass I had made of myself.

"Anyway," Mom was saying. "Maybe you should come home. Maybe I should just wait for Daniel to come back on his own. Or call the police. I don't know. I'm not sure."

Eliza didn't do uncertainty well. It ran counter to her central currents.

"Look, Mom, I wouldn't be doing this if I—"

"It's just that Elliot has brought up the time I left Glenn. And you children."

I stubbed out my cigarette in the Subaru's burgeoning ashtray. The damned thing was always burgeoning. It was as though it came from the factory that way—pre-burgeoning.

"Are you there?" my mother was asking me.

"Yeah," I said. "I'm here."

A long pause. "Elliot has always wondered why I left the way I did," Mom said slowly. "It's always been a . . . a sticking point between us. He doesn't find that my explanation is fully . . . that he can understand why things happened the way they did."

My exit was coming up.

"He feels that it's emblematic of our family as a whole," she was continuing. "He wants to *get* us, and in a good way. He's very supportive and positive, but he doesn't understand what makes us tick. The five of us. The family."

I wished she would stop. I *so* wished that she would stop.

"And I can't fully explain. There is so much in the past that I think really needs to stay there, and I simply can't dredge all of it up right now. I just want to know that Daniel is all right."

Her voice broke. She was weeping.

"Mom, it's all right," I said. "Elliot will get over it."

Silence on her end. I pulled off the freeway and got in line before a red light about ten cars ahead of me. It felt as though the world around me was too *sloooow*; it needed to speed up to match my pace.

"We don't have to fix everything from the past," I said. "That's the beauty of it. It's done. We'll get Daniel home and have that wine tonight, out on the back porch."

"I'm sorry," she said, very quietly.

"Don't be," I told her. "I'll call you soon. Call if you hear from him."

I hung up. I drove. I tried to replace thoughts of my family splitting up with amorous flashes of Lida, with degrees of success. Because I kept remembering, as hard as I tried to forget, that I still didn't understand why my mother had left us ten years before. Left *me*.

●　■　●

I still hadn't worked out the Kurt/Kirk matter; vague memories returned to me when I assayed the resolutely plain marquee over the Abyss (what were they supposed to do? Paint an abyss there? It's like describing a void—can't be done). The theater's locale off University Avenue was torpid with summertime vacancy. I fumbled to take off my sunglasses when I went inside; it was pitch dark after the yellow, blaring sun.

After taking in a sequence of spots and orbs telescoping and jitterbugging across my field of vision, I walked past an empty ticket booth and down a long hallway. I couldn't remember ever being in an empty theater in the middle of the day; it was like walking a ghost ship, without the back-and-forth motion.

I reached the theater itself: quite small, maybe one hundred seats, dimly lit. Onstage was a set, half-constructed—what appeared to be a seedy motel room (wallpaper strategically stained, bed unkempt and cheapo), next to a patch of artificial grass that looked ready for outdoor scenes.

"Are you here for tickets?" said a voice behind me. "We're not opening for two weeks yet, but I can take your money. None of the performances are sold out."

He was my height, maybe five or so years older than me, and had embraced the onset of his premature baldness by keeping his middling brown hair shorn close to the scalp. He was holding a hammer, which was alarming until I realized that he had been working on the set.

"I'm not here for tickets," I told him. "I don't like theater very much."

He gave me a pitying look and I regretted blurting out my quasi-insulting comment. I wasn't firing on all cylinders. I wasn't entirely myself.

"Matt," he said, shifting the hammer and making to shake hands.

"Sam," I said. My hand was bigger than his. "I'm sorry about what I said. It's just that—"

"You know, when people say they don't like theater, it's usually because the theater they've been exposed to wasn't very good," Matt said. "They think it's their fault. But they saw something plastic, or phony, or incompetent. They don't realize their negative reaction was a *good* thing."

"Sometimes I think I'm a born philistine," I said.

Matt took a step away. One hand made its way up to cover his mouth. This guy had to be an actor. He looked as though I had made some deep and shocking admission. I meant it, though. Compared to the rest of my family, I was an ardent consumer of the pursuits of brain-dead mouth-breathers: reality TV, country music (mostly from the seventies—my soul missed its temporal mark by a few decades), airport novels. Dad's treasured Schubert and Mahler were too much bother for too little payoff. So much left me cold and numb.

"Then why are you *here*?" Matt asked gently.

"It's just that I have this *situation*, and I was hoping—"

Matt touched me on the elbow and led me to an empty seat. We sat front-row center, facing the stage. His head was haloed by a light shining from above. It made it hard to get a read on his expression.

Then I spilled the woe. By the time I was done, I was barely aware of what I had said. A great wave of worry swelled up inside me. Matt waited after I finished, staring at me as though making sure that another tide of confession wasn't going to hit shore.

"I know Daniel," he finally said.

"You *do*?"

"He helped me build the set for the Jordan Harrison play we did last season. He was in here painting for a solid week." Matt winced. "I liked the play. We lost money."

"When's the last time you saw him?"

"Daniel wants to act," he said, with a dry air of diplomacy. "But we haven't had any roles for someone his age. I suggested he start auditioning around town, getting *real*. But Daniel doesn't seem like someone who wants to do things the hard way."

"You sound like you know him pretty well," I said.

"We weren't *dating* or anything like that," Matt flushed. "He's still in high school, for God's sake. I'm not looking for *that* kind of trouble."

"Look, I wouldn't care if you were," I said. "I just need to—"

"The last time I saw Daniel was a couple of days ago," Matt said slowly. "It was over at Spyhouse."

"The coffee shop?"

"No, CIA headquarters." Matt grinned without much humor. "Of course the coffeehouse. I was in there for the WiFi. Daniel came in with a couple of—"

"On Hennepin," I interrupted. "Over by where my mom—I'm sorry. I just talked over you. I'm hyper. I'm worried."

"I know you are," Matt said patiently. "You have good reason to be."

"What do you mean?" Something kicked inside my chest.

"Daniel was really whacked out on something. It was the middle of the day. I think it was a school day. His pupils were big enough to dive into. He didn't even recognize me at first, but when he did, he came over to my table and made some bitchy remark."

"Bitchy—"

"About me being old and bald." Matt showed me his teeth. "Bald, sure. But I'm hardly old."

"You look distinguished," I said. "Pretty hot, actually."

Matt looked at me for signs of sarcasm. "Anyway. He and his friends left, and then about ten minutes later Daniel came back alone. He started apologizing, telling me he loved me, crying. I told him he was a mess. I told him to go home. He said he couldn't."

"He couldn't? Why not?"

"Because he said he can't stand his family," Matt said. He cocked his head, examining me, clearly wondering what we had done. "He said he hates you. All of you, every single one."

In the brief pall of quiet that enshrouded the two of us, I wondered about my own crimes, my own intolerability. I couldn't help but entertain the notion that, perhaps, there's truth to the notion that each of us gets precisely what we deserve.

7

THEORIES OF GOD DIFFICULT TO COMPREHEND

MY FATHER USED TO TELL ANYONE WHO WOULD LISTEN that children had innate psychic abilities. Reality was hyper-linked, he liked to say once, or sometimes I thought before, the term came into common usage. Consciousness is an aspect of the whole. Our minds can travel, and apprehend more than the limited input of the senses (this occurred on some quantum level, according to my father, though he was sketchy on the details). The mind can see things that it isn't supposed to see, things that are there but don't fit the standard model of reality. Children intuit this, according to Glenn, but the process of growing up, going to school, and accepting the common paradigm of reality dampens those talents until they wither and die.

That was the beginning, Glenn would say, of the long process of our eventual, individualized deaths. That's the way the universe, as much as we can comprehend it, works: you shine, you fade, you die, perhaps you shine again. Dad would also mention that there were esoteric representations of these things, which might in fact prepare the soul for higher understanding upon death, the possibility of controlling what happened next. But he never got into specifics. I had the sense that he was *working on it*.

Glenn used to say a lot of things. He didn't say quite as much recently as he used to, which bothered me whenever I noticed him passing up an opportunity to drop a timely philosophical mind bomb. I would watch his eyes glaze, and I could see him considering his moment to strike. Then he would move on, his arrows still in their quiver. Glenn didn't care as much as he used to. My father wasn't fighting nearly as hard. Too many years had passed, and his children had grown.

I used to overhear him talking to my mother about time elapsing. I had a sense that he was holding on with cracked and bloody fingernails, that he was describing to Eliza a fight against the pull of vast and infinite darkness (he reminded us children that time was the adversary no one could ever defeat). I wasn't supposed to overhear such things, of course, but the start of every new school year plunged him into a panicky, agitated gloom after those golden idylls of summer, drenched in sunshine free time. I liked to think that he drew inspiration from us when we were small, when he could unwrap facets of the world and hold them up to his light at just the perfect angle to elicit our wonder.

It had been years since Dad went on about his psychic children thing. Probably he would revive it once grandchildren came into the picture, although Daniel didn't seem the fatherly type, and Kevin's sperm were surely addled and lethargic from marijuana bombardment, and I planned to forestall reproduction until at least several lifetimes forward in my Karmic cycle.

Daniel was, to hear Dad tell it, more special than

Kevin or me, at least in terms of the psychic sweepstakes (I always thought of it in terms of Cracker Jacks—clairvoyant abilities in every fiftieth box). When Daniel was a little boy, he was *jazzed*. He was clued in. He knew more than any of us, about all the hidden *stuff*.

Or so went the mythology. I was never sure what my mother thought about any of this transcendent business. I knew this was one aspect of why my father thrilled her, his willingness to embrace ideas unlikely or apparently insane. To her, Glenn had *credibility*. He could dive into an ocean of nuttiness and come out with a gleaming pearl of truth. He thought he just might understand UFOs— he had a box of books in his office on the subject. He had theories of God that were very hard to comprehend, yet they were enticing in their gossamery elusiveness, and what a thrill just to watch him stumble over his tongue trying to express them. Glenn *went there*.

I assume that this quality became less attractive to Eliza over time (his false lurches into questionable conclusions, the recurring despair), particularly during those stretches when he seemed tortured by his own mind, isolated, seemingly willfully alone and stubbornly refusing reassurance (although she finally got him to start taking medication). I think these traits also became less attractive to Glenn himself, though in recent years I sensed him looking back and wondering if it might be possible to return to the way he once was. He was looking for inspiration. He wasn't the only one, though he was one of the few people I knew with the arrogance to assume that inspiration was somehow his right and not a rare, temporary, and capricious gift.

Glenn's case for Daniel's uniqueness boiled down

to two incidents—Dad claimed there were many more,
but these were the gaudy ones he shared with those in
the most inner circle. In the first, he took Daniel to the
Children's Theater by the Art Institute. Once inside, the
toddler Daniel took off running down the aisle. Dad
shouted after him, undoubtedly cursing under his breath,
then got the tickets out of his pocket to see where he and
his wayward son were supposed to be seated. He found
the seat and, to his astonishment, found Daniel there
waiting for him.

"No problem," Daniel told him. "I just listened to
what you were thinking so you didn't have to tell me
where to go."

Dad, to hear him tell it, had his view of the universe
nicely reinforced by this occurrence (barely stirred, not
shaken, not Glenn) and sat down to enjoy the show.

Daniel was a little older the next time. He and Dad
were walking to SuperAmerica, the Mecca of all things
sugarcoated, salt-infused, frozen, microwaved. It was a
spring afternoon, a weekend, and they walked the short
block and a half from our house.

"Dad," Daniel reportedly said. "Can cars drive on
the sidewalk?"

Glenn pondered this. "Well, theoretically they can,"
he told his preschool son. "But, by and large, it's frowned
upon. The sidewalk is for pedestrians. The street is for
cars. That's the way of things."

And so they continued to walk; they passed an ivied
brick apartment building, the long cavernous alley that
ran alongside it, then the death-trap parking lot of our
family convenience store and gas station. There they
had a view of Hennepin Avenue and, across the street,

a lineup of police cars, a fire truck, and an ambulance. Red lights flashed, strobed. The boulevard vibed with danger aftershocks.

Once they were inside SuperAmerica, Dad quizzed the clerk about the fuss across the way.

"A car just jumped the curb," the clerk said, deadpan and matter-of-fact in my mental movie. "Hit someone on the sidewalk just a couple of minutes ago. It was the freakiest damn thing."

More evidence. Daniel was something *special*. Glenn used to talk about consciousness as the great cosmic frequency—our brains were radios, receptors rather than generators of thoughts and ideas. Some of our radios were a little more tuned in than others, and that's how you got psychics, geniuses, and weirdos.

Naturally, having this stuff laid upon me from my earliest memories, I wondered which category described me. Or any of us. I couldn't speak for my brothers (no, really, I couldn't), but more and more I felt this ambient buzzing of restless, unshakeable disappointment. Not my father's, no, he was too fundamentally generous to ever heap disapproval upon any of us. It was as though I was disappointing the universe somehow, the great collective cosmic sphere that had supposedly bestowed upon us three siblings gifts and powers. I now had a Lit degree and little desire to do anything with it. Kevin seemed nearly ready to be done with it all, though knowing him, that probably entailed six decades of passivity and indifference before he went on to What Comes Next.

And Daniel . . . he was the strangest of us, for all his charm and magnetism. I couldn't remember the last time he seemed happy, or consumed with wishing to become something, or achieve anything. I didn't know what pleased him. And what a fucking cliché, to lay it all at my mother's feet, to blame Eliza's rejection of my father for what had become of Daniel. But inside, in a place I preferred to keep buried, I held her responsible.

"Sam?" Matt was saying. "You still here?"

"I'm trying to wrap my mind around all this. About Daniel hating us. I . . . never would have used that word."

"He's *young*," Matt said. "You try on all kinds of crazy ideas at that age. Not to get all pop-psychology on you or anything, but he's probably afraid of how much you mean to him. He says he hates you because his love is so strong that it frightens him."

Matt was wrong about Daniel. Here the simplest explanation was the truest. Daniel did hate us. He had felt that way since he was a little boy sitting in the backseat of what was now my car, seething and refusing to speak, eavesdropping on our squabbles and recriminations and wishing upon the stars outside that he could be rid of us.

"Maybe you're right," I said.

A door creaked open down the hall, in the darkness. I straightened in my seat as a pair emerged purposefully into the light by the stage, squinting at us. It was a man and a woman. I had a quick vision of glamour and attractiveness. Each had a pen tucked behind one ear in unconscious symmetry.

"Matt," said the man, about forty, with long black hair, an attractively protuberant nose, and the sort of rumpled chic that took an effort to maintain. He sized me up. I didn't particularly like it.

"This is Sam," Matt said. "Sam, this is Henderson. And Robie."

Robie was closer in age to me, and short next to Henderson—no call on whether this was his first or last name. She had her arms folded and a wary look in her eyes; she did the thing of exhaling with her lower lip extended to blow away a lock of short blond bangs that had strayed down her forehead.

"We've already cast the show," Robie said. "Auditions are over."

"She's not here to audition," Matt told her. "She's not an actress."

Henderson took a couple of steps closer. He made a show of looking over my face, lingering for a long time on my eyes.

"You could be," he said.

"I could be what?"

"An actress," he said, as though bestowing the highest possible compliment. "You have the face for it."

"I think it takes more than a face to act in a play," I said.

Robie looked at me again, up and down, with a tight-lipped weariness that seemed designed to shoot down any illusions I might have harbored about my ability to charm her. I found myself smiling. Why I wanted to please her, I couldn't say.

"Sam's looking for her brother," Matt said. "He's been missing a couple of days."

"And why are you looking for him here?" asked Henderson with a decent helping of icy condescension; apparently he felt rebuffed. He struck me as fundamentally insecure, the sort of man who goes around attempting to hide his combination of massive ego and equally colossal self-loathing.

I could have been wrong. Maybe I was just thinking of myself.

"Her brother is Daniel Burns."

"Daniel," Robie said. "Thin, not very tall? And sort of . . . pretty?"

I shifted forward in my seat. "So you know him?" I said.

"He auditioned for our last show," said Robie, who had glasses with very small frames that hung from a chain around her neck. "He was too young. He looks even younger than he is. Is he in trouble?"

"I'm not sure I know," I told her. "I'm only just beginning to grasp that no one in my family knows him very well at all."

"That means you're normal," Henderson said, somehow conveying superiority rather than sympathy.

Matt and Robie shot him simultaneous glares. Henderson shrugged. If that's how his pearls of wisdom were to be received, then we were welcome to wallow in our witless ignorance.

"Daniel hangs out with some people I know," Robie said, making it very obvious that she was choosing her words with care. "Not his high-school crowd. I don't know much about his peer group. But he also spends time with some older people. More my age."

"Ancient, in other words," Henderson said, in an awkward attempt at a joke.

Robie ignored him. "Wait here," she said. "Let me make a call or two."

With that, she disappeared down the hall, fishing her phone from her pocket. I reflexively looked down at my own. No messages.

I got up and looked around the half-finished set. It was like a dream that had yet to find proper shape, waiting for dreamers to invest it with meaning and weight. It seemed like just about everyone's life.

"I don't know much about your brother," Matt said. "But he strikes me as pretty secretive. It kind of comes with the territory."

"What territory?" I asked.

"Being a gay teenager," Matt said. "Things are better these days. But it still isn't always easy. Has he come out to your family?"

I took a long time before saying anything. I could feel Henderson scrutinizing me. This was what always annoyed, or discomfited me, about artistic types. They behaved as though they deserved the privilege of holding back, watching, burning others' reality for self-serving fuel. Meanwhile the rest of us were supposed to keep on living as though we were some kind of exhibition for their enjoyment, just characters reciting lines. I went home with a guy once who, twice in one night, pulled a notebook out of his pocket and wrote something in it without telling me what it was. I decided that his penis would also remain a mystery to me.

"Look, I have a weird family, all right?" I said.

"The genius clan," Matt said flatly. "Daniel mentioned it once or twice. I think it's a lot for him to live up to."

"Don't blame me," I said. "It's just that . . . we all had a sense of being unusual. And Daniel was unusual even within that," I said. I looked to Matt. "And yes, because he's gay, but also not because of it. I mean, how do you separate that aspect of a person's whole being and say how that makes them what they are?"

"I've downed many a bottle of wine trying to work that one out," Matt said.

"And no, Daniel hasn't come out to our family," I added. "But there's a lot more to *that* than being gay. I mean, we're about the most gay-friendly family imaginable. It's like telling us he's gay would be letting us in, letting go of all the grudges he's holding against us. He's lived a parallel life, on his own as much and for as long as he's been able. Sexuality is only part of that."

"I came out when I was his age," Matt said. "My dad was cool with it. My mother kept suggesting I go out for dinner with her friends' daughters."

"Did you?" Henderson asked.

"A couple of times." Matt nodded down the hall. "Robie was one of them."

"Too bad you couldn't swing for the other team," Henderson said dryly. "Maybe you could have saved her a lot of trouble."

The two men went silent, suggesting a river of turbulence and intrigue.

"We would have murdered each other," Matt said, almost cheerily.

"Each coupling eventually will end in homicide," Henderson pronounced. "That's why we have divorce, split-ups, and, when all else fails, the grave."

"Spoken like a man with two ex-wives," Matt said.

Robie emerged again, as composed and circumspect as before but with an expression of delicacy. Or restraint. Or simply not wanting to tell me something.

"I tried," she said. "I called a couple of people. But no one has seen him in the last week or so."

"Who did you call?" I blurted out.

Robie held up a hand. She had very long fingers, and her nails were chipped and unadorned.

"I don't want to get involved," she said. "I tried to help, and couldn't. Let's leave it at that."

"Come on," I said. "Give me the number. Give me something to go on."

"That's not going to happen," she said. "But listen. You have to know something. It sounds like he's not in very good shape."

"In what way?"

Robie looked down. "Daniel showed up at my friend's house about a week ago. He didn't seem to have slept in a while. He wasn't making sense. My friend wanted to call your family but Daniel was insistent that he didn't. Apparently he got himself together and eventually headed home."

"So this is about drugs?" I asked. "We're talking about drugs?"

Robie held up her hands in a this-is-all-I-know gesture.

Then my phone rang. It was Kevin.

"I'd better take this," I said.

I made to leave, making a gesture of farewell, but by then the trio had moved on. It was obvious that they were glad to be rid of me. After all, who needs other people's problems, especially when they remind us of our own?

8

A LONG TIME SINCE WE WENT AT ONE ANOTHER

I IDLED THE SUBARU A HALF-BLOCK FROM THE ABYSS, LETTING the fans blow hot air over me and interfere with the proper burning of my latest Marlboro Light. Kevin sounded far different than just a few hours before; his voice chimed with a sharp tang of gloating.

"So you *found* him?" I said, unable to believe that the disengaged slob I thought I knew had transformed himself. "Did you bring him home?"

"Slow down," Kevin said. "You're talking very fast."

"Sorry," I said, breathing dragon fire. "Where is he? What happened—"

"I was in the kitchen getting something to eat when the phone rang," Kevin said, very sure of himself, and I realized I had to enter into a bargain: he had done something affirmative, something difficult for him. I had to pay him respect.

"Mom and Elliot were out back arguing. I could see them through the window. He had his arms folded, and Mom was running her hands through her hair and getting way too close to him."

"I can picture it," I said.

"And I don't like to answer the phone," Kevin said. "You know, I kind of just realized it in that moment: I don't like to answer the phone. I don't ever want to talk to anyone. Isn't that kind of fucked up?"

"Not unreasonable, but yes."

"But I said fuck it, and I just picked it up." Kevin paused. "It was a guy wanting to talk to Mom. I lied and said she wasn't around. You know, I could tell he was kind of stressed out, and Mom was out there railing on Elliot, so I figured I'd see if I could sort of *handle* things."

There was no doubt in my mind that I loved my little brother very much. There was no one else in the world to whom he would confess how much this little breakthrough meant to him. This was the Kevin that used to make me feel joy, even when I was insulting him and pushing him away.

"And?"

"It was this guy named Ben," Kevin continued. "Daniel showed up at his place yesterday. I guess they're friends. Daniel didn't want anyone to contact Eliza or Glenn, but I guess he finally fell asleep so Ben called here. We can pick him up any time. I have the address and everything."

"What kind of shape is he in?"

"I didn't really ask," Kevin said. "I was just so glad to find him. And I haven't told Mom. You need to be the one to go get him. That's what he would want."

Damn it, it was true.

"Okay, I'll do it," I said. I stubbed out the cigarette. Kevin gave me the address. It was on Lake of the Isles, mansion territory. Somehow it didn't surprise me that Daniel had picked such an opulent place in which to break down (yes, it was uncharitable of me, but now that I knew he was safe, I allowed myself the luxury of feeling pissed off).

"Crashing and burning among the highest of property values," Kevin observed, sounding droll. "That's our little brother."

"The thought crossed my mind."

"I know it did," said Kevin.

I started to say something about how good he sounded, and how he was reminding me of the way things used to be, but before I could summon the words, he interrupted with an anxious cluck.

"Eliza's heading back toward the house," he said. "I'm going to have to run."

"Don't tell her," I said.

"Wouldn't think of it. Bring him home. I can't wait to see you."

Kevin hung up. And as improbable as the sentiment would have seemed to me scant minutes before, I shared it. The idea that there was hope for Kevin was one that I was willing to welcome, shine, and burnish. If I were one for prayer, I would have beseeched the infinite that this was the start of a lasting transformation, though another aspect of my mind leapt in, warning me against disappointment.

For the moment, though, I had to perform some speedy calculation. I had the address where I could find Daniel. The question was how best to act. I could drive there solo; it was little more than ten minutes away. But then what? I had no idea who this friend of Daniel's was, or what kind of shape my brother was in.

More worrying was the prospect that the lakeside

friend might have played a part in Daniel's condition. Daniel was hiding things. It sounded clear that drugs were involved. Lake of the Isles was a very upscale address. There was a particular variety of very wealthy people for whom chemical indulgence was part of the general terrain. I had made it a point to hang out with some of them.

Messy. It was all so messy. I didn't want to deal with this alone. But I didn't want my mother anywhere near this situation, which reeked of illegality. On a whim, I punched up the contact roster on my cell phone and dialed Elliot. I waited, listened.

"You have reached Elliot's voicemail," I heard. "Leave me a message, and I will get back to you as soon as I'm able."

I allowed myself to luxuriate in that voice for a moment: concise, to the point, delivered in a deep tone that oozed reassurance and solidity. Elliot was just the guy I needed in this situation: strong, calm, cool, devoid of judgment.

But he wasn't picking up his fucking phone. It was probably sitting in his study, while he was out in the garden taking out his extravagant hostilities on the rosebushes. Elliot was nowhere nearly as uncomplicated as he liked to pretend.

It was well into the afternoon, and the high beams of the sun had begun the slow process of self-muting, descending through levels of filtration that evoked the ghosts of rush hour, the specters of dinnertime. I still hadn't eaten anything, and I needed to make something happen.

"Yes? Sam? What is it?" my father barked, picking up

his phone after a single ring.

I sighed. I already knew that I would regret drawing Glenn into this.

"I think I've found him," I said. "I have an address."

"An address? Where?"

"Lake of the Isles."

"Give it to me," he said. "I can be there in minutes. How did—"

So I gave Dad the abridged version, though he was certainly smart enough to intuit what lay behind my diplomatic interpretation. On the whole, he seemed appropriately disturbed.

"The address," he commanded. "Give it to me."

"Dad, I don't want you going over there alone."

"The address, Princess."

My father hadn't called me that in at least a decade; it felt primal and instinctual, him trying to assert his patriarchal force. He should have realized that I would react the way I always had.

"No way," I said. "I hear that tone in your voice. You're all worked up and looking for an excuse to do something crazy."

A pause. "All right, you have something there," he allowed. "I am worried. I am anxious. I want to get my son back home. I am worried that my ex-wife feels that I am irresponsible and unreliable. So there is an element of saving face here. But I am by no means eager to do 'something crazy.' If anything, I am trying to reassert some measure of *sanity*."

"The calmer you sound, the crazier I know you are," I told him.

He started to laugh, but caught himself. "That's kind

of mean," he said in a hollow and mournful voice.

"Look, I didn't mean to be hurtful."

"I'm not necessarily disagreeing with you," he said. "But I *am* trying to stay cool. I don't plan on doing anything crazy. But I intend to go get Daniel."

"Wait for me," I said. "I can be there within ten minutes. We'll go together."

"I'm not sure I want that," Dad said. I heard his telltale grunt that signaled he was putting on his shoes.

"I'm not giving you a choice," I said. "I have the address. You have to wait for me."

"Oh, Sam," Dad said, and this time he allowed himself to laugh. "It's been a long time since we went at one another, hasn't it?"

"Let's not start," I told him. "Just hang tight. I'll be right there. And then we'll get this over with."

I put down the phone in the passenger seat as though it was a hot coal. I pulled into traffic, locating the source of my irritation: Glenn had wanted to go get Daniel himself, *after* farming out the Daniel-locating duties to me. My father's motivations were always gnarled and complex, but here I sniffed a hint of the glory hound. He wanted to rush into the unknown, snatch Daniel from consequence, and make things right again. And I figured this was some oblique way of making a point for my mother.

What point, exactly? That she shouldn't have left him, that she shouldn't have married Elliot?

Irritation can transform into sympathy. Peel away the ulterior motives, and Glenn probably simply wanted to be Dad again, not the single guy with the succession of girlfriends whom his grown children indulge with a visit from time to time. He never mentioned it, but Dad was the one who was *left*, the one who had launched us across the continent in an effort to keep our family together. Dad was the one who wasn't living the way he intended.

The traffic on I-94 slowed to a typically retarded crawl just east of downtown, giving me a focus for my nervy state that didn't involve diving deep into the inky rabbit hole of my family's knotted reality. Because, yes, I did feel for my father. It was terrible, what my mother did: *there*, there's the kind of truth that can't be voiced. But whatever her reasons for what she made come to pass, I had faith that they were good. Even if she never told me why. Even if she left me guessing.

Yeah, Dad had it rough. But in that, at least, he wasn't alone.

● ■ ●

Naturally, he was standing outside his building waiting when I pulled up. He was in the same rumpled professorial getup I'd seen him in earlier, along with a corduroy jacket in all defiance of the heat, and he was smoking a cigarette as though he was intent on *destroying* it, angrily reducing it to its component atoms and defiantly redistributing them into his lungs. He spotted me coming up the street in his old car, threw down the butt without stamping it out, and held out his hand as though he was flagging down a taxi.

Dad hurled his body into the Subaru and clamped on his seat belt as though it had done him wrong. I pulled out of my double-parked place and slowly made my way in the direction of our old elementary school. It was empty, of course, on summertime hiatus, its halls darkening as the afternoon bled into the tracings of nighttime.

"Tell me what's going on," Dad said, barely un-clenching his teeth in doing so, staring through the car's streaked windshield, which I hadn't cleaned since somewhere in western Wisconsin.

I gave him the expanded rundown, tracing the chronology of the day since I had seen him last, from my chat with Katrina (Glenn furled his brow), to my visit to the White Flame (Glenn stared in mute incomprehension), all the way to the Abyss (which seemed to ring a bell). The account ended with Kevin's phone call, which Dad pondered mutely before letting out a whistle of appreciation.

"Jesus," he said. "You're like some kind of postmodern Nancy Drew or something. No wonder your mother has so much faith in you."

"I'm a resourceful girl," I said.

"These people, at this theater," Dad said, pausing to choose his words. "They seemed to feel that Daniel was *troubled*. He has that kind of reputation?"

"I wouldn't go that far," I said. I had deliberately omitted the part about Daniel declaring his undying enmity for his closest relations. It was hard enough for me to deal with it. Dad would have been crushed.

"You wouldn't go that far," Dad repeated.

"Limited information," I said. "You always told me about the dangers of leaping to dire conclusions based on limited knowledge."

Dad leaned back in his seat, one hand coming to rest on his forehead.

"That I did," he said.

We drove past Jefferson School now, its sunken asphalt parking lot empty and chained off, its concrete stairways and mortar edifice in stately mourning for the past, perhaps even for the future. I could feel my father's energy churning next to me, and I knew him well enough to understand that the day's events were charged with import and symbolism. Dad was a fundamentally lonely man who had a tendency to get too heavy, to let the load in his heart drag him down when his energy flagged and he could no longer hold it up to the light. I wished I were a lot less like him.

We caught a red light at Hennepin. The four lanes of cross traffic were thick and congested, a regular chest cold of traffic, vehicular tuberculosis. My father and I smoked, knowing we shouldn't.

"It's going to be all right, you know," he said without looking at me. "Daniel. You, me, everything. I have a firm sense at this very moment that everything is going to work out for the best."

"Did you know anything about Daniel doing drugs?" I asked.

Dad stared at the burning end of his cigarette. "We smoke pot together once in a while. Not so often. Just a bit of father-son bonding."

I let it go. The unspoken knowledge that passed between us, of course, was that this information would have made my mother furious.

"I thought he looked a little stoned a couple of times the past few months," Dad added. "But nothing terrible. Not out of control or anything. And, you know, it's just not in my nature to pay close attention to that sort of thing. I always figure that if people in my life are doing an adequate job of keeping from me the things they don't want me to know, then those things don't need to impact me."

This was a graciously shortened version of the same speech Dad had given all of us kids many times, presumably in order to demonstrate what a great guy he was and that small transgressions would be overlooked. I knew that, in my case at least, this sentiment had made me feel that Dad couldn't be bothered with the details of my life. He liked me as a concept, as a grand theme, while loving me furiously, and occasionally he would thunder into the minutiae of my life, sensing perhaps that I was drifting away. But I knew that, in Daniel's case, my little brother could have been nursing anything up to and perhaps including a full-blown addiction, and it wouldn't have taken much energy to hide it from Glenn.

"Maybe I should have been more hands-on with him," Dad muttered as we crossed the road. "Maybe. I'm not sure. I'm also not sure that I know how to go about the whole parent-as-police-officer thing."

He sounded alarmingly fatigued. I could have pointed out that there was almost surely a middle ground between emulating Stalin and toking out with his teenage son, but this was a more mature me, and it wasn't fun anymore to pick apart my father's fractured logic—it hadn't been any fun when I was a girl, either, but it had satisfied a deep-seated need that no longer nagged at me.

Dad glanced over. I couldn't be sure, but I thought I sensed disappointment from his end of things, that I hadn't taken the bait and started a fight. At least that would have comprised familiar territory, I supposed. Instead I kept my mouth shut as we neared the lake— I realized that I had unconsciously taken a circuitous route, to avoid driving past Mom and Elliot's place—and fished the scrap of paper with the address out of my pocket.

" . . . whether this represents some kind of isolated incident, or whether there's a whole pattern here to which I've been blissfully oblivious," Dad was saying, leaning forward in his seat as I pulled up to a stop sign. "Of course I would like to know the answer to that question. But here's the thing: I might never know. I'm in triage territory now. Staunch the bleeding. Get him back home in one piece. Get him away from these *people*."

I made a turn onto the parkway. Lake of the Isles was always quieter than the jam-packed singles' bar of Lake Calhoun, or the more square Lake Harriett. Still, it was late in the afternoon on a summer's day, and people lolled on blankets next to the water, while the runners churned past. The uninhabited island in the center of the lake slouched in casual abandon, ringed by some of the most expensive and adorned houses in the city. It was a mishmash, with the outsized houses pushing close to one another on treasured lakefront real estate, stately old brick abutting fresh construction, great expanses of glass to maximize the view.

"Wait a minute," I said. "What do you mean by *these people?*"

Dad looked around conspiratorially. "Well, I don't precisely know," he said. "Again, that's the worst part of it. He's hanging around with rich people. I had no idea. Rich people are often bored. More ways to get in trouble. More car crashes, more heavy drugs. The primary difference is that they can buy their way out of trouble. They can't bribe death, of course, but their circumstances often allow them to begin to think they can."

"We don't know anything about the people who have taken Daniel in," I pointed out. "For all we know, they're

Quaker pacifists who volunteer at homeless shelters and rescue kittens from trees."

"We'll find out," Dad said cryptically. "How far to go?"

I drove around a bend in the road. A couple of guys sped the other way on bicycles. I wondered, as I always do, why people on bicycles are so attractive.

"Don't worry," I said. "I'll get us there."

"I don't expect trouble," Dad added. "I don't *want* trouble. I just want to get in and get out. I'll take Daniel back to my place and stall Eliza until he's sober enough to be presentable."

As though inspired by the mention of her name, my phone rang and her name appeared on my screen. I plucked it off the dash.

"It's Mom."

My father flashed a look of terror. "Don't answer it," he said.

"Oh, come on," I said, pushing the button that accepted the call.

"Sam."

"Mom."

"Where are you? Have you—"

"Daniel's all right, Mom," I said. My father was glaring at me and shaking his head, as though I had committed an inexcusable breach of protocol.

"You know that for a fact?" She sounded as though my fragmentary news had done nothing but deepen her alarm. "Then where *is* he?"

"I talked to some people who know where he is," I said. "I'm going to follow up. It might take a little while."

Now Dad was nodding. It was one of his many passions, this deep thirst for secrecy; I could tell that I had entered into a two-person cabal with him, with Daniel soon to make it three. The mission: *keep Eliza in the dark.* Come to think of it, it wasn't a terrible idea. Mom would be upset, and she would almost surely go into her mode of making something happen right away in the legitimate sphere of things: calling the cops, checking Daniel into rehab, or some other cut-and-dried way of taking action that would probably imbalance things even more than they already were.

"You're holding back," she said. Mom was no slouch as a mind reader, though she wasn't going to get this one out of me.

"A little, but not much," I said. "Daniel is safe. I'll figure out where he is, then I'll come back for that bottle of wine."

"Can I relax?" Mom asked. "I don't need to know every detail. I really don't. Just let me know: can I relax? Even a little?"

"I think you should relax as much as you possibly can," I told her. "Take a walk or something. Hang out with Elliot."

"He's so mad at me."

"Make it up to him." I couldn't say anything, obviously, with my father sitting right next to me, but it seemed that Mom and Elliot were perfect candidates for a bout of anxiety/anger sex—one of my personal favorites.

"That sounds dirty," Mom said.

I laughed. "Take it any way you want to," I told her.

My father was staring at me. "Anyway, I have to go," I told Mom. "I'll be in touch really soon. Don't worry."

"Thank you," my mother said. "I'll have to find some way to make this up to you."

I switched off the phone and tucked it in my pocket. My ass-kicking boots rode the brake as we circled the lake, slowed by a carload in front of us, driving slow, taking in the sights.

"Don't mention it," I said under my breath.

"Come again?" Dad said.

"Nothing."

"Eliza didn't seem to press for too many details," Dad noted.

"I think she might be playing this one smart," I said. "As long as Daniel's all right, there might be things she's better off not knowing."

"Because she's a judge," Dad said, with a whimsical note in his voice that I didn't care for at all.

"Because she's a judge," I repeated.

"Fair enough." Dad looked out the window. "It's all so poetic, in a way. I certainly always felt that she was more than capable of judging me."

I pulled the car over and stopped.

"What the fuck?" I said.

Dad looked wounded, curious, although anything but contrite. "Mind telling me why you're putting our little rescue mission on hiatus?"

"Because we're walking into the unknown here, and you're availing yourself of a gratuitous opportunity to take digs at your ex-wife. My mother. I'm pulling over because I want to ask you, in all seriousness and sincerity, when are you going to acquire a sense of fucking *proportion*?"

Dad put his hands on the dashboard and looked away. "You shouldn't take that tone with me," he said.

"I shouldn't—" I would have laughed; it would have been merely ironic, though, not truly funny. "What is it,

Dad? Seriously, what's your problem? You act like you're still in a relationship with her, like you have to prove—"

"I *am* still in a relationship with her!" Dad said; when he turned to face me, his eyes were shining. "We have children together!"

"It's more than that," I said. And there we were, back in the Subaru, with me unable to back down, pushing him toward places he didn't want to travel.

Motioning at the road, Dad said, "Well? Are we going or not?"

"Dad, you're *not* still in a relationship with her," I told him.

He bit his lip and stared at the road. "Right. Let's go. *Vámonos.*"

"She's very jealous of your girlfriends," I told him, not knowing why but feeling as though I should offer him comfort.

If it helped, he certainly hid it well. "You don't say."

"She tries not to show it," I added. "But she can barely say Katrina's name."

"Well, it's not all *that* difficult to pronounce," he said.

"You miss her."

Dad looked at me, his twin brown eyes swimming behind a film of moisture.

"You have a knack, Princess," he said.

"I guess I didn't realize."

"I screwed things up and made it impossible for her to stay with me any longer," Dad said, very precisely. "No matter how many other women I meet, or know, none of them can compare to her. Maybe it was because we got together when we were so young, I don't know. It doesn't matter. While I enjoy aspects of the freedom my current life affords me, the past ten years have been hollowed out, and I feel like a ghost moving from one inconsequential scene to the next."

He let that one hang there for a while.

"And the worst part, the most terrible thing," he added, as somber as I'd ever heard him. "Is that I suspect she has really and truly moved on. I'm sure her thing with Elliot isn't nearly as intense as life with me, but I think she's made her adjustment to that. She's found happiness. She left me, and then she found happiness. And here I am. Wondering what the fuck happened that I should be in this position."

It was all coming back, of course: the Christmases, the summer days, the dinnertimes and the smells of food, the harried weekdays, and the shared moments that constitute deep, pre-verbal familial connection. I could see them together, Glenn and Eliza: tall, shining, dynamic, with their three impossibly precocious, verbal, gifted children. The world must have seen them as an unassailable edifice, an arrangement so steeped in sturdy logic that nothing could change it or lay it low. But something had altered it, and it would never be again.

"Dad, what happened?" I asked.

He was in a reverie of his own; I wondered if he was remembering some of the same sights, sounds, smells.

"In all honesty, Princess, I am still spending an inordinate amount of time trying to answer that very question for myself."

"Not in general," I said. "Specifically."

He looked at me flat, fatigued, as though he had just returned from a long march through exhaustingly hazardous territory.

"Why?" I said. "Why did Mom leave you?"

"We had issues," he began. "Things build up. We were together for a very long time. Family life is as much a hardship as it is a joy, and you begin to associate the other person more with work, and tasks, than remembering the connection that brought you together in the first place."

I let him finish. "You're telling me the truth, I know," I told him. "But it's not all the truth. Why would a married woman walk out on her family? It's always the father who has to go, or who *wants* to go. But not the mother."

Dad stared at me.

"Was it something you did?" I asked.

Nothing.

"Was it something *we* did?"

"You must never think that," Dad said seriously. "You children did nothing to harm the relationship between your mother and myself. If anything, you made it possible for us to have whatever tattered connection still exists between us."

And that was it. I could see that he had clammed up. I lit up one more cigarette, let out a stream of profanity, and tried to get my anger to subside as we made our way around the lake, to find my brother, to rescue him, to save him, to intervene with him, or whatever it was that Glenn and I thought we were doing.

9

IT WAS SHAPING UP

THE HOUSE WAS VERY BIG. IT HUDDLED CLOSE TO ITS NEIGH-bors, the lakefront land doled out in stingy parcels, the side windows of the wealthy staring at each other un-blinking, their status requiring a foregoing of privacy paralleling that of the ninety-nine.

Or else they just bought fancy curtains.

The house was much larger than the one in which I had grown up, at least twice, two-and-a-half times as big, with Mom and Elliot's Kenwood pile somewhere in between. It wasn't ostentatious. It was tasteful, with clean lines and a big window looking out over the blue water.

It wasn't trying to draw attention to itself. *I'm so out of your league*, it was saying to me, *but let's not make too big a deal about it.*

Glenn was standing on the bottom step, looking up. He had his hands jammed in his blazer pockets. A breeze drew and rearranged his salt-and-pepper situation. He scowled. Out here in the natural light, it occurred to me that he was finally starting to look his age.

"You need to put on a few pounds," I told him.

He gave me his that's-all-I-need-to-hear look. As we made our way up the steps, he tucked in his shirt and fiddled with his blazer. I glanced back; a couple of older guys were on the lake in a canoe, paddling away obliviously. For them, for just about everyone, this was nothing more or less than an ordinary day. It eluded me why so many of my days seemed to require a part in other people's dramas. I wanted a glass of wine. I wanted something to eat.

The front door was a sturdy screen, dark wood behind it. The afternoon sun reflected off the big windows, making it difficult to discern much of anything inside: I saw angles that might have been furniture, or a bomb-making factory, or a sadomasochistic dungeon.

Dad was looking at me. "What?" I said.

"You do the honors," he said, motioning at the door. His hands were back in his blazer pockets, shoved deep, distorting the lines of his lapels.

"If you want something done right," I said to no one at all, and then pressed on the doorbell. I didn't hear anything, so I pressed it again. While my finger was still on the button, the door opened.

Behind the screen was a man in the vicinity of fifty, but unlike the bohemian splendor that my father had carried well into middle age, the first impression he gave was one of vigorous tidiness. He was shorter than me, in a white buttoned-up shirt and with cropped, wavy white hair. He looked out at us as though we were diplomats freshly arrived from some barbarous nation, with unpredictable natures but bearing business that required we be treated with respect.

"You're Daniel's family," he said in a surprisingly rich, deep voice.

"I'm Glenn Burns, and this here is my daughter,

Samantha," Dad said, very stiffly.

"I'm Ben,"

"Is Daniel here?" my father said.

"Yes, of course. I talked to your other son. I understand you've been worried."

Ben pushed open the screen to let us in. When I passed him, he seemed very compact, a man who gave an impression of efficiency. He radiated calm, control, and an unmistakable sense that he was more than a little frightened of us.

I scanned Ben for guilt. But he stood stolid on a Persian rug in the middle of his living room, as placid as the waters outside on a windless afternoon. Which it wasn't, as it turned out, but still.

The living room, if that was what its inhabitants called it, was commodious to the point of having uncertain borders; to one side the space receded into a dining area, and in the back a drop in ceiling height seemed to signal a transition into a walled patio that I could barely glimpse through a thicket of arts-and-crafts furniture and extremely tasteful lighting fixtures: copper, brass, all the old-time metals. The place was clean to the point of austerity.

"He's sleeping it off in the spare room," Ben said in a placating tone.

Dad still had his hands in his jacket pocket. He was hunching, his jaw out as he stared at Ben; it gave my father an unfortunate simian aspect.

"Why did he come here?" Dad asked.

Ben frowned. "I'm on the board at the Abyss. We've gotten to know each other a little over there. Apparently he found out where we live. He's never been to this house before—you should know that."

Dad unleashed a look of outsized skepticism that was theatrical on its own, but before he could open his mouth another man came into the room. He was tall, as tall as Dad, and about as thin. He had a beard and a baseball cap and a plain white T-shirt, none of which did much to hide that he was as old as Ben, if not older.

"I'm Stan," he said, a hand outstretched for my Dad to shake. "I'm Ben's partner. We're so glad you're here. You must have been terribly worried."

While quick-and-dirty mutual introductions got made (Stan gripped my hand and conveyed an elemental empathy that took me aback), I watched my father. His body language was hard to read.

As far as I was concerned, this situation was shaping up much better than I had any reason to expect. Daniel had washed up at the shores of some rich guys whom he knew through the Abyss, and they had given him a place to sleep off whatever chemical hurricane had been coursing through him. We'd pick him up, scrape the crust off of him, and bring him back to friendly family confines in no time.

"I still don't get why he came here," Dad said, shaking his head.

"Pardon?" Stan said.

"Why he's here," Dad repeated. "I don't know how it adds up. Apparently Daniel was in some kind of trouble. When we're in trouble, we go to people we care about."

"Dad," I said.

"Glenn, we can only tell you what we know." Ben paused. "Do you want a cup of coffee or something?"

"I'll have a cup," I said. Stan gave me a grateful smile

and made off for the kitchen.

But Dad wasn't having it. "Well, you've given shelter to a minor," he said after Stan made his momentary escape. "And you've done so without notifying his family. Doesn't that strike you as unusual?"

"It's unusual as *hell*," Ben agreed. "Daniel begged us to let him get some rest before he went home. He went on and on about how his mother is a judge, and how his father doesn't understand . . . "

Ben caught himself. He gave a disappointed sigh, as though things that should remain unspoken had a tendency to launch themselves from his lips.

"Look, he said all kinds of things." Ben sighed. "He was pretty high."

"What was he taking?" Dad asked.

"I don't know," Ben said.

"You don't know," Dad repeated. "What about you? Have you ever done drugs with my son?"

Ben folded his arms and looked at the floor. "Look, Glenn, I understand that you're having concerns."

"Dad, come on," I said.

"Just answer the question," Dad said. He had his hands pressed together in front of him, his beak out like an aggressive blackbird.

"I don't use drugs, Glenn," Ben said very deliberately and with a growing undercurrent of disdain in his voice. "And I don't socialize with minors. I didn't invite your son into my home. He showed up in need of help."

Dad turned away. He stared transfixed for a grateful moment—I was grateful, anyway—by the view of the lake out the window. A slow procession of cars came around the bend, stopping one by one at the posted octagon, a ballet of vehicular politeness.

No one was saying anything. I heard rustling from the next room. "It's been a really hard day," I said. "Hard for everyone."

Ben regarded me with a sternness that he hadn't displayed when we first arrived. "I can understand that," he said. "And I'm not looking for sympathy from either of you, but this has been a rather strange and somewhat stressful situation for me and Stan as well. Just so you know, Stan thought we should phone you right away. I was the one who decided to do what Daniel asked, and give him the chance to sleep a few hours."

"Why?" Dad asked, looking from the window with the startled wonder of someone yanked unwillingly from a dream. "Why did you do that? You could have saved us all kinds of worry. Sam's been going all over the city looking for Daniel."

Ben shot me a look, one of mixed surprise and inquiry; I shook my head slightly, signaling him not to dig into the situation. This was no time to begin outlining the intricacies of the Burns family dynamic.

"I did as Daniel asked," Ben said to my father, "because when I was his age, I was a lot like him."

"How so?" Dad asked, still making everything sound like an accusation.

"I was unhappy," Ben said, his gaze locked onto my father's. "I took risks and did things that I shouldn't have. And a lot of it was because my family and myself were having a uselessly difficult time coming to terms with me. And, I suppose, the fact that I was gay didn't help communication much at all."

Stan appeared, a tray in his hand with four cups of

coffee and a little ceramic cow with a hole in its mouth to dispense milk.

"Nice cow," I said.

"I know," Stan agreed, putting down the tray on a round wooden table with a rich, dark finish. In my family, any piece of furniture of its ilk would have long ago been brought low by nicks and scratches.

"Why don't we sit down," Ben said, motioning to an area that contained about fifteen or twenty seating options amid various sofas, chairs, ottomans, and pillowed surfaces. My father accepted a cup of coffee like a man in a daze. I took one too, since my stomach had long since stopped grumbling for food and had locked down for an extended period of malnourishment.

"Your boots are awesome," Stan whispered as he passed me.

"Your timing is cool," I told him. I felt like an appealing human being again.

Stan and I sat next to each other; he gave off a pleasing, minty smell. I knew I reeked of cigarettes. Ben and my father plopped down across from us, Glenn shaking his head slightly.

"I don't think it's that," Dad said, his voice low, slightly strained.

"You don't think what's what?" I asked.

"Being gay," Dad said delicately, as though voicing the sentiment was difficult for him. "I don't think that it's at the root of what's going on."

"I don't presume to know," Ben said. He was the model of somber rectitude. "I can only tell you that I see a lot of myself in him. The insecurity, never feeling accepted, feeling as though I always had something to hide."

"We're very progressive," Dad said flatly. "We live *here*. Sexuality isn't something that is even an issue with our friends—gay, straight, in between, what have you. I mean, you know, unless someone is making a *joke*."

"Dad, stop," I said. The coffee was very hot in my hands; the place was cooled by gratifyingly efficient air conditioning.

"What, Sam?" Dad stared at me with a look of total innocence.

"Dad, when have we ever discussed Daniel being gay?"

My father stared at me for a long time. Stan cleared his throat. Everyone was waiting for the big guy to provide an answer.

"Well, it . . . I suppose it hasn't been something that we've particularly *needed* to talk about."

"Everyone avoids it," I said firmly. "And Daniel does his mind tricks to keep us from bringing it up. He's in a lot of pain, Dad, and he checked out on us a long time ago. He doesn't look at us as people he goes to for help, or understanding, or anything."

"Now that's . . . " Dad trailed off.

"And because we think of ourselves as somehow fundamentally different, the genius Burns family, we chalk Daniel's situation up to our general eccentricity." I paused. "But it isn't just that. Daniel's always been different from the rest of us, he's always set himself apart."

"We're all *different*," Dad said. "All five of us."

I couldn't have elucidated precisely why I was saying these things to my father; until the words came out, these were thoughts that I had never definitively formed even in the privacy of my own head, and now I was sharing them in front of strangers—which typically would have appalled Glenn, but he was so taken aback that few of his normal defenses seemed to be online. And I was off my own game, by hearing him refer to the "five of us." It never ended for him, I understood with nauseating certainty. It was Glenn, Eliza, and the kids. He would never be able to let go.

"*Everybody* is strange in some way," Stan said helpfully. "It's the nature of things."

Ben gave Stan the sort of look that I've noticed is the result of long-term domestic cohabitation. "He's a young gay man," Ben said. "And he's in a crisis. I just recommend that you look at the situation starting from that viewpoint."

"It's not as though I'm not open——" Dad began.

"Yet about five minutes ago," Ben interrupted, "you were ready to believe that we were seducing your son, or plying him with drugs, or some other awful, immoral, and illegal thing. Would you have done that if Stan was a woman?"

"Why do I always have to be the woman?" asked Stan of no one in particular.

My father looked forlorn and stung by the truth of what Ben had said. This clearly shook him. Glenn, whose entire identity was based upon rabid and cosmic open-mindedness, had been demonstrably revealed as hung up about who his son really was. He hadn't properly processed the information, hadn't integrated it into the glowing electric flow of things—the way he should have, long ago. Not that I had done much better, mind you, but on this score I was happy to embrace the traditional hierarchy: parents were required to set the tone. Eliza and Glenn had, in their separate ways, allowed Daniel to slip away.

"And he's the youngest," Ben added. "Are you and his mother still together?"

"No," Dad replied.

"How old was he when you divorced?"

Dad thought for a moment. "Young. Still in elementary school."

"He was *six*, Dad."

Ben nodded. "I was the youngest, too," he said. "It tends to make you pissed off. The older siblings got to enjoy the glory days, when there were just three of you, or then four. No matter how things really were, the youngest always feels cheated. Throw in a divorce and, well, you know . . . "

Realization washed over me. I was back in that Subaru, on the interstate, with Daniel glowering in the backseat. The world had exploded into fragments for all of us, but it had to be worst of all for him, the last born. He was the last to join the club, and he was different from the rest of us. He hated us because he had never felt that he was truly one of us. Or else he was a selfish little self-absorbed shit. It depended on how you wanted to look at it.

"Thank you," Dad said to Ben, with a simplicity and sincerity that startled me. "Thank you for your decency and your understanding. I'm going to try to change things."

"Daniel is a shining young man, from what I know of him," Ben said. "He just needs to stay away from the fucking drugs."

"My ears are burning," said a raspy voice from behind us. "How long have you all been talking about me?"

The first thought that popped into my head was

incredulity that the voice I had just heard had come from my little brother; he sounded as though he had applied a ball of steel wool against his larynx for the better part of a day. The second was the observation that Daniel had dyed his hair blond since I had last seen him. Bieber Burns. With this obvious artificial coloration, against his dark eyebrows, the overall effect was to frame his baby face, his thin nose and bowed lips, evoking the boy he had so recently been.

My father then said his son's name in a trembling voice as he made his way across the room to hug him. It was an awkward embrace, with the smaller Daniel looking momentarily confused, surely uncertain how much trouble he might be in, and not apprised of the terrain now that we had showed up here at the house of a couple he apparently knew really very little.

"How are you feeling?" Dad asked, his hands on Daniel's shoulders, holding him at arm's length and with a look of uncomplicated, unmediated relief.

Daniel didn't look particularly well, in fact—the whites of his eyes were puffy and red, and his pale skin was acned as though something had abraded it and left it half-healed. But he was still Daniel, and so he was beautiful. His delicacy bordered on translucence, his lithe frame outlined in jeans and a threadbare T-shirt. He looked like royalty fallen on hard times.

"I feel okay," he said. "What's going on?" He peered at me, then looked pointedly at Ben. "Did you call him?"

"At first I did as you asked," Ben said, rising slowly. "Although now I feel perfectly shitty about it. I broke down and called your house. I spoke to your brother."

"You guys have been talking?" Daniel asked warily.

"What were you on?" Dad asked him.

Daniel folded his arms.

"Never mind," Dad said. "We can talk about it later."

Daniel stared at the floor.

"Thank you guys for looking after him," Dad said, shaking Ben's hand, then Stan's. They both did the don't-mention-it thing, although I'm sure they meant it literally, as in, they would have preferred that Dad leave them out of his retelling of this story. "I really mean it. I'm profoundly glad that we met and had a chance to speak."

"Come by for a barbecue sometime," Stan said, causing Ben to give him a look of mortified horror.

"We should do that." Dad turned to Daniel. "We should probably clear out and let these guys get on with their lives."

I could see Daniel trying to summon up a sullen reaction, but he had essentially been busted for drugs and for running away, and at least so far my father hadn't responded with anger or hysteria. Even my little brother had to understand that he was very much ahead of the game.

Ben gave Daniel an affectionate hug as we left, which my father watched impassively in the foyer. He had shoved his hands deep in his blazer pockets again, and he suddenly looked deeply exhausted. I was well into an out-of-body experience of my own, buzzing from the latest cup of coffee and craving a cigarette though it would probably send me into tachycardia.

"Ready to go?" Dad asked.

"Yeah. Sure." Daniel paused, and we exchanged a glance. "Look, can we go to your place?" I don't feel like dealing with Mom right now."

"I guess——" Dad began.

Dad was interrupted by a loud pop, a metallic sound; he cried out, his legs buckled, and he dropped to the floor. He closed his eyes in agony, and a weird, devilish smell filled my nostrils.

"Jesus Christ!" Stan shouted.

Daniel looked as though he was about to vomit. On the floor, around my father's thighs, an alarming pool of dark red was beginning to form.

I got down on my knees. Dad's hands had made their way out of the jacket to his upper leg, where he pressed hard while contorting his face with pain.

"You brought a *gun*?" I shouted.

"Shut up. Shut up," he hissed.

"Of all the idiotic——" I barked.

"He shot himself?" Ben said, so calm as to give the impression that this was a predictable turn of events.

"What were you going to——" I began.

"Go to the kitchen and get a towel," Ben commanded Stan, who was very happy to comply; during the events of the previous moments he had stood apart, his mouth forming a perfect O, his hands comically draped across his cheeks like a terrified heroine in a Wild West movie.

Ben took his cell phone out of his pocket. He got an emergency operator on the line, gave his address, and informed them that there was a man down. My father continued to bleed, and when he shifted he smeared crimson all across the marble foyer.

He looked up at me sheepishly.

"Jesus, Dad."

Daniel looked as though he couldn't be sure that what he had witnessed was verifiably real. Ben shook his head, swore under his breath, and then went to see what the fuck was taking Stan so long in accomplishing the simple but apparently overly demanding task of fetching a towel to deal with the bleeding guest who had arrived uninvited into their previously, presumably, calm, sane, and orderly household.

10

I'D MELT THE THING DOWN TO SLAG

WHAT TRANSPIRED THROUGH WHAT SHOULD HAVE BEEN THE dinner hour did so with a strange, timeless inevitability. After the initial shock, it was as though my father's shooting himself in the leg was the most natural thing in the world. Never mind that I had never known him to own a gun and, had I even stopped to contemplate the matter, would have thought the notion absurd. After all, there isn't much you can do with a gun, other than shoot someone, or yourself.

I couldn't say whether my father had been seriously contemplating the first course of action, but he was a blinding success in the second. He shot himself right in the meat of his thigh. During the ambulance ride to the county hospital, he slipped into a delirium during which he seemed to think I was Katrina.

"I won't be able to make it over later, like I said I would," he slurred. "But I have the most amazing excuse. Really."

The EMT, a woman several years older than me and about half my size, stared at me over my father's prostrate form.

"I'll bet you hear some amazing things," I said to her.

She held my father's wrist in one hand, checking his pulse. "That's one way of looking at it," she said.

"It's not that I don't love you," Dad said, his eyes unfocused.

"It's not you," the EMT pronounced without a trace of obvious humor. "It's me."

"I just need some space," I told her.

"Anybody would be lucky to have you," she said.

"It's just not the right time," I added.

The EMT looked up through the divider that separated us from the driver. The siren shrieked throatily above us. The confined space was packed with machinery and all manner of rubber and latex, as though prepared to fight against an overpowering river of blood. What with the flashing lights and a series of daredevil maneuvers down Third Avenue into downtown, we had gotten from Lake of the Isles to HCMC in about five minutes. Now Glenn was making a grand entrance.

It turned out that arriving at the emergency room with a bullet in one's thigh made for a no-wait proposition. There was a brief intermission during which my father was whisked away on a gurney; I availed myself of a can of Coke from a vending machine, which tasted like pithy battery acid when I poured it down my parched throat. Out in the waiting room was a stolidly purgatorial crowd in various states of distress, waiting in long rows of chairs as though waiting was what they *did*, the act of passive anticipation having become a meaning in and of itself.

Then people started showing up. Whatever discretion Dad or Daniel had hoped to shroud over the events of the day was well and truly fucked. First through the sliding lobby doors were a pair of cops, both about a decade older than me, eyes darting around the room with an apparent readiness for things to go very crazy in a very short time. Their uniforms were in tones of blue; their big belts culminated in wide gun holsters. They talked to the older woman behind the desk, who had tried to catch my eye once or twice (I figured she looked to corral me with paperwork; it wasn't really in my job description).

"Are you Glenn Burns's daughter?" one of the cops said by way of introduction. He was tall, more than six feet, and sported a goatee.

"Depends who's asking," I told him.

The other cop, blond, shorter, and chubby, seemed to think this was funny. I guessed it was a line of work that entailed a lot of ambient humor, if one were inclined to tune into that frequency.

The first officer gave me a cut-the-shit look and tapped his finger on his badge. I wasn't feeling particularly compliant to authority, but clearly these two had a job to do.

"My name's Sam," I told them.

"Short for Samantha," said the first cop, evidently the alpha to the other's beta.

"And Glenn is my dad," I added.

The cop, who had the name "Pender" on a pin over one breast pocket, took out a pad of paper and a very small pencil, which was a bit of a trick, for he had a thick manila envelope tucked into one armpit. His hands were big, and veiny, and the effort he took in applying his tiny utensil was inexplicably touching.

"I had no idea he had a gun," I said. "But the shooting was a complete accident. He had it in his jacket pocket, he shoved his hands in there, and the thing went off. Total fucking foolishness."

The second cop smiled at me again. I was his kind of girl, evidently. It occurred to me that I had never seriously considered dating a police officer. But I didn't think I would start with this one, his wedding band notwithstanding—he was giving me the once-over without realizing that I could tell he was doing it. I didn't mind having my ass checked out, I just preferred some measure of subtlety.

"That checks out with what we heard at the scene," Pender said. It took me a moment to realize that "the scene" referred to Ben and Stan's place.

"Is everything all right there?" I asked.

Pender sized me up, in a manner that was considerably less complimentary than his partner's. I got the sense that Pender would have liked to expand the scope of criminality to things that he simply didn't like, such as smart-ass girls in big lace-up boots that he didn't stand a chance of ever fucking.

"Everything checks out," Pender said.

"Is my dad in trouble?"

Pender bit his lip, as though it would please him very much to inform me that Glenn was indeed in deep shit; instead his partner shrugged to convey that there were surely many worse things occurring as we spoke.

"The gun is registered," Pender said. "Although your dad doesn't have a conceal-carry permit. We'll write him up a citation. But other than that, it looks like there was no serious harm done."

"Other than to his leg," I said.

"And probably to his ego," offered the second cop, twinkling in a manner that stopped just short of winking.

"Well, we have all his info," Pender said, his palpable disappointment leading him to snap shut his notebook and cast a look around, perhaps in search of some concrete malfeasance to which he could apply his disdain and impatience.

"Any word on how he's doing?" asked the partner.

"They said he'd be fine." That was a relief to pronounce, although my father was currently out of sight and, I presumed, undergoing a bullet-removal procedure that surely wouldn't be painless or without side effects.

Pender released the envelope that he'd had stuffed under his arm, and from its bulge I realized that it contained the gun. *Dad's* gun.

"Do me a favor and don't give that back to him," I said.

Flipping the package a half-rotation in his sizable hand, Pender granted me the gift of a gruff chuckle. "That won't be up to me," he said. "But if it was, I'd melt the thing down to slag. There are too many fucking crazy people out there. Take it from me."

Of course he was talking about Glenn, and I wasn't inclined to take issue with Pender's assessment. My day was enough of a wild card without introducing firearms into the equation.

"I have to ask," Pender said. "Why was he carrying it?"

A very fine question, I had to admit. Even if Daniel had been waylaid into a den of vice and iniquity, it was very hard to imagine Glenn blasting his way out of the situation. The greatest likelihood was what indeed had happened—Dad planting a bullet in himself.

"I seriously doubt there was a thought-out plan involved," I said.

"Look, it's none of my business," Pender said, not very convincingly. "Those two guys told me about your brother, and the runaway thing. I don't think they gave me the whole story, if you know what I mean."

"And what part would they be leaving out?" I asked.

Pender pursed his lips, a gesture of surprising delicacy, as though an odor slightly askew had glanced his nostrils.

"It's not my problem," he finally said. "Tell your father we'll be in touch if it's necessary. It's not exactly a Federal case."

"Not to you, at least," I said.

Pender nodded to this, so affirmatively that I got the feeling it was the first sensible thing he'd heard all day. His partner gave me a dopey grin as they made to leave, their departure coinciding with the arrival that I'd been dreading: my mother's.

Eliza had changed clothes, into a long skirt and blouse that looked functional but sleek and elegant. For a moment I wondered whether she regarded this as some sort of public appearance, related to her judgeship and her election coming up next year. Then I realized that I really should stop being so hard on my mother.

She took me in her arms. Trailing her, still in jeans, looking around like an astronaut who had just made land, was Elliot. He looked at me over my mother's shoulder, slightly shaking his head, conveying that he understood the essential nuttiness of what I'd been through since I saw him last.

"Where is Daniel?" I asked.

"At home." My mother raised a hand and brushed my hair off my forehead. "Sleeping off whatever he was on. I picked him up at that house on the lake."

"You met Ben and Stan?" I asked.

"Ben I already knew. He's a lawyer. He's been in my court before."

"Oh," I said, the sound escaping me involuntarily, with me already wondering what sorts of complications this news entailed.

"It doesn't matter," Mom said, her hand to my forehead, ironing out the worry lines. "Everything's all right. You're so good, Sam. You're so *good*."

I was never more intensely aware of my insatiable craving for my mother's approval than on the occasions when she lavished it upon me. I thanked her, I turned away. I looked at Elliot. I worked very hard to keep tears from flowing into my eyes. Elliot shoved his hands in his pockets, looking very much like a man standing in an emergency room waiting for word of his wife's first husband's condition.

"Dad's going to be fine," I said.

"They told you that?" Mom asked.

I nodded. My mother glanced back at Elliot, clearly calibrating how much relief she should demonstrate in her new swain's presence. Elliot cleared his throat.

"I'm going to go see about some coffee," he said. He put a hand on my mother's shoulder and glanced between the two of us. "Anyone need anything?"

My mother and I both said no, releasing him from the drama. I wouldn't have disapproved if he opted to travel to North Dakota for that coffee; Elliot, for all his forbearance and depth, crackled with tension, as though he had long ago lived through awful scenes of his own (of his own doing, in fact, which I would learn years later) and no longer had the stomach for further tribulation. I guessed that it was one of the qualities that attracted Eliza to him.

Before he escaped, Elliot surprised me by bending over me and planting a kiss on my cheek.

"Say hi to Glenn for me," he said. "And maybe explain the part about guns where you flip on the safety switch."

That was about as close to a criticism of my father that Elliot would ever venture and, as usual, it was pitch-perfect and appropriate. Elliot vanished down the hallway, his big lumbering form improbably graceful, a hint of jauntiness in his step.

"I'm going to spare you the interrogation you probably think I want to put you through," my mother said after we sat down in an uninhabited zone of sadistically unpadded chairs. "I'm just grateful to you for finding Daniel. It feels like so long since we've had this kind of . . . *upheaval*. It's a funny thing, Sam. You live long enough, and you feel as though you might have worked out a thing or two. But then something happens, and you're right back the way you were. Uncertain. *Scared*. Unable to know what the right thing is . . . "

There really wasn't much I could think of to say. I was still holding a can of Coke, half-full, gone warm. I got up and chucked it, and when I came back to my mother she was staring into space. I loved looking at her when she wasn't looking at me: the curve of her nose, the stray hairs that poked out along her neckline from where she had carelessly, hurriedly, gathered her hair. She had a grace that I knew better than to try to emulate. It was easy for me to see why my father loved her. I wondered, of course, what she would think had she heard the things he had said to me about her earlier in the day. And earlier, when he had been going into surgery, when the drugs had kicked in and he didn't know who he was talking to, he kept saying her name and mumbling that no one had or could replace her—but that was firmly in the category of things that should not be repeated. There had been enough disturbances, too much turbulence, and worst of all, I dreaded the prospect of how she might react.

We sat together for more than an hour, barely speaking, watching the slow-motion rituals of the afflicted arriving, filling out forms, waiting. An old woman rolled in with a flurry of activity, dislodged from an ambulance with her disheveled white hair peeking out from a sheet pulled up to her neck; she was greeted with grim efficiency by the hospital staff, whisked away to whatever fate.

I spotted Elliot through the glass doors; he clapped his first two fingers together inquisitively—universal smoker's sign language. I nodded back and left my mother alone with the thoughts that swirled through her mind.

"What a day," he said.

"Nonstop fun and games," I replied.

He took a long drag. "Can I just say, I've been fairly pissed off since this morning."

"I got that idea," I replied.

Elliot glanced at me with surprise, as though unaware that I took his impressions or opinions into consideration at all.

"I don't think you should have been drawn into this," he said. "Christ, you just got back from college. You graduated. You need time to catch your breath."

"I'll catch my breath," I told him. "Really. Don't worry about me."

Elliot squinted at me with a skepticism that was unusual for him. "That *really* sounds believable."

I flicked the ash off the end of my smoke. "Okay, look. I'll be as well adjusted and fine as anyone else. Reverting to the mean. How's that?"

Elliot glared up at the sky. "And, might I add, your brothers really piss me off."

This was sort of thrilling, actually. By Elliot's usual standards, this was tantamount to a thundering tantrum.

"Go on," I said.

"They're so fucking alike in so many ways." Elliot's voice rose, the tone of a man who had bottled up a great deal of sentiment and words that he didn't dare voice. "They both act like the world owes them something, but neither one of them can be bothered to do the things normal people do—act nice, speak when spoken to, put some goddamned *effort* into things. And they both treat Eliza as though she did something terribly wrong which they're going to hold against her until the fucking earth falls into the fucking sun—"

"Elliot—"

"Let me finish," he said. "You and me, we get along. We have an understanding. That's all I want. I *like* your brothers. They're good, fascinating people. But all of this *shit*, and now Glenn with his—"

Elliot broke off; coming up the street toward us, slouching and scowling, was my brother Kevin. His overall demeanor suggested someone who had been interrupted from something of far greater interest than these distasteful proceedings. I gave him a long hug and smelled the vapors of marijuana that wafted from his wrinkled shirt.

Elliot stubbed out his cigarette on the curb. "How's Daniel?" he asked.

"In his room," Kevin said. "Quiet."

"Good," Elliot said. "Quiet is good."

I gave Kevin the status report on Dad; Elliot took out another Camel and contemplated it wistfully, glancing back toward the doors as though wondering whether Eliza could see him. Kevin and I made to go back inside.

"If it's all the same to you guys," Elliot said. "I'm going to stay out here for a little while longer."

"Don't blame you," Kevin said, floating ahead of me.

I stopped, just for a moment, and locked eyes with Elliot. I tried to let him know that I understood, that he had just needed a moment in which to speak in plain English about that which was propelling the angst in this phase of his life, things that he knew he couldn't solve (things in which he had no place to meddle). He probably wished all the time that he could have had Eliza without Glenn, without my brothers, probably even without me. But he couldn't. Perhaps he wished that he could have had an Eliza entirely unaltered by her life with us, with her first family, with her original shot at lasting happiness: the Eliza of her youth. It wasn't to be, not ever. Poor Elliot. But then I also knew that Elliot had sins of his own, things he had done and things he should have done but had not, and that he had been just as buffeted and bruised as Eliza, and Glenn, and eventually myself.

But I loved Elliot, and I think he knew that. I gave him as much of a smile as I could muster, and he returned it. Then he motioned for me to go inside, back to a place where he didn't belong, and for which I sensed he enjoyed immeasurable relief over his status as an alien and an outcast.

Before we went in, I grabbed Kevin's elbow. His head jerked back.

"What?" he asked, annoyed, defensive.

"You did good, taking that call and getting in touch with me," I told him. "It means a lot. I know you don't want to deal with any of this shit, but you did."

Kevin's frown unfolded, very easily, and he gave my shoulder a squeeze. "I was thinking of you. That's why I did what I did."

"I know it," I told him. "And I love you."

Kevin's mouth locked into a straight line, and there he was again, the boy I used to know, full of feeling and soul and trying so very hard not to be carried away by it all.

"You're all right," he said quietly. "You know, you are every kind of all right."

Then, we got the news that Glenn was in post-op. His surgeon, a tall, skinny man with a mane of luxurious silvery hair that unfurled from a paper cap, informed us that the procedure had been "relatively easy." Apparently Dad's gun didn't pack enough pop to sink the bullet life-threateningly deep into the tissues of his thigh, and for all his profound idiocy he had managed not to damage his femur or pierce the big artery that ran alongside it.

"I'd say he was lucky," said the doctor in a parched, dusty voice. "But given the circumstances, I don't know exactly what to call him."

This made my mother erupt with an unfamiliar bark of a laugh; she raised both hands to cover her mouth, her eyes wide and glistening, her body coiled with the force of involuntary reaction.

"Will he recover all the way?" I asked the doctor, ignoring my mother, instinctively wanting to keep matters in the realm of the here and now, the practical and not the loony.

The doctor shrugged as though it wasn't really his problem. "He'll be on crutches for a while, then a cane," he said. "After that, he'll limp for a while. It's really up to him. If he follows his physical therapy with diligence, he should be getting around fine before too long."

Sure. And since following regimens that included discomfort and taking orders from others were in perfect alignment with my father's personality, things were going to be peachy keen.

"Can we see him?" asked Eliza.

"He's awake," the doctor said. "But he was under sedation during the procedure. Don't be surprised if he says some weird things."

"That wouldn't surprise me one teeny bit," I said. The doctor looked at me, perhaps about to give utterance to something that he then decided to keep to himself. He gave us an insincere smile and moved off, presumably to cut and slice some other piece of semi-anonymous flesh.

"You don't have to go in there if you don't want to," I said. "I can handle it."

"You've been made to handle enough," my mother said with a look of regret. "In fact, you can stay out here if you want to. I can check on him and then we can all go home."

Kevin had already voted with his feet, leaving as soon as word came down that Dad was out of surgery.

Elliot was still trekking someplace downtown, I imagined in widening circles until he was sufficiently steeled to return to his wife.

"No, I'll go in," I said. "Maybe he'll say something really stupid or insane that I can use to embarrass him at a later date."

"*Sam!*" said my mother, unable to hide a streak of delight.

"I'm just saying."

Dad was in a bay of six beds, only two of which were occupied. In the other, an elderly man lay propped up with an oxygen mask on his face, his eyes open but staring vacantly into the middle distance. Glenn's bed linens were all white, and he had a blanket pulled up over his waist; beneath it was a big, long protrusion, his leg dressed up in bandages. I observed the entirely unwelcome information that Glenn's chest hair had gone largely white.

"Eliza," he said, sitting up a little straighter. "Sam. They told me you were still here."

"We know where the action is," I said.

He looked at me, puzzled. He smacked his lips absently, then smiled.

"I shot myself," he said.

Mom took the chair next to his bed. I remained standing, trying to muster up the will to be pissed off at him. He looked very thin, though, and weak, his hair gone slack and greasy and pressed in odd whorls to the sides of his head.

"Everyone has noticed," I said.

Glenn looked up at me like a child who had been caught doing something irrationally naughty, something for which there was no good reason.

"You're mad at me," he said.

"Just gobsmacked, really," I said. "Damn it, Dad. And this is one of the better versions of the way things could have played out."

"I'm not enjoying it all that much," he said, avoiding looking at my mother.

"And how long have you had a fucking *gun*—"

"Sam," Mom said.

"Really, I want to know." It turned out it wasn't all that difficult at all, getting pissed off at Glenn. "Did you have that thing around when we were *kids*?"

Now he looked at my mother; their eyes locked, and they turned away the next instant, as though something had compelled them to seek understanding in each other, a pact that led to the necessity of silence.

"I saw that!" I said. "What, did you *know*?" I asked my mother.

The nurse at the other end of the room stopped what she was doing. My mother raised a hand to wave at her, signaling that things were not going to deteriorate any further.

"Stop it, Sam," Mom said. "Stop it now. You can interrogate your father to your heart's content after he gets out of this place. For now, he's been injured, and we have to let him rest. Even if his actions have been entirely beyond the pale."

Dad looked at my mother fondly. "Beyond the pale," he said. "You know, there's an interesting origin to that particular phrase—"

"Yes, and I know it already," my mother interrupted. "It has to do with boundaries, and places like Ireland where they used to always be shooting one another. The phrase is positively *rich* with meanings."

Now Glenn was beaming at her. "It's so much *fun* when you talk to me like that," he said, and it took me a moment to realize that he was entirely sincere and not sarcastic in the slightest. He made a move as though to take her hand, but she shifted in her chair to make it impossible.

"Don't," she said.

"The police have your gun," I said. "I told them not to give it back to you."

"I'm sure they listened." Now Dad aimed that goofy grin at me, as full of happy affection as a dog's. "And that's fine. I think that gun and I have come to a turning point in our relationship."

Mom smiled, clearly in spite of herself. "You'll have to do physical therapy," she said.

"Only the physical kind?" Dad laughed. "I think I'm getting off easy, then."

"Those drugs they have you on are really good, aren't they?" I asked.

Dad shot me a sidelong look of conspiracy. "Indeed," he said. "It almost makes it all worth it. Almost."

"Well, you have one more leg left to shoot," I said.

Dad beamed even more as an idea transparently entered his mind. "You know what this means, don't you?" he asked. "Now I can't be drafted."

"I'm sure the army will be very disappointed," I told him. "You were just the sort of specimen they drool over when they're recruiting for the Special Forces."

Dad gave me his classic that-stings look, the one he always flashed me when I suggested that he was anything other than an exemplar of red-blooded, mainstream, strapping American manhood. It was comforting in its familiarity, even if the grin plastered to his face was beginning to put me on edge.

"Well, it doesn't matter." His gaze alternated between my mother and me; a stray clump of hair had detached itself from the pack, and wobbled like an antenna whenever he moved his head. "Before too long I'll be as good as new. Back to the old routine of climbing taverns and fighting mountains."

I guessed it didn't matter much whether the drugs were talking, or if Glenn would have said such a thing unaided. He and the drugs clearly made an advantageous pair.

"And thank you, Sam," he added. "For everything. I am so happy you've finished college, and that you've come back. I'm so grateful to have you around, to be able to talk to you when I feel like it. When I get out of here, let's go get *wasted* together."

I had to laugh. "I think you need to come down off whatever you're on first."

Dad pointed at me. "And you always *think* that that kind of remark directed toward me is going to be a buzz-kill, but it isn't." He squinted at me. "Because I *know* you. You love nothing more than to get a rise out of me, but today it isn't going to happen. Because I love you too much. And because I'm high as a kite."

My father laughed uproariously at this, as though he had just uttered the wittiest thing in the history of witty things. He laughed and laughed, seeming not to notice my mother and I looking at each other, shaking our heads in incredulity. Finally he began to calm himself, wiping his eyes with his hospital gown; our comrade two beds down still stared into space, showing no sign of being aware of anything, much less my father's chemical repartee.

"Can you wait outside?" Dad asked. I looked back and realized that he was talking to me. "Just for a minute. I want to speak to your mother alone."

Mom did a pretty good job of hiding her utter horror; if I hadn't known her the way I did, I might have taken the horizontal tightness of her lips for patience, or forbearance. But it was neither. I couldn't remember the last time the two of them had spoken one-on-one, save for planning logistics over the phone. The prevalence of the text message, with its haikus of terse declamation, had been a godsend for the overtime period of their relationship.

"Okay," I said. My mother blinked, and I knew that she had been hoping I would throw her a lifeline. It wasn't my job, though. Glenn and Eliza had set in motion all sorts of things. If Glenn wanted a word alone, even given the state he was in, it wasn't my place to get in the way. Besides, I was beginning to resent them both anew for letting me ping-pong around the city by myself all day. The less charitable part of my self felt that they deserved each other.

"See you around," Dad said. "Come give me a kiss." I did as he asked, on the forehead, and he reached up with his big hands and lightly touched my shoulders.

"I love you very much," I whispered in his ear.

He nodded, dabbing at his eyes.

I left the two of them there, with Glenn clearing his throat, with Eliza leaning close to listen. I had no idea what business Glenn intended to conduct just then, or even if he would later remember anything that he was about to say. I went out in the hallway and immediately encountered Katrina.

"Oh, God," she said, having arrived in a panic, the narrative of her own drama far more hectic than the embers of my own. I let her take me in a big emotional hug and spoke into her lush red hair.

"He's fine," I said several times. "Katrina, they said he's going to be fine."

Katrina blew her nose very loudly and leaned hard against the wall. "I was so afraid," she said. She had a lovely chin, which I hadn't really noticed before. She was so benign, so *good*. I would have told her to run for it, to get away from Glenn, from me, from my brothers, but it wouldn't have done any good. She loved my father, I could see that very clearly. Before long he was going to break her heart. Maybe it would be worth it.

"Can I see him?" she asked.

"Give him a minute or two," I told her. "He's in there with my mother. They're talking."

Katrina nodded, resigned, though I saw in her the same yearning that Elliot evinced: the wish to have this person somehow separate, to remake the world into one in which they could be together unencumbered by everything that had come before. It was the weight of things that they both felt, events that they had nothing to do with, regrets that weren't their own, and swings of the heart ever and eternally beyond their influence or even their recognition. Things were going to go on, the combinations helixing and, hopefully, coming out in everybody's favor. There should be more happiness, always more happiness. But it would arise and fall like the waves on the ocean, while the causes of things that happened in the past—mine, theirs, everyone's—might well remain submerged in a deep dark that never allowed more than the most fleeting and fragmentary illumination.

I craved a drink, most sincerely and with a total absence of humor or condition. After that, I needed a break from myself. My first wish was tantalizingly near to happening. As for the second, I was very unsure.

BEFORE SUNRISE THE NEXT DAY,
WHEN MANY OF THESE THOUGHTS
WILL BEGIN THE PROCESS
OF BEING FORGOTTEN FOREVER

THIS WICKER CHAIR—WHOSE IDEA WAS IT? ISN'T THAT FUNNY, I've begun to forget which things I brought into the marriage and the new house, and which were Elliot's. Not that he had all that much when we moved here—that high-rise condo of his had been the epitome of bachelor Spartan splendor, all gleaming countertops and spotless hardwood floors. I remember going over there for the first time, in the afternoon, the way the sun shone on the floor in the languorous living room, the window looking down on the city, me knowing I was doing something wrong.

You'd never have known Elliot would transform himself into such a thorough homebody, always out in the yard with his garden, building shelves, sheds, all sorts of masculine monuments. Cashing in his business stakes has certainly freed him, changed him. He's further away from me, more distant . . . he's totally secure now, set for life. I wonder what that makes him think. At times I sense him quietly watching me, and I really have no idea what is firing inside his head. The usual things, I suppose: who *is* this woman? What have I gotten myself into? He likes his life neat and tidy, and for a time when we were first together I felt that I shared his urge. But a flatline existence is only sporadically available to me, it turns out. I try to indulge Elliot his quiet, his serene reserve, but the messy details of my first forty-plus years have a stubborn tendency to break the calm.

Not that I am remotely begrudging, of course. It's all firmly in the realm of the things we can't talk about, though: Elliot's blatant resentment of Glenn and my boys, the way he's cast Sam as the *sane* one. Of course Glenn hasn't done much to smooth matters, but I can't really expect him to. Still, I don't think my former husband realizes how injurious to me is his smug, patronizing manner toward Elliot. Or how much I understand that it's a furious attempt to mask Glenn's jealousy over Elliot's worldly success.

Glenn, the great martyr. The unrealized genius. In his bachelor pad, with his succession of devoted women whom he routinely dispatches as though moth-eaten and inevitably qualified for the discard pile. Casting his hairy eyeball across Hennepin Avenue at my new house, my new life with all its trappings. Well, I didn't plan any of this, not that Glenn would ever concede such a basic point—in his mind, my life is a grand conspiracy, with me ever falling upward, never mind how hard *I've* worked, or entertaining the possibility that *I* might ever suffer.

Jesus. I'm fighting with Glenn and he's not even here. You'd think the conflict would stop, ten years after ending the relationship. It hasn't. Glenn is with me every hour of every day. He probably has no idea.

"How does this make you feel?" asks the inner shrink.

Bad. Conditionally good, processing the past. Complicated. Maybe that's what Elliot is thinking when he's silently staring at me: he's wondering if I'm thinking of Glenn. More often than not, I probably am not, but sometimes I surely am.

It's so late. And I hate this wicker chair. Every time I shift my body, it lets out these grating creaking noises, and Sam is sleeping across the table from me and I desperately don't want to wake her. I want to watch her for a while longer, in the cool of the night, the sky outside the porch screens moonlit, the exhausted silence all around me like a blanket. Everything feels right: tenuously, delicately right.

Sam is beautiful. I was so glad earlier when she got out of those god-awful dominatrix boots, and she tucked into a sandwich I made for her and then finally joined me out here. The wine is almost gone—a very nice Bordeaux, our mother-daughter reunion finally coming to pass.

She's on her side, her face pressed against the pillow I fetched. I covered her with a sheet about fifteen minutes ago, when I was sure that she had gone down for the count. I stare at her perfect nose, the curve of her lips in profile—the same side view from the ultrasound image all those years ago, when she was still inside me, when she was all mine and would be forever.

Well, things change. That's what they *do*. I don't need a Buddhist rant from Glenn to comprehend that. And while I'm not welcoming it, now I remember him that day of the ultrasound, his handsome face lit up, his eyes wet with tears. We were going to be together for the rest of our lives. We were going to make something as solid as anything could be in a world of suffering and impermanence. Well, we did for a while.

The day she was born it felt as though time stopped entirely (I vaguely remember the pain, blinding, seemingly infinite, past the point of sensation into a place in which I didn't know my body, but of course it doesn't matter now). Glenn kept congratulating me, praising me, to the point at which it got annoying, but I remember trying to focus on his joy. A joyful Glenn is a silly Glenn. Of course those were probably the times when I loved him the most.

What is it about wine, the way it turns on you? My mouth feels far too parched. I'd get up for a glass of water (there's a pitcher on the table, but it's all gone), but I don't want to wake her. I want to keep things from changing for as long as possible. The backyard is bathed in moon glow. Light from the sun is reflecting off the surface of the moon, traveling all those million miles, and caressing the forehead of my oldest child. I see her as a girl, a woman, even the old person she will one day become. I don't want to let her go; I have the luxury of not doing so, not yet.

For fuck's sake! The things she was telling me! She apparently detonated her relationship with that David (who, admittedly, I knew wasn't right for her, not capable of her, but he was easy enough to be around) by sleeping around with a girl friend (girlfriend?), then apparently behaving quite heartlessly when she was found out. Now it sounds as though the friendship with the girl is shot to shit as well, which is the aspect that most disturbs me—the cavalier way she described that falling out. People her age have no idea how difficult lasting friendships are to find; it's as though they think suitable, reasonable, compatible people are surrounding them like low-hanging fruit.

It isn't that way. So terribly often these days I feel friendless. Oh, I have any number of female names in my iPhone whom I can call for a coffee or a play. But the number of people in whom I can confide has dwindled alarmingly. It doesn't help that Elliot is so self-sufficient. Maybe that's what people think about me: that I don't need anyone. It's probably true that people tell me about their problems more than I share mine with them, but is that such a bad thing? Maybe it is. But what am I supposed to do, invent some kind of dramatic travail? Things are fine for me, by and large.

It pisses me off. I know how people see me: the judge, the rock, the one who's always particular about everything, the one who never lets down her guard.

Maybe I know too much about how letting down my guard gets me all fucked up. That's probably something people should consider when they're viewing me as this uptight, controlling person.

Let it go. Look at Sam. Oh, and the way she talked about that girl in that New Age shop. She didn't say anything as clichéd as "love at first sight," but she might as well have and gotten it over with. I just sat and listened, taking it all in without uttering anything that could be construed as judgment. Of course, I also knew my silence would in and of itself be construed as a form of judgment, or disapproval, or *something*. I couldn't win. So I sipped my wine, *drank* it, actually, while my daughter informed me that her first order of post-college-graduation business was to stalk a female clerk in a hokum factory, presumably in order to engage in some hot girl-on-girl action (at times, surely, in my house), followed by weeks or months of obsession, betrayal, text messaging, and broken promises that will end up with one of them heartbroken and the other a bit more cautious.

What the fuck. I could see the appeal. I just hope that Sam's the one who comes away more wary. I know she had her heart broken once or twice while off at school, but she never let me witness the direct effects. I don't want to. I can't stand the sight of my children being sad. Are they sad already, sad now? I don't know. Sometimes I think so. Daniel obviously has problems that I will have to begin dealing with first thing tomorrow morning. Oh, he's so unreachable, so remote. Sometimes I think he has some vast unspoken grudge against all of us, a cauldron of poison that's going to spill out one day, blaming us all, indicting us in the crimes that made him who he is.

And who could conceivably win a trial such as that one? Our lives intertwined, we see each other at our best and worst. It feels as though we can't *escape* one another. Every family must feel this, the paradoxical snare of what makes us whole (or scatters us). When Glenn and I were together, he was my frame of reference; I filtered every facet of reality through him. The arrival of the children diluted that, of course, but he loomed, for good and ill (mostly good, I still think). I placed him in that position. I *wanted* him there.

Until it all became impossible. Until he . . .

Someone's stirring inside. I hear the sound of the refrigerator door closing. Probably Kevin, in the midst of one of his all-night computer and grass binges. He's getting chubby. He's becoming less masculine. I remember reading somewhere that pot does that to men: it reduces their testosterone levels. I should find the article, clip it, and leave it on his pillow. Then I'd be a lock for mother of the year.

Elliot has never really been the center of my universe. Maybe it's because I can tell he doesn't want to be. He's at a point in his life at which the pressure would be unwelcome. We orbit each other, but I don't know where the center is located. I know he loves me, though, with that quiet stolidity of his. We're getting old together. This seems the way things are intended.

At times I think Elliot appealed to me because he reminds me of my father: both big, hulking guys with a delicacy of manner, both radiating a don't-tread-on-me rectitude. Of course Dad slaved in an office all his adult life, barely making enough for car vacations in the summer, while Elliot's wealth quietly infuses his self-perception (and contributes, I suspect, to his easygoing generosity). Dad's been dead for, what, seventeen years now? Eighteen? I used to be able to hear his voice in my mind, if I was in a quiet place and could relax into the stream of memory. That stopped being available to me years ago.

I should probably get up. Sam seems pretty comfortable. I can just let her sleep out here. If I fall asleep in this fucking chair, however, I will be so stiff in the morning that I won't be able to walk. I'm not due in court for two more days. God, I'm glad for that. I compartmentalize my job, all the sad stories and infuriating self-inflicted disasters, I push it all to one side into a territory into which I'm neither a mother, a wife, or an ex-wife. But it takes a toll. Elliot knows it, although he never says anything. He skirts around the issue, pointing out when I'm negative, or harsh, or, God forbid, *judgmental.*

Glenn used to point out the same tendencies in me. So I must have them. I by and large keep to myself how Elliot's reserve can at times feel like a cudgel. And I used to cut Glenn all manner of slack, at least in my opinion. He's chaotic, he's sloppy, he's in love with the thoughts in his head and the sound of his voice.

He is also, or at least used to be, a better lover than Elliot. I wouldn't know now, not having indulged since our
split. And not that Elliot is a bad lay, not at all, but that
maniac passion of Glenn's translated very well when he
was inside me. He used to come so quietly, hardly making
a sound (even if he had been moaning and swearing the
moment before, which was usually the case), as though it
was a holy moment. Elliot is certainly more straightfor-
ward, although he gets me off, so I can't complain. I can't
say that I feel more passion for him than he does for me.
Passions cool. What's left, hopefully, is what works.

Shit. I think Glenn and I fucked up the kids by splitting up. I try to look at things from the good side: I have a
husband other women covet, my three children are alive,
and reasonably healthy, and terribly interesting. But the
five of us, back then, were golden. We were brilliant, and
our winning streak was going to extend into infinity.

And right now, I'm filled with the sense that things
have gone terribly wrong. Daniel is a mess—if he hates
us as much as I suspect he does, how strong is his enmity
toward himself? As for Kevin, how long does a parent
have to continually deny, in the dark rooms of secret
thoughts, that she simply doesn't *like* one of her children?

I am a terrible person. Sam is stirring. I send her a
psychic wave: *don't wake up.* I don't want her to see me
like this, with tears running down my face. I don't want
to have to explain to her what's going on.

Glenn and I fucked up the kids. For all our expec-
tations of them, and all our love and support, we failed
them. We didn't keep things together. And now I'm a
judge, living in a big house with an opulent garden, with
a husband who might well be seething with resentment

much of the time, and three fucked-up young adult children spiraling in diseased orbits out into the world (that is, if Kevin ever chooses to actually *participate* in the world, an open-ended question at this point), and I'm still conditionally in love with my ex-husband.

I can't even say whether or not I like Glenn, not at this point, after all the years spent with him and then without him. Most of all, I miss his intensity, the gleam in his eye, the way he thought things that no one else would think. I miss his craziness, the way that some part of his mind seemed to be permanently detached and wandering somewhere in the vicinity of the asteroid belt.

Glenn wasn't always nice to me. I certainly wasn't nice enough to him—I fully comprehend that now. But we were *young* when we established our patterns. We're just people, two intense and willful spirits who clashed and loved, until it fell apart. He's probably happier now, anyway. He cycles through those girlfriends every couple of years or so, hitting the reset button and lavishing his outsized attention on the next. Sometimes I think he picks them just to appall me, to prove a point. Like this Katrina, whom I loathe entirely, a half-assed Earth mama who thinks she can keep up with him, that he won't grow bored after he's banged her a couple of hundred times, that he'll still be listening to her New Age drivel once her tits start to sag.

Well. That's very charitable of me, isn't it? Truly, fuck it. Well and truly fuck it. Glenn can do what he wants, that's the deal. I don't have to like it.

I feel cheated. I worked so hard. I gave birth to three children. I considered myself a person living with an open heart.

I stare at the moon long enough to watch it move a fraction across the sky. There's no sign of life from inside the house. I'd like to know what time it is, but I left my watch on the kitchen counter. If Elliot wakes, he might come looking for me. Or he might not. He's very considerate about giving me space. He knows how often I feel pressed upon from all sides.

Glenn was the opposite, of course: always coming at me, always craving my attention, my approval, wanting to tell me the next astonishing thing, or how wonderfully crazy the children were, or trying to get me into bed. It was flattering, on good days, but at times the intensity made me feel as though I was going to explode like a water balloon, only filled with blood, spattering everyone with my depressurized worries and besiegement.

By the time I left Glenn (by the time I *had* to leave Glenn), I had already drifted into a form of infatuation with Elliot. It's something I hate to admit; even now, in the quiet (save for the creaky chair underneath me), the thought makes my guts lurch with nausea. Those were the long months before I caught that flight to LA, when Glenn's normal moodiness had hardened and darkened into something else, a cloudy thing that hovered over all of us. He and I had slipped into parallel tracks, immersing ourselves in our work, loving in our best moments, glacially distant in others. The children occupied the great majority of our shared interests, which was easy in those days of straight-A report cards and laughably high, record-setting test scores.

"We're raising a little mobile genius army," Glenn said to me one day, dripping with that false irony of his. "I can't wait to set them loose on the world."

Elliot had hired one of my associates on a land deal, which required him to come to the firm pretty often for a period of about six weeks. He was long divorced by then, and when we met I noticed his glance drifting to my wedding ring (as well as elsewhere). We ran into each other in the parking lot a couple of weeks later, around lunchtime, and we were both hungry. We went to Pete's Diner and talked about our work, a bit about our children, where we'd lived. We didn't talk about Glenn, nor did I mention that lunch when I got home that night.

There were a few more lunches after that, a few phone calls off work time. (Had I seen the new show at the Guthrie? *Yes*. Could I recommend it, considering that he respected my taste?) I didn't feel anything changing, or anything slipping. Of course Glenn was slipping all over the place, and I didn't realize it, so I suppose there was something wrong there. But things felt solid. I remember that. Things felt solid.

I love the quiet around here. In our old neighborhood, Friday night meant young drunks bellowing down the streets after closing time, vomiting in the bushes, leaving beer bottles in our yard (we lived in a hip neighborhood, okay, but did that necessarily include degradation?). It felt like such an invasion, a gesture of such profound barbarous disrespect. Sometimes Glenn would get out of bed and go confront them, which usually ended with them skulking away like reprimanded Labrador retrievers; when Glenn gets righteous, he's very difficult to contend with. And quite sexy. I wonder if he still gets that way. Judging from earlier today, it seems as though he's lost a bit of his edge.

And *how* hard am I trying not to think of those things

he said to me in the hospital, once he got me alone. He was higher than hell—*I* could have used some of what *he* was on, especially once he got talking.

He knew how happy I was with Elliot, he said. He understood clearly that I had moved on. Stoned as he was, Glenn talked to me in the most serious, hushed way, selecting his words with difficulty, if obvious care.

Elliot and I started dating seriously a few months after I left Glenn. Nothing physical had happened between us until then, but I felt Elliot's presence all the time. I visited his condo downtown once . . . once before things between Glenn and me became impossible. Elliot planned to paint his living room, or rather hire someone to do it for him. He wanted me to look at some color samples, help him make up his mind. The backs of our hands brushed against each other a few times, and there were silences that weren't at all awkward.

I hope he mows the lawn tomorrow (I guess it's tomorrow already). The grass is getting long. Soon it will be mosquito season, with the little bloodsuckers lurking everywhere. I like the smell of bug spray, though. I like it wafting up from my neck, chemical and otherworldly.

It had been a big deal to me, how to present the situation with Elliot to the children. I thought he and I were getting involved at an unseemly pace, but it simply *felt* right. Once Glenn had moved out, and we began the process of splitting our finances, our time, all the details of the life in which we had just recently been so entrenched, I found myself with a startling amount of freedom—Glenn and I agreed to split custody of the children equally, a typical aspect of a divorce that had been much like our marriage, a series of sensible, agreed-upon decisions at which we mutually arrived with a minimum of discussion or conflict.

I downplayed Elliot to the kids, and to Glenn, for as long as I could. But it was a heavy romance, admittedly an unlikely one, and one that demanded enough of me that it soon became impractical to pretend it wasn't happening. Glenn knew who Elliot was, and managed to maintain a great amount of silent dignity on the topic. And Elliot and I waited another six months before negotiating moving in together, long enough for the children to become used to the idea of two separate households, long enough for them to gradually stop asking when things were going to return to the way they once were.

Sam looks so much like her father, in this light. She radiates intensity from the depths of slumber. The two of them are really so much alike—willful, acute, too sensitive for their consistent good. Glenn and Sam have fought more than any two members of the family over the years (a calculation that includes Glenn and myself), but in some ways they've been the closest. There's always been something unspoken between them, a comity, an understanding. It never made me feel jealous, or left out. I'm just glad the two of them have each other.

You're happy with Elliot, Glenn kept saying, lying in that hospital bed with his hair all straw-like and matted to his head.

"I want you to be happy," he added. "Which is why I generally try to stay out of your way. I guess it's affection by omission, or something."

Glenn tried to laugh, but of course, it really wasn't all that funny.

"You still have the gun," I said. He went silent.

"You told me you had gotten rid of it."

"I *did*," Glenn explained. "It just kind of returned to me."

What followed was a convoluted explanation that I barely bothered following. Apparently Glenn had passed the gun on to Carson Willis, an old friend in the newspaper business, and Carson had kept it in his home for a while, until he had gotten divorced, and taken up with a new woman who vehemently preferred a lack of the presence of firearms in her home. The details didn't really matter to me. What mattered was the fact that Glenn had a gun.

"You know you shouldn't," I said.

"Evidently," he said.

I told Glenn that I should be going, and with that he made another attempt on my hand, this one successful. He locked those big brown eyes on mine, and I felt a rush of bewilderment. It had been some time since we had looked into each other's gaze with this kind of intimacy.

"There's been no one since you," he said.

"Glenn," I laughed. "There's been ample evidence to the contrary. Should I start listing names?"

He shook his head in that furious way of his, whenever I frustrated him by not grasping the meaning of what he was saying. His grip on my hand tightened.

"I just want you to know," he said. "I haven't found anything that approaches what we had together. I figure I'll never get up the nerve to tell you this again, and it's probably inappropriate as all hell, but it's the truth. What we had will never happen again. At least for me."

I said his name, very quietly. Funny, we rarely called each other by our names when we were married. Mostly when we were angry, then the name took on the tinge of an epithet. He said my name back to me then, barely audible. My nose itches. I'm going to be so fucking *useless* tomorrow. I have to deal with Daniel, try to unpack his parcel of woe. Maybe we can do something outdoors. Whatever happens, it's not going to be particularly easy or relaxing. I have all three of my children under one roof. It's been a while. I wish I didn't have to be here tomorrow.

It was so like Glenn to lay something like that at my feet. There hasn't been anyone but me. Nice, fine, lovely, very romantic. And probably true, sure, but what did he want? An admission of the same from me? Well, he wasn't going to get it—because it was impossible. In some remote corner of his mind, did he think I would take him back after everything that's happened? How would that even be possible? How, exactly, I wanted to ask him, would that work?

When I left him, I wrote him a note. Knowing Glenn, he probably still has it. It was the most difficult thing I'd ever done. Physically leaving was relatively easy: booking the flight, getting to the airport, going to the gate, ending up at Alayne's. But the note flummoxed me. I remember feeling as though I was writing the most stilted, thoughtless thing. And I knew Glenn would parse my every word, limning my subtexts, probably shouting and reading the thing to the children. I didn't know what else to do. Glenn had backed me into a corner, and he should have known it. Instead, I go into history as the mother who broke up her family.

Maybe that's too harsh. In reality, Glenn stood behind me in spirit once he realized that it was truly over. He allotted blame for the state of things on our shared

relationship, usually adding a remark about how everyone knew how impossible he was. Few of our friends
even knew that it was me who had left. For public consumption, we invented a tale of mutual, almost friendly
and shared intent to put an end to things between us.

None of which helped me with the children, of
course, who had probably heard all sorts of things during
that mad car ride out to California (I didn't think Glenn
would do that. I thought he had more sense. It was impossible for me to understand at the time that he held out
genuine hope for things returning to their previous state).
It's the great thing that's never said: the time I left, unannounced. Sam had come the closest to interrogating me
outright over what happened, but I was (and will always
be) sufficiently protective of Glenn not to tell her. It's left
us with a nagging mystery between us, but sometimes
these are the sorts of things that life produces. We simply
have to live with them.

Oh, God, I remember seeing that Subaru pulling up
in the driveway, that golden LA light, Glenn shooting out
of the car and spotting me in the window. I'm amazed
I didn't faint, just collapse right then and there.

I remember what I said: "Of all the . . ."

But then I stopped myself, because then I was surrounded by the children, which elated me to no end
despite everything, and this had been what Glenn
wanted: to present the children, and himself, to me, to
demonstrate the bonds, the essential way in which all of
our lives are and always will be connected. He wanted to
back in, and buy in again.

It wasn't enough to save the marriage. Not after what
I had seen.

I couldn't get angry with Glenn. Well, no, I could, I was angry with him all the time, but never in a meaningful way. But for him to drive all that way . . . we left for Minnesota the next day. And what a drive that was. Glenn full of good cheer, optimism, making every gas station and souvenir stand out to be some glorious wonder, the funniest thing he had ever seen, the epitome of all that was wonderful and amazing about what we were doing.

It made me feel so cold. I couldn't read the children much of the time. No doubt it was traumatic in a very fundamental way. I simply wasn't able to fake it. I didn't want to be around Glenn. I was too full of frustration, and fear, and betrayal to pretend that nothing had happened.

"No more guns," I said to Glenn, in the hospital, unable and unwilling to respond to his declaration. He nodded. He knew what I meant.

The day of the night I left him, ten years ago, I came home early and unexpectedly from work. There had been a big partners' meeting planned that was scuttled for one reason or another, and I don't remember why, but I didn't think to call and let Glenn know I was coming. I didn't want to surprise him, or expect to catch him in anything, nothing like that. I just didn't think. I came home early and let myself inside. I wasn't even sure he was there.

In the next moment I knew for sure. Glenn was in his study, blaring Wagner. Wagner had a lot to answer for, as far as I was concerned—his operas worked Glenn up, or else he listened to them when he was worked up, whatever. The effect was the same: blasting Wagner meant that Glenn was in a mood.

I waited outside his door, listening. Then I turned the knob and took a step inside.

Glenn was sitting at his desk. He wore an old T-shirt with a map of Puerto Rico on it. The music was deafening. I looked on the desk. Atop a stack of paper, dull, emphatic in its banality, was a handgun. We didn't own a gun, as far as I knew.

The things that happened next were a terrible, scorching blur. Glenn had a pen in his hand, and was scribbling on a piece of paper. It was a note to me. It was an apology. I don't remember exactly what it said (I would never *save* such a thing), but it was a good-bye. To me. And to everyone.

My initial reaction was that I didn't know this man at all. Then I realized that indeed I *did* and that this made terrible sense. I loved him. What he was apparently about to do was such an act of violence, psychic brutality, that my disorientation eclipsed even my compassion for him, or the pain he was going through. I remember staggering, hitting my head on the door frame trying to get out, out, out, that music still roaring and Glenn shouting. His initial facial expression, when I walked in on him, had been mixed: sheepish, ashamed. And disappointed.

I ran out to the car, with Glenn calling to me from the open front door, and I started driving. I drove round the lakes, got onto a freeway, kept going aimlessly for a couple of hours. It was almost beyond me to think coherently, but a couple of pressing matters grabbed most of my attention.

The first was that I had to find some way to stop Glenn from killing the father of my children.

The second was that I could not be married to him anymore.

So I came back later, parked around the corner, and slipped inside. I could hear their voices upstairs, all four of them. I already had my plane ticket. I had already called my sister. I think I may have mouthed the word *good-bye* before I made it back to my car, my legs about to buckle, my hands violently shaking.

He couldn't kill himself if he was alone with the children. He wouldn't do it. He loved them too much. He would keep himself alive for them.

In the hospital, earlier today, I made him let go of my hand. And then I leaned forward and gave him a long, sincere kiss on the forehead. I knew he meant well. And I knew what he meant. There just shouldn't be a vocabulary for these sorts of thoughts, not now. It doesn't work. It isn't particularly easy, but you have to learn how to banish the impossible.

The sky in the east is starting to lighten, just a shade. Shit, how long have I been sitting here? Long enough for a lifetime.

Oh, the children aren't *that* screwed up, not any more than everyone else. When I was Sam's age, I was everybody's favorite, the hardest worker, always thinking of everyone else first. How many of those years did I waste, in a sense, thinking that I wasn't good enough, that I wasn't pretty, that I didn't deserve anything but that which came from tireless work and sacrifice.

Love takes work, and sacrifice, but not as much as maybe it should. Maybe we would appreciate it more if its costs were presented to us up front. Maybe we wouldn't throw it away when it becomes inconvenient, or when the world recombines in ways that make it impossible.

Of course I am contradicting myself. You *do* have to learn to banish the impossible. At least I think you do.

And very soon it will be morning, and I will be this person people know as Eliza, and whatever I do or say, nothing will entirely triumph over the preconceptions and assumptions of others. The people who love me will love a version of myself that they, in part, create, one that I might well not recognize if she were presented to me in all her naked truth.

But then it's entirely possible that the Eliza they love is truer than the one that I know. Maybe their ability to organize me, comprehend me, is the real truth, the real me. I certainly hope so, because she's the one they love. The Eliza in here, right now, I feel as though I hardly know.

Sam is shifting, nestling. She looks incredibly comfortable. She must have been exhausted, after all that driving, all that pressure and insanity. I'll run her out of the house once she's eaten and gotten her feet under her. I'll give her money, tell her to go someplace and do something entirely for herself.

And then I'll get even older, with Elliot, in this house that used to belong to someone else, and in which one day someone else will live, perhaps with children, maybe not, another set of souls living a moment that feels wholly original and distinct. And we will all be gone—me, Glenn, Elliot, the children—to that great scattering and recombining of which we're only dimly aware, having been fragmentary aspects of events and emotions that spiral on and on. Another woman may well sit in a creaking chair, in the middle of the night, worrying about her men and her children, wondering how things went wrong, where they went right, what she could possibly have done differently. If any aspect of myself survives then, a whisper of a thought, a fleeting feeling, I will impart it to her: everything, all these things, from the most minute to the nauseatingly vast, will truly be *all right.*

Thanks to Natasha and Gabriel for endless inspiration, and to Richard and Joyce. Thanks to Michael Croy and Colleen Dunn Bates for their belief in my work.

ABOUT THE AUTHOR

Quinton Skinner is the author of the novels *Amnesia Nights* and *14 Degrees Below Zero*, as well as the nonfiction books *Do I Look Like a Daddy to You? A Survival Guide for First-Time Fathers* and *VH1 Behind the Music: Casualties of Rock*. He has written for such publications as *Variety, Glamour,* and *American Theatre*, as well as a number of newspapers. He lives in Columbia Heights, Minnesota.